A NOVEL WAY TO DIE

NEVERMORE BOOKSHOP MYSTERIES, BOOK 6

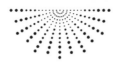

STEFFANIE HOLMES

BACCHANALIA HOUSE

ISBN: 978-1-99-115040-0

⭐ Created with Vellum

A NOVEL WAY TO DIE

Mina Wilde – bookstore owner, girlfriend to three of the hottest heroes of literature, and now... reluctant vampire hunter.

In the sixth novel in the Nevermore Bookshop Mysteries, Mina, Heathcliff, Morrie, and Quoth face off against their ultimate enemy.

Add meddling villagers, an army of fictional characters to wrangle, Mina's mother's latest get-rich-quick-scheme, and a curious dog into the mix, and Mina's got her hands full.

But Nevermore Bookshop still has secrets to reveal. Mina and her men are ready for an epic showdown worthy of a Homeric poem... *if* they survive.

The Nevermore Bookshop Mysteries are what you get when all your book boyfriends come to life. Join a brooding antihero, a master criminal, a cheeky raven, and a heroine with a big heart (and an even bigger book collection) in this steamy reverse harem paranormal mystery series by *USA Today* bestselling author Steffanie Holmes.

Grab a free copy *Cabinet of Curiosities* – a Steffanie Holmes compendium of short stories and bonus scenes, including one from Quoth's POV – when you sign up for updates with the Steffanie Holmes newsletter.

JOIN THE NEWSLETTER FOR UPDATES

*W*ant a free bonus scene from Quoth's point of view? Grab a free copy of *Cabinet of Curiosities* – a Steffanie Holmes compendium of short stories and bonus scenes – when you sign up for updates with the Steffanie Holmes newsletter.

www.steffanieholmes.com/newsletter

Every week in my newsletter I talk about the true-life hauntings, strange happenings, crumbling ruins, and creepy facts that inspire my stories. You'll also get newsletter-exclusive bonus scenes and updates. I love to talk to my readers, so come join us for some spooky fun :)

*To all the book boyfriends
who keep me up at night.*

"They are given to all kinds of marvelous beliefs, are subject to trances and visions, and frequently see strange sights, and hear music and voices in the air. The whole neighborhood abounds with local tales, haunted spots, and twilight superstitions..."
    – Washington Irving, *The Legend of Sleepy Hollow.*

"I have crossed oceans of time to find you."
    – Bram Stoker, *Dracula.*

ARGLETON GAZETTE

THIRD GRISLY MURDER BY THE SUSPECTED DRACULA KILLER

*H*alloween may be just around the corner, but Argleton residents are advised to lock their doors and avoid trick-or-treating after the body of Debbie Malcolm was found on the grounds of the Argleton Presbyterian Church, her body drained of blood.

The serial killer terrorizing the village has been dubbed the Dracula Killer, as his attacks mimic vampiric killings from mythology and literature. Many speculate his nocturnal activities may be linked to a series of grave robberies at the Argleton Presbyterian Cemetery. Police report that they don't believe the crimes are related.

Sylvia Blume and Helen Wilde, who manage the local crystal and tarot-reading store which mysteriously exploded earlier this year, believe the killer may in fact be a real vampire. "He's been lured to our world for All Hallows' Eve celebrations, when the veil between heaven and hell and the living world is thinnest," explains Ms. Wilde. "I've made a new healing tea that will help you to ward off psychic attacks. Only £12 for a box. Can I interest you in one?"

Mabel Ellis, head of Argleton's Spirit Seekers Society, agrees that the killings have a supernatural origin. "At my age, I've seen lots of murders in the village, but never anything like this. The ritual nature of them, the fact one victim was found in the graveyard, the time of year – it all points toward a killer not of this world. It's all very exciting. But don't let it stop you enjoying the first annual Argleton Halloween Festival – we promise no murders, only spooky good fun."

The Spirit Seekers Society is sponsoring our Halloween festival, and for the month of October they're offering discounted paranormal investigations for any Argleton resident who finds themselves unsettled by strange occurrences in their home or business.

This reporter remains skeptical, but arcane superstition aside, it's clear the Dracula Killer continues to hunt in Argleton. Who will be his next victim? Will the Spirit Seekers exorcise the demon in our midst? Will our local constabulary or amateur bookstore sleuths save the day?

CHAPTER ONE

"Oh, great." Morrie rolled his eyes at the architectural monstrosity towering over us. "Another human fishbowl. Why can't our favorite bloodsucker's assistant buy blocks of pokey terraced houses where no one will notice us breaking and entering?"

"It does look like *Grand Designs* had a baby with Alcatraz," I ventured. In the gloom, all I could discern were vague shapes, which made the house seem even more sinister. Who wanted to live in a place like this, all sharp corners and jutting steel? Give me a homely fire in a pokey upstairs flat with a cat on my lap, a book in my hand, and ghosts in the walls, and I was perfectly happy.

Especially if the chair opposite me contained the brooding figure of Heathcliff Earnshaw, and a lanky Moriarty bent down to hand me a plate of roast beef with lust in his eyes, while the kind fire-rimmed eyes of Quoth the raven burned into me from the shadows.

That was exactly where I wanted to be right now – back at Nevermore Bookshop, tucked up in front of the fire with a mug of Quoth's amazing hot chocolate warming my fingers. Not freezing my arse off in the crisp October air, about to commit *yet another* crime, all in the name of freeing the world from a blood-thirsty vampire.

How is this my life?

It had been nearly a year since I came back to Argleton from New York City to lick my wounds and figure out the person I'd be after I lost my eyesight. I never expected that person to be the vampire-hunting, murder mystery-solving, book-slinging daughter of Homer with three gorgeous boyfriends and a cat for a grandmother. Nevermore Bookshop had the last laugh on that one.

Over the last few months, I'd added 'cat burglar' to the list as Morrie and I sought out the boxes of Romanian dirt Dracula hid to ensure his immortality. If he was killed and his servant buried him in dirt from his homeland, he would regenerate. We couldn't go after him until we'd made sure every last one of those dirt boxes was destroyed.

I drummed my fingers nervously on the skintight black catsuit I wore. At least cat-burgling outfits were *fierce*.

We rounded the edge of the building. All was in darkness, save for the bright moon that hung over us, reflecting dappled light from the steel front door. To be fair, most things were in darkness for me these days. In the months since I cleared Morrie of murder charges, my eyesight deteriorated to the point where my night vision was now only shapes and shadows.

I was basically the worst cat burglar in the world. Luckily I had the Napoleon of Crime at my side.

Morrie pulled out his lock-picking kit and got to work on the door while I stared over my shoulder at the bright moon, letting my eyes adjust to make out the rough shapes of the minimalist front garden, the street beyond, and the woods of King's Copse edging the property. My guide dog Oscar sat at my heels, his ears pricked for movement. He'd gotten awfully good at navigating in the dead of night, thanks to our recent nocturnal adventures.

Poor Oscar. I'm sorry I made you into a criminal. I should probably start calling myself a dog burglar.

"We're in, gorgeous." Morrie's rich voice broke the silence.

I heard the door click open. Morrie went inside first, using an app on his phone to disable the alarm. I waved Oscar in after him, hoping he didn't have mud on his paws that would leave prints behind. Not that it mattered – the man who owned this house, Grey Lachlan, rarely spent any time at his properties. He was too busy renovating the flat across the street from the bookshop and making our lives miserable.

"What's the layout of—*ow.*" Something hard and metal slammed into my forehead, sending me sprawling backward. My tailbone cracked against the hard tiles. Oscar barked with distress. He was supposed to lead me around obstacles, but he was a dog and he was not perfect and he probably got lost in the dark, which was something I could relate to.

"Ssssh, boy." I wrapped my arms around Oscar, nuzzling his neck until he licked my face. Morrie helped me to my feet. He flicked on the light, revealing the shape of a random steel sculpture with eight spindly arms like spider's legs that attached to the walls with bungee cords.

"Who puts a medieval torture device in their bloody entrance hall?" I growled, giving the thing a kick with my cherry-red Doc. The steel arms wobbled, and Oscar shied away.

"Someone who wants to impale a blind burglar." Morrie rubbed his chin. "Come on, gorgeous. The sooner we find the dirt, the sooner we can get out of here before you accidentally put your head through a Constable."

"Urgh, don't remind me." Three houses ago, I tripped over the edge of a rug. Only instead of landing on said rug, which was quite soft and snuggly, I slammed into the wall and knocked a priceless artwork onto my head. Now, we turn the lights on and Morrie inspects carefully for trip hazards.

Once Morrie declared the property Mina-proof, we spread

out. Morrie took the living room while I hunted through the kitchen cupboards, feeling over the empty shelves and pushing my fingers into the show-home designer teacups. I pulled the back off the coffee machine, but it wasn't filled with dirt. In the book, Dracula had large wooden crates filled with Transylvanian earth, but all the stashes we've found have been relatively small – he must only need a little for his regeneration.

"Ah-*hah*," Morrie yelled.

I spun around. Morrie barreled into the kitchen. I could just make out a rectangular object in his hands and the long cord dragging across the carpet behind him.

"What's that?"

"I have no idea. It was plugged into the telly. It might be some kind of DVD player, but look at the size of this hole." Morrie poked his fingers into a wide slot. When he removed them and held them up to my nose, I saw they were covered in dirt.

Transylvanian dirt.

"I think that's a VCR." I fumbled in my bag for my vial of holy water. We were running low, which meant we'd need to add 'stealing from a Catholic church...again' to our long list of indiscretions. "Mum used to have one when I was little. You watch videos, which are on spools of magnetic tape. You have to hold down a button to fast forward or rewind, and you couldn't skip around scenes. But you could use them to record programs off the telly so you didn't miss anything."

Morrie looked confused. "You mean, you couldn't just select a show and push play?"

"Nope. The newspaper published a list of what programs were and their times, and you had to show up at that time or miss out. Unless you had a VCR, of course."

"How quaint." Morrie looked at the machine with such unrivaled disgust I fell in love with him a tiny bit more. James Moriarty needed the best of everything in life, and that included the latest technology.

And he needs me. The thought sent a thrill racing through my veins. There was a reason I came with Morrie on these burglaries. He could probably do them on his own, and sometimes, like the time with the Constable, I was more of a liability. But the way he smiled at me when I pulled on my catsuit and snuck through the countryside with him did delicious things to my insides. Morrie tended to view most interactions with humans as exercises in lower-brain functions, but he was never afraid to be completely himself around me, even when his true self was manipulating an innocent with his charms or gleefully committing property damage.

If I had to be truly honest, I got a thrill out of every moment we spent together, walking a tightrope edge of being caught. My master criminal had rubbed off on me more than I'd like to admit.

Morrie held the flap of the VCR open while I sprinkled the dirt inside with holy water. For good measure, I tossed in a broken piece of communion wafer. If my life was a movie, something magical would happen to indicate the dirt was no longer useable by Dracula, but this wasn't a movie, so nothing sparkled and there were no shimmering sound effects.

We just had to hope like hell we'd done the job.

Far too much of our plan revolved around 'hope like hell' for my liking.

Morrie tossed the VCR down on the table. "While we're here, I want to have a peek around this place. I wonder if it's as ghastly as that last flat, with the gold bathtub? I've been thinking about getting a place of my own, and I wouldn't mind something modern and elegant like this. My temporary bedroom doesn't have room for my toys."

I could see Morrie living here, creepy modern sculptures and all. It definitely suited him more than our current arrangement. Morrie gave up his bedroom in the flat so I could have a space of my own. He'd been sleeping in the first-floor storage room, but that was only big enough for his bed. All his 'toys' – his various BDSM accouterments and computer equipment – were still in my room, taking up valuable space I needed for my record player and shoe collection. The truth was, we were all falling over one another in the cramped flat, but with Morrie having to refund several clients after winding down his death-faking business, we didn't have the funds for more renovations—

A noise caught the edge of my conscious – a rustle in the trees outside. My heart thudded against my chest.

"Maybe we should leave…"

"Nonsense. We can't leave until I've measured the bedroom for my stockade and that puppy has taken a shit in the toaster. A little gift from us to Grey for keeping us up all night with his hammering. Oh, and I might grab a bottle of wine. Grey always has exceptional taste."

Morrie moved to the kitchen, his long fingers dancing over the bottles in the rack. This was the problem with breaking and entering with a man who wasn't afraid of the law. Morrie always wanted to hang about and make mischief. I was keen to get home to my hot chocolate and my Quoth.

Another noise sent my heart hammering. "Are you positive that no one lives in this block of flats? I swear I heard—"

I jumped as a long, low howl echoed outside, followed by the sounds of snarling, snapping teeth. Oscar pawed at the rug and whimpered.

"They've unleashed the hounds," Morrie whispered.

"You didn't tell me there were hounds!"

"You never asked." Morrie dared one of his sheepish grins.

"We have to go." I pictured the three of us cowering in here with vicious dogs barking outside when Hayes and Wilson showed up. I wouldn't be able to do much about Dracula from a jail cell.

"An excellent deduction." Morrie tucked the pilfered bottle of Château Lafite under his arm. I tucked my hand into the crook of his arm, and he led me around the sculpture. We stepped outside. The snarling drew closer, the bushes rustling as vicious beasts closed the distance to the house. Morrie slammed the door and tugged me forward as I yelled at Oscar to run. My brave doggo barked at the beasts as Morrie led us into the woods at a sprint.

I screwed my eyes shut with terror. Tree branches scraped my arms. I tripped and skidded over gnarled branches and loose stones. I focused on holding Oscar's harness as tight as I dared. Morrie and Oscar would never steer me wrong. I trusted them with my life.

The snarling grew closer. Fear squeezed my heart as the dogs rounded us, closing in. Hot breath tickled the backs of my legs. I screamed and kicked forward, lunging after Morrie into the darkness.

Behind the dogs came another sound – a rhythmic clatter as if of horses' hooves, carrying with it an oppressive terror that settled low in my chest. My limbs ached, my lungs screamed for air. It wouldn't be long before I couldn't run any longer. The sound drew closer and closer and—

THUD.

A dull tremble, horribly close, shuddered through my body. Then a whimper and a receding rustle. Paws crunched in the falling leaves, stampeding *away* from us. *What in Isis' name happened?*

I opened my eyes.

The action was pointless. In the dark, away from the streetlights, I had no hope of seeing more than rough shapes. But I could hear the dogs whimpering, whining, slinking away. Oscar burrowed his head into my shoulder, his whole body trembling. *What's going on?*

"Mina, look." Morrie turned my head and pointed. "I think that's who scared the dogs away."

The moon shone through a gap in the trees, casting enough light that I could make out the silhouette of a man sitting on top of a monstrous black horse. Steam pooled from the animal's nostrils as it snorted, stomping an enormous black hoof against the ground. I'd never seen a horse like that before, so huge and mean with its yellow glowing eyes. But that wasn't what stilled my heart and dried the saliva on my tongue.

"Is it just me," I managed to choke out, "or does that rider... have no head?"

CHAPTER TWO

*M*orrie seemed completely nonplussed, but his fingers tightened around mine, and I knew he was frightened, too. "Yup. He looks pretty headless to me."

The rider inclined its torso stump toward me, then directed the horse to trot away into the trees. I buried my face in Oscar's fur as a groan welled up inside me.

The Headless Horseman.

From Washington Irving's *The Legend of Sleepy Hollow.*

This isn't good.

How'd he get all the way out here?

I was too annoyed to be scared anymore. A cranially-challenged rider jaunting around Argleton could only have come from one place, which made him the third new literature character who'd appeared in Nevermore Bookshop this week. We now had Socrates sleeping on a rollout bed in the Philosophy room, and Dr. Victor Frankenstein had taken over the cellar for his laboratory. Nevermore felt less like a bookshop and more like a halfway house for the literarily depraved.

I set Oscar down and gave him the signal to lead me through the trees after the horse.

"What are you doing?" Morrie jogged after me.

"We can't just leave him wandering all over Argleton. Someone might see him."

"So?"

"So...we have enough problems to deal with right now without the villagers discovering their favorite local bookshop brings literary characters to life."

"Relax, gorgeous. They'll think he's part of the Halloween madness."

Morrie did have a point. It was October, and in a country that didn't officially celebrate the holiday, Argleton village had gone a little Halloween mad. My old neighbor, Mrs. Ellis, decided the village needed something fun to take our minds off the serial killer in our midst, so she organized a week-long Halloween festival. Seeing all the decorations in the shop windows and pumpkins lining the garden paths made me nostalgic about my four years in New York City. Every year, Ashley and I would spend months designing each other's costumes as a kind of creative challenge. We'd reveal our creations to wear to Marcus Ribald's epic Halloween party. America was one crazy-ass country, but they did Halloween up RIGHT.

Argleton couldn't quite match Marcus' gritty elegance, but they were more than making up for that with reckless enthusiasm. The festival didn't officially begin for another few days, but so many people were wandering around in costume, I doubt our decapitated jockey would stir much fuss.

But still.

"I'm going after him. Are you coming or not?" I didn't wait for Morrie's reply. Oscar had picked up the horse's scent. He trotted along at a decent clip, steering me around the trees and bushes in my way. He stopped at a low dry stone wall so I could clamber over, then took off again, his nose close to the ground.

Oscar and I had become quite a team in the few months we'd been together. He knew every corner of Nevermore Bookshop intimately, so much so that sometimes I attached a kiddie trailer filled with books to his harness and got him to wheel it to the appropriate shelf. I'd even caught him snuggled up in front of the fire with Heathcliff after a busy day. He'd become an intrinsic part of our strange little family.

And I was turning him into a criminal.

If I didn't have Oscar with me on these dangerous midnight missions, I'd be going in completely blind (pun intended). And I wasn't going to sit around at home and wait for Morrie and Heathcliff and Quoth to take out Dracula for me.

I was Mina Wilde, daughter of Homer. Somehow, I was responsible for what came out of Nevermore Bookshop. I wouldn't shirk that responsibility, which was why I crashed and stumbled my way through the woods after the Headless Horseman.

We emerged into a clearing. Moonlight gleamed off a large, circular pool. We'd reached the duck pond at the edge of the council estate where I used to live with my mum. I came here as a kid sometimes to read under the gazebo and escape having to be slave labor for Helen Wilde's latest get-rich-quick scheme.

Horse and rider circled the duck pond. The rider's cloak billowed in the stiff breeze. The horse bent its neck to the water. At that moment my mind imagined all kinds of sinister and ghostly tricks – the water boiling, the ducks' heads flying off, a demonic face rising from the depths...

"Oh, he's having a drink." I breathed in relief as loud slurps echoed through the trees.

"I guess even spectral horses of pure evil need to hydrate." Morrie appeared beside me. "Maybe he—Mina, what are you doing?"

I squared my shoulders and stepped out of the trees, gripping Oscar's harness tight between my fingers. I cleared my throat.

The horse continued to drink, but the rider turned his body toward me. Even though I couldn't see much more than his silhouette, any movement of a silhouette without a head was freaky as fuck.

Terror bit at my throat. My heart battered against my ribs. Even though I knew horse and rider were characters in a book, I also knew they had the same motivations and desires as they did inside the pages. Encountering this beastly duo hadn't ended so well for Ichabod Crane.

"Hi." I waved. "I'm Mina. I wanted to say thanks for saving us."

The rider kind of bobbed in his saddle. I guessed that was Headless Horseman talk for, *'you're welcome.'*

I continued. "So...I don't know if you noticed, but you're not in Sleepy Hollow anymore. It's kind of a long story, but you probably don't want to be wandering aimlessly around all night long. If you follow us, I'll take you somewhere safe and maybe get some stabling for your horse."

I turned to leave, gesturing for Oscar and Morrie to head toward the road. Horse and rider continued to stand there. I felt the itch of eyeless eyes watching me.

"I said, you can follow us." I stepped behind the horse to try and encourage it to move. I waved my arms, but the horse remained rooted in place, so I stepped closer. *How do you get a spectral horse to move? I can't exactly feed it an apple—*

"Ah...Mina." Morrie looked like he was trying very hard not to laugh. I opened my mouth to ask him what was so funny when a stream of foul-smelling water drenched the front of my clothes.

"Argh!" I leaped back. Oscar barked with excitement. He thought it was great fun.

The horse wasn't moving because he was taking a piss.

All over my brand new catsuit.

"Yuck." I limped over to Morrie. "You might've warned me."

"And miss the delighted expression on your face? Never." Morrie's finger stroked my chin, tilting my head up. He leaned in close, giving me a moonlit view of the aristocratic planes of his face and those cheekbones made of razor blades. His voice rasped. "Besides, I heard a rumor horse piss is actually an aphrodisiac."

He tipped my head back with his thumb to claim my lips. I forgot about the Headless Horseman and the very real, very smelly piss staining my best cat-burglarizing outfit. We poured all the adrenaline and fear of the evening into the kiss, and it burned with our need for each other—

Okay, maybe I didn't entirely forget about the horse piss. I pulled back, wrinkling my nose. "Can we revisit this later, when I don't reek of equine urine?"

"As you wish." Morrie wrapped his arm around my shoulder as we trudged back along the wide path toward the village, the clop-clop of hooves behind us as the Headless Horseman fell in line. Oscar tugged on his lead, keen to return to the bookshop.

We walked past the old train station where the homeless population of Argleton hung out. It looked as though they were having a rager – a fire blazed from an old oil drum beside the tracks, and I heard a chorus of voices singing bawdy folk songs along with a screeching fiddle.

As we trudged past, Earl Larson leaned out the window of an old carriage. "Hullo, Mina, Morrie."

"Hi, Earl. How's your kitten?"

"Oh, he's a right piece of mischief; got us kicked out of the cafe the other day for stealing kippers." Just then, Oscar perked up, and I knew a tiny black kitten face had popped up beside Earl. "Would you like to stay for a cup of tea?"

"Um, I can't stop now." My heart pattered against my chest. We needed to move on before Earl noticed our decapitated friend. I also badly wanted to get out of my piss-stained catsuit.

"You should come by the bookshop next week," Morrie piped up. "Heathcliff's got some new books set aside for you, and we're having a bunch of little events for the festival. Oliver's making Halloween cookies."

I elbowed Morrie in the ribs. *Are we just going to stand here making chitchat and pretending the rider behind me has all his bodily appendages?*

"Might do, might do." There's a pause, then Earl said, "Doesn't talk much, does he?"

"Who?"

"Your jockey friend." Earl nodded to the Headless Horseman.

I wasn't sure whether to laugh or cry. "No. Not so much."

Earl waved a flask at us. "Well, you know where to find me if you need a little of Earl's drum-cider to loosen his tongue."

We waved goodbye to Earl and led horse and rider up the hill, past darkened terraced houses and the crumbling village skateboard park. As we turned onto Butcher Street and dodged around Lachlan Enterprises' scaffolding, I couldn't help but glance toward Mrs. Ellis' old flat. It was shrouded in darkness like the rest of the village, but something about this particular darkness sent a shiver down my spine.

As we trudged up the steps, Heathcliff leaned out the shop window. "What time do you call this?"

"Time for oscillating our unmentionables, you saucy specimen of manhood," Morrie called back.

Even though I couldn't make out his face, I knew Heathcliff was glowering. He'd been in a near-constant state of glower ever since he'd rescued Morrie from the Barset Reach falls and the three of us shared an intense kiss. I thought that kiss meant he'd *finally* be able to acknowledge his feelings for Morrie, but instead, Heathcliff had retreated from both of us, which of course spurred Morrie to even greater heights of provocation. The resulting standoff added yet another item to my growing list of 'shit Mina needs to deal with while she's trying to save the world from a bloodthirsty fictional vampire.'

"Heathcliff, my love," I asked sweetly. "Did you happen to notice a black horse with a headless rider hanging out in the shop this evening?"

Heathcliff grunted. "The walking glue factory showed up after you left. The fellow riding it was agreeable enough, but that long-faced bastard shat on the rug. I shoved them both out the door and said they'd better find you."

"Well, they did." I stepped aside, giving Heathcliff a view of our new friends. The horse lowered its head and snorted at Heathcliff, while the rider jiggled in his saddle, as if to say, *'Don't let that surly bastard torment me again.'*

"Get lost." Heathcliff brandished the broom out the window, waving it in the horse's face. "We don't need your type here."

The horse reared up as the rider yanked on the reins.

"Stop it." I reached out and grabbed the broom. I wanted to laugh, but that would only encourage Heathcliff. "You *know* we can't have him running around the village."

"Why not?"

"Because he doesn't have a head."

"Well, he can't stay in the bloody shop. The rider might be a spectral ghoul, but the horse smell is tangible as fuck." Heathcliff screwed up his face.

"Tell me about it." I caught a whiff of myself on the breeze, and it was not pretty. "Where in this village can we hide a horse?"

"There's that old stable block around the back of the pub," Morrie suggested.

The village pub, the Rose & Wimple, was over five hundred years old. It was a rabbit warren of thick beams, low ceilings, and crooked floors, and included some of the original Tudor outbuildings. I knew the landlord Richard was using the old still to brew his craft cider, but as far as I knew the stables were empty...and far enough away from the pub building that they were unlikely to be visited. It was as good a place as any to keep our truncated terror and his steed.

Heathcliff glared at the rider. "I don't care where he goes, just as long as it's not in the shop."

The rider slid off the saddle. His feet made no sound as they touched the cobbles. He picked up the reins and indicated with an incline of his neck that he'd follow me. The horse's hooves made a *clop-clopping* sound as he turned around, but the Headless Horseman seemed to float over the ground without touching it.

I was used to seeing odd things in my line of work, but a headless specter and his beast were another matter entirely. And they were an all-too present reminder of the supernatural evil we were fighting.

Oscar led the way, marching across the deserted village green, ducking and weaving between the half-built carnival stalls and the bonfire preparations. I tied the horse up in the stables. The Headless Horseman bent down and stroked his steed's face. The horse whinnied. I thought the horseman would remain with his beast, but with a final nuzzle, the rider turned away and followed us back to the shop. Morrie held the door open and I trudged inside.

As soon as I passed along the narrow hallway crowded with books, my fear and stress slipped away. Nevermore Bookshop had that effect on me. I wasn't sure if it was the shop's magic or a reflection of how comfortable I felt here. Nevermore was my home in all the ways that mattered.

Heathcliff had turned on all the lamps for me, so the shop glowed with enough light to enable me to discern shelves, furniture, stairs, even individual books. Just when I thought I couldn't take his distance and grumpiness any longer, he showed me how he still cared about me, how he thought of me always.

Oscar waited while I removed his harness. Inside the shop, I was able to let him off duty. He scampered ahead of us, heading straight for his food and water bowls. My stomach rumbled, but I had a vitally-important matter to attend to first – a shower.

Heathcliff appeared in the hallway, wearing a black shirt that set off his dark eyes and the scowl he usually reserved for customers. I threw my arms around him, burrowing my face into his neck and breathing in his earthy scent. There was something about Heathcliff that was so grounding, so steadying. After a moment of stiffness, he gave into the embrace, curling his body around me and squeezing so tight he could fuse our atoms together.

"You smell like horse piss," he murmured, but he didn't pull away.

"I sure do. I missed you tonight."

"You're home now." Heathcliff's voice rasped with emotion as he crushed my spine in his grip. He was closing himself off from me, not saying what he wanted to say, and I worried about him. I worried that he'd hold back so much that he'd burn up in the inferno of his repressed passions. But then he embraced me like *this*, his whole body thrumming on the knife-edge of losing control, and I could read his mind and his heart as though they were my own.

"I'll get our guest settled and I'll be right upstairs." I brushed my lips lightly on Heathcliff's cheek. His eyes fluttered closed and his whole body stiffened. He jerked away from me as though I might burn him. *I hate this.* My touch moved him, but it was destroying him, too, and I didn't understand why, and he wouldn't tell me, and I wanted to throttle him and also hold him and never let him go.

Heathcliff turned to the stairs. "I'll run you a bath and make ready the hot chocolate." He didn't look back at me as he disappeared into the gloom. He hadn't acknowledged Morrie at all.

"I brought the wine." Morrie held up the bottle he'd stolen from Grey's showhome. "No need to thank me."

No response from Heathcliff. Not even a grunt.

"I see Lord Peevish of Peevleton is in fine form tonight." Morrie's voice was bright, but I could tell by the way he studied the spine of a Dan Brown novel like it held the secrets to the universe (it didn't) that Heathcliff hurt him deeply.

That makes two of us.

"I'm sure he's just desperate to escape my delightful perfume," I said with faux brightness.

The Headless Horseman floated up behind Morrie. He raised his hand. My chest tightened. *What's he going to—*

The decapitated specter patted Morrie's shoulder, inclining his stump.

"Great." Morrie moaned. "Even the resident ghoul is feeling sorry for me."

"Morrie—"

But he'd disappeared deeper into the shop. I didn't blame him. He'd been battling with the Heathcliff situation for months, and I *did* smell rather foul.

"You'd better follow me," I gestured to the horseman. "I'm afraid we're a little short on beds. If you're staying at the shop, you'll have to share." I led him up to the first floor and pushed open the door labeled 'KEEP OUT: SPRAYING FOR INSECTS.' I flicked on the light, revealing the inflatable mattress set up on the floor. "You'll be sharing this room with...hey, what happened in here?"

Someone had divested the bed I'd made up this morning of its sheets, and turned the room upside down. Books lay scattered across the floor, their covers torn off, their pages creased and crumpled. One had been stabbed through with a kitchen knife and was now pinned to the wall.

The someone whom I assumed responsible for this destruction hopped across the sofa, a whirlwind of wrinkled skin and righteous indignation, his knobbly knees sticking out in all directions and his eyes bugging out as he gesticulated at the page of a book. The bedsheet pinned over one bony shoulder drooped dangerously, revealing a pasty chest covered with downy silver hairs.

"I never said that!" he raved, jabbing at the book with his finger. "I never said, 'beware the barrenness of a busy life.' I did once tell my student Plato that my *wife* spent so much time thinking up ways to infuriate me that she had not a minute to spare for child-making, thus rendering her barren by circum-stance, but I hardly think that's a teachable lesson—"

"Gah." I held up my hands as Socrates kicked out a bony leg, sending his sheet flying and offering far too much wrinkly skin for display.

It's times like this I wish I had no vision left at all.

Socrates had been the first recent arrival – an interesting addi-tion, considering he wasn't technically *fictional*. But Mr. Simson – my father, Homer – had insisted on stocking some of the staples of Greek and Roman literature on the Classics shelves; his own works, Ovid, Herodotus, Plutarch, Plato, Aristophanes, etc. So we assumed that explained Socrates' loud-but-generally-harmless presence in the shop. Hopefully, he wouldn't be followed by Nero or Caligula.

"And I *never* said this nonsense about slander being the tool of a loser. I love a good slander! I slander with the best of them. Hmmph, all I did was ask questions and let others make up their own stupid minds, and look what a fool history has made of me." Socrates threw the book to the floor and stomped on it, his sheet flying up around his bony arms.

"Socrates, this is the Headless Horseman. Headless, meet your roommate, Socrates, the greatest philosopher that ever lived. I'm sure you two will get along great. Be grateful you don't have ears," I muttered as I slammed the door in the horseman's not-face.

"Pre-bath drink?" Heathcliff held out a glass for me as I trudged upstairs to our private flat. Morrie was already at his computer desk, adding details of tonight's raid into our Dracula database. Our cat (and my grandmother), Grimalkin, curled around his narrow shoulders.

I downed the glass on my way to the shower. In the bath-room, I flung open the window and tossed my catsuit outside into the alley below, probably missing the rubbish bin by miles.

So much for my fierce cat-burglaring outfit.

After rubbing my skin raw and dousing myself with seven gallons of vanilla-scented perfume, I collapsed into the chair opposite the fire and accepted another drink. My vision from earlier rushed back to me, and I felt the stress from the night slip away. So what if Dracula was still out there and Heathcliff was being a shithead and we now had to contend with yet another fictional character, this one without a head? Here I was in my chair by the fire. The world's hottest gothic antihero was devouring my body with his smoldering eyes while a lanky criminal mastermind rose from his computer to rustle up a midnight snack in the kitchen. All I needed was some hot chocolate and my favorite raven and...

"Hey, where's Quoth?"

"He's not back from his *private lesson*," Heathcliff grumped. "Morrie's hot chocolate is vastly inferior. He doesn't put in nearly enough whisky."

I raised an eyebrow. Quoth had been invited by Mrs. Ellis to exhibit his paintings in the village's first-ever All Souls Day art walk for the final day of the festival. It was like a trick-or-treat path for adults – visitors could walk to different locations in the village to experience spooky art and performance pieces and buy treats from local artisans. It was a neat idea. The date was fast looming, and Quoth couldn't think of much else. He was either at his school's art studio or having private tutorials with his new favorite teacher, Professor Sang. When he was at home, he spent every spare moment hunched over a canvas in his attic room, refusing to let me see any of his creations.

Even so, I was surprised he was still out. It was well past midnight. Surely the school had health and safety regulations that prevented students and teachers camping over? And Quoth *knew* Morrie and I would be going after the next box of earth tonight. I pulled out my phone and checked the messages. He hadn't even replied to my texts. I couldn't help the hurt welling inside me that Quoth hadn't even checked that we got home safe.

That's not fair. This exhibition is important to him, and you know he needs this. It's so hard for him to come out of his shell and be around people. If he can speak through his artwork, it's one step closer to him feeling truly free.

Heathcliff touched his hand to my knee, his thumb moving over the fabric. "No message from the little birdie?" His eyes met mine with intensity. I knew for all he griped about Quoth, he was worried about him, too.

At least, I thought he was worried. It was hard to tell with Duke Pricklebum. The more Heathcliff pulled back from Morrie and me, the less I was sure about anything.

"Nothing." I tossed my phone on the rug. Grimalkin leaped from Morrie's shoulders and dashed across the room to jab it with her paw.

"He'll be back crapping all over the shop in no time. How was the break-in?" Heathcliff sounded like he was asking about the weather. He hadn't even commented about my delightful horsey scent. Did he truly want to be part of this relationship, or had he gone along with it because he needed a distraction from losing Cathy?

Cathy. I knew she was a fictional character, but I *hated* her and her perfect Cathy-ness. The greatest love story ever written was about Heathcliff and Cathy, not Heathcliff and Mina and Morrie and Quoth. I'd fallen hard for Heathcliff because of the way he loved me, intensely and possessively, but every time he drew away, I wondered if he was saving a piece of himself for his doomed ex-lover, hoping that maybe one day she'd appear in the shop.

It wasn't fair on either of us, but you couldn't help the way you feel, especially when someone who once told you he'd be with you always went cold. I swallowed a lump in my throat.

"We managed to get the box, but then we were chased by vicious dogs. Luckily, the Headless Horseman showed up and scared them away, but now he's *our* problem." I shuddered as a bang sounded from downstairs, followed by Socrates yelling something incomprehensible in Ancient Greek. "Why are there so many more fictional characters appearing now?"

Even though I couldn't barely see his features in the gloom, I felt Heathcliff's glare boring into me.

"What?" I flicked my dark hair over my shoulder and glared right back at him.

"Isn't it obvious? They're attracted to you," he said. "The waters of Meles flow in your veins. These bastards are attracted to it like Morrie to my whisky stash."

"But my father was here for years, and things were never this bad, were they?"

"No," Heathcliff admitted. "According to his records, it was a couple of fictional characters a year at most. It's been the same since I took over the shop."

"So what's changed? And why did it have to change *now?* We've got enough on our hands with Dracula and Mrs. Ellis' bloody Halloween extravaganza without turning the shop into a halfway house for literature layabouts."

"And don't forget your dad's mysterious note," Morrie piped up.

That's right. Dad's note. The note he asked Sherlock Holmes to deliver. The note that had chased me across space and time to impart vital information.

The note that read simply:

BRING THE WINE

By Hathor, WTF, Dad?

I clutched my head in my hands. "Bring the wine? What does it even mean? Which wine? Where am I bringing it? It sounds more like a text from Jo than a vital clue from my dear departed time-traveling father."

"I guess it's another mystery for the great Mina Wilde to solve."

"Not tonight." I yawned. Grimalkin's body hummed with bliss as she settled herself into a ball on my lap. "The great Mina Wilde needs sleep."

And to get away from Heathcliff and his indifference.

I cradled a sleepy Grimalkin on my shoulder and clambered up the rickety stairs to Quoth's room. His bed lay under the window, the covers strewn all about. When I first saw his attic bedroom, it made me sad. Why should Quoth be hidden away up here in the smallest, pokiest room in the house? Now that Quoth was going to art school and being in the world more, he needed his room to be a sanctuary – a place where he could be completely himself. So we made it beautiful. The four of us repainted the walls and built a bird gym in the corner, with a swing and a tunnel and a little box for his favorite berries. His artwork adorned the walls, and Morrie even gifted him with a sound system so he could play his favorite post-punk music while he painted.

I paused in front of Quoth's easel. It held a large, square canvas covered in a grey sheet, tacked down at the edges so no one could peek. My fingers itched to tear away the sheet and see what my beautiful artist was working on. I shook my head. I wouldn't do that to Quoth, not when he'd asked us to respect his desire to keep the paintings a surprise.

The string of garlic around Quoth's window had fallen down again. I found it in the corner and tacked it up. I didn't have to see out the window to know that across the street a bat hung in the window.

Dracula's eyes bridged the darkness between us, watching me, biding his time.

I drew the curtains with more force than I intended and lay down on the bed, sliding Grimalkin's sleeping body onto my feet. I breathed deep as Quoth's light, crisp scent rose from the sheets.

I had everything I could possibly want, right here in this bookshop. But that meant I had so much to lose. On the other side of the street loomed the greatest danger humankind had ever known, and I was responsible for stopping him.

"Mina. Miiiiina…"

He hissed my name through the darkness – the nightly taunt that only I could hear. This was his game when the moon rose him from his daily slumber – to ensure that even in sleep I could not escape the looming terror of his presence.

"I have crossed eons of time to find you, Miiiiina. Soon, I will taste your sweet blood and we will be together for all eternity."

CHAPTER THREE

*H*eathcliff's mouth hung open, his booming cry made mute by the blood burbling from the jagged wound in his throat. He staggered back, his dark eyes wide with fear, his hands clasping the gash as if he could push the blood back into his body.

No, please no.

I tried to will myself to run to him, to hold him in my arms. But my limbs remained frozen. All I could do was glance down at my hands, stained with dark blood. *Heathcliff's blood.*

And I knew. The sickening truth slammed into me.

I did this…I killed Heathcliff.

"M…mmm…mmminaaaaaa…" Heathcliff tried to speak. With one last surge of effort, he launched himself at me, but he slipped in his own blood and crashed to the ground. His glassy eyes blinked, once, twice, then no more. Their light dimmed. I licked his blood from my fingers. It tasted like the finest whisky.

I killed Heathcliff.

I drank of Heathcliff.

I am Heathcliff. I am...

I bolted upright. "Fuck."

Sunlight poured in the window, casting a beam of light across the narrow bed. But in my head I was still standing over Heathcliff's body, sucking every last drop of blood from my fingers. *I can taste him on my lips...*

My heart clattered against my ribs. I held up my hand in the light. No blood. Not a drop. I wiped my clammy forehead as soft lips touched my shoulder. A warm arm closed around my waist, drawing me back to press against a hard body. Kisses feathered along my collarbone.

"Waking up next to you is a beautiful gift."

Quoth. No one else spoke like poetry.

My body responded to his words. Warmth pooled in my belly, spreading out through my limbs.

"You were having the dream again."

"It's just a dream. He can't hurt me in my dreams if I have you protecting me. When did you get in?" I reached up to run my fingers through his hair. Quoth had the kind of arse-length, thick, shimmering hair that shampoo companies envied. It fell through my fingers like silk, and where it brushed my skin, it left a trail of fire.

In his arms, Dracula's dream threats couldn't touch me.

"I think it was about 3AM. You were sound asleep." Quoth's lips brushed against my earlobe as his fingers slid into my panties, finding my clit and stroking it softly, slowly. "I crawled in beside you and you grunted at me and stole all the blankets."

I stroked his face as he touched me. The light hit him in such a way that his skin seemed even paler than usual, luminous like spun gold. His hair spilled over his shoulders, grazing my bare skin. I pulled his lips to mine as his fingers worked their magic on me, dipping and swirling, teasing a delicious ache in my belly. Within moments, I shuddered and gasped in his arms.

After I was done, Quoth pulled me back into his arms, nuzzling his head into the crook of my shoulder. My gaze fell on the canvas covered with the sheet. "I can't wait to see your artwork."

Quoth's breath hitched. He still struggled with the idea of sharing who he was with the world, even with me. He made himself vulnerable through his art – with every stroke of the brush he feared he wasn't good enough, he didn't belong, he should be hiding away instead of baring his beautiful soul to the world. It'd been hard enough for him having some of his paintings on sale in the shop, even though they were a big hit with our slightly strange clientele. It was a huge deal for him to exhibit for the public like this – to be in the room while people judged him.

But I wasn't people, I was his girlfriend. He knew I loved everything he did. I didn't understand what he could possibly be nervous about.

"I can't wait for you to see them, too," he whispered against my ear. "You're going to be so surprised."

"Good surprised, right?"

Quoth chuckled, kissing the sensitive skin on the back of my neck. And I wasn't thinking about paintings or Dracula anymore.

I left Quoth sleeping, the covers pulled up over his head, and padded downstairs. Oscar followed me, and I let him out the back door into the alley so he could do his business.

I tiptoed downstairs and peeked into the storage closet, aka Morrie's room. His bed was already empty and neatly made with hospital corners. He'd probably gone out for coffee. Heathcliff had thrown our machine against the wall after Morrie pinched his arse the other week, and we hadn't replaced it yet, and the Napoleon of Crime couldn't function without his morning latte. I heard a thump from the Philosophy room, but I didn't want to deal with Socrates without coffee, so I headed back upstairs.

Heathcliff slumped in his chair beside the dead fire, his head flopped against his shoulder, and his big hands wrapped around Grimalkin's body as she slept contentedly in his lap. He looked so peaceful and at ease, so unlike my Heathcliff of late.

I bent down and brushed my lips over his, breathing in the woody, heathen scent that never failed to do magical things to my insides. Heathcliff cracked open one eye, training the wine-dark orb on me.

"Morning," he murmured. I stared into the inky depths of him and didn't know how I'd ever doubted his love. I'd caught him before his morning coffee, before he had time to pull on his mask of indifference, and he was full to bursting with savage need.

Also, very definitely not bleeding to death from a wound on his neck, which was how I prefer my men.

I grinned and held my finger to my lips. I dumped Grimalkin on the floor and gave her a nudge with my boot. She shot me a filthy look as she padded downstairs, Oscar at her heels.

You're one to judge, Grandma. I heard you and Mr. Hartford's tomcat getting up to all sorts of kinky shenanigans behind the rubbish bins last night.

Heathcliff's eyes were wide open now, hard and hungry, every trace of indifference wiped away. I straddled the armchair, lifting my skirt to settle myself on top of Heathcliff's thighs. His fingers slid over my skin, drawing out the wild animal inside me, the one who didn't know if she wanted to fight or fuck.

One thing that'd been amazing about losing my sight was how much more time I spent noticing other sensations. Before, just the sight of Heathcliff's possessive scowl would turn me weak at the knees. Now, it was the brush of his bristly beard against my skin, or the way his fingers dug into me a little too hard, as if he was terrified that if he let me go I'd float away. And his taste... that glorious bite of whisky-laced sin that could only be Heathcliff Earnshaw.

I tasted him now, my lips devouring him. He shoved up my Sex Pistols tee and palmed my breast, squeezing the sensitive flesh until I moaned against his lips. There was no pretense here. Heathcliff didn't play games like Morrie, and he didn't wait for permission like Quoth. He growled, low in his throat, a man possessed by need of me. That was so damn addictive.

I raised myself up on my knees to tug off his boxers, then lowered myself onto his cock. He hadn't touched me in so long, and now he was inside me, and he felt *amazing*. I wriggled my hips, a smile playing on my lips as he touched the dark, secret places inside me.

Heathcliff made this choking sound that pooled heat in my belly. He thrust inside me with a force that nearly bucked me off the chair. *Yes, please.* His hand clamped behind my neck, holding me in place while his whole body raged into mine. This was what it meant to love Heathcliff Earnshaw, to love a tsunami as it crashed over you and dragged you under.

I ground my hips, meeting every thrust with my own power. My clit pounded him as the pressure inside me built and built. I dug my nails into his shoulders. My head fell back. For a moment, I was nothing but stars exploding from the depths of his fathomless eyes.

I breathed him in until my body was made of him, pieces of Heathcliff inside me, driving me mad, loving me always.

He came with a bellow that shook the house. I rested my forehead against his, tracing the planes of his face with my fingers. His eyes were so dark they sucked in the light, except for the stars in the heart of them that burned for me. I relished this picture of him, the vision of him as he truly was. I knew one day it would be gone for me. I wasn't sad about losing my sight anymore, but I was determined to enjoy my vision while I could.

I was also determined that now I had Heathcliff alone and somewhat under my spell, I'd confront him about the way he'd been acting. I pulled back from him and folded my arms across my chest. "What's been going on with you?"

"The usual. Vampires threatening us, customers existing,

Grimalkin coughing up hairballs on my face." He wriggled his hips, trying to slide out from under me, but I held firm. Instead, he grabbed my thighs, lifted me off him like I was a light summer sweater, and deposited me roughly on the chair opposite him.

"Oh, no you don't." I caught his wrist as he tried to escape toward the kitchen. "You've been acting strange lately. Cold. Aloof."

"Nonsense. I'm trying to be more positive every day." Heathcliff forced a smile that looked more like a grimace. "Today I'm positive everyone's a wanker."

"I'm serious, Heathcliff. We're all tired and stressed, but this is more than that for you. I don't get it. I thought you and Morrie sorted your shit out that night at the falls. Or is this not about Morrie? Is it me? Have your feelings about me changed? Because if you can't love me the way you loved Cathy, then I understand—"

"It's not you," he growled with a fierceness that pierced my soul. "You're everything. I could no sooner forget you than my existence."

"Then what? I'm on edge all the time, thinking that any moment Dracula will sneak up behind me and sink his teeth into my neck. I could really use you – *all* of you, not these cold pieces you have on display. And so could Morrie."

"I'm right here."

A tear fell from the corner of my eye. Heathcliff touched it with his thumb, wiping it away before it scoured its way down my cheek. "You're not here. You've gone somewhere else."

Heathcliff opened his mouth, shut it again. His coal-black eyes swiveled to the ceiling, and he stared for a long time at some object out of my sight. I hold my breath, daring to hope he would break down and free himself from whatever darkness caged his heart.

"It's nearly 9AM," he murmured. "Customers will be waiting outside."

I resisted the urge to throttle him. "Heathcliff, why can't—"

"Go open up the shop," he muttered. "I'll take a shower."

"*I* should have the shower. I'm the one with your cum running down my leg—"

"Don't," he whispered. "I love knowing that you're working with my seed inside you."

I folded my arms. "That's hot in mafia romance books, but in the real world, it's sticky and gross, *especially* when you're acting all emotionally-stunted. I'll only be a minute, and then the shower's yours."

Heathcliff lunged for me, but I sprung off him and darted away.

"Come back here," he howled. "You know you won't be a minute. Between you and Morrie and that poxy lot downstairs, there won't be a drop of hot water left for me."

"Then perhaps you should consider installing that second bathroom. Or showering with Morrie," I yelled over my shoulder as I slammed the door behind me.

I turned on the water, shoving the dial right to the end to get as much water as possible, which was nothing but a limp, lukewarm trickle. The boys redid the bathroom as a surprise for me when I moved into the shop. It was beautiful, but Heathcliff was right. Lately, the hot water hadn't been lasting long, the flow had slowed to a dribble, and sometimes the sink didn't drain well. I'd also noticed a few loose floorboards in front of the Classics shelves, and a kind of general aura of *dampness* in the shop. When I mentioned calling in a plumber to Heathcliff, the resulting temper tantrum was so obscene I didn't bother again. Nevermore Bookshop was falling apart at the seams and he was fine with it, and I had too many other problems.

Freshly showered and with my makeup applied (how does a blind woman do her makeup? Braille labels on my eyeshadows, tattooed brows and mascara, which hurt like a bitch but now I look fierce 24/7, and lots of asking Morrie if I look like a drunken circus act), I poked my head into the kitchen. Morrie wasn't back yet and Heathcliff was locked in a heated argument with the toaster. I grabbed a snack bar from the tin and headed downstairs to let Oscar in and open up.

I peeled back the wrapper and took a big bite as I crossed the first-floor landing. I could hear Oscar scrabbling at the door. *I wonder if he—*

"Look alive, m'lady!"

I had just enough time to duck as an arrow soared over my head and embedded itself into the wall behind me.

CHAPTER FOUR

"**W**hat the fuck?"

My body slammed into the balustrade. My knee cracked on the stair, and my heart hammered against my chest. I couldn't see a thing in the gloom, but I knew I'd never heard that voice before. I felt along the wall until my fingers closed around the light switch. I flicked it on, illuminating a weedy man wearing a skintight pair of leggings and a green doublet. In his hands, he held what looked suspiciously like an... archery bow?

By Isis, not another one.

"My apologies, fair maiden." The green-clad archer gave an apologetic bow. "I was attempting to lend my bow to solving your vermin problem, but my shot went a little wide."

"Don't listen to him." A genteel voice with a faint Swiss accent snapped from behind me on the stairs. He'd be a perfectly benign figure if not for the sack over his shoulder that bore the distinct odor of grave-dirt and decay. "That rapscallion wasn't aiming for a mouse. He intended to pierce my skull."

"Upon my honor, 'tis not true." The archer looked shame-faced, but he drew another arrow and aimed his bow at my companion.

"Honor?" The man pushed past me on the stairs, dropping his disgusting sack onto the rug so he could pull on a white lab coat. "You're an outlaw. What good is your honor?"

"It's better than the honor of a crazed doctor," the archer shot back. "At least I only steal from the rich to give to the poor. I saw you stealing from the graves of the innocent to create your aberration—"

"Gentlemen, *please.*" I held up my hands. "It's too early in the morning for this, and I haven't had my coffee yet. Victor, take your night's findings down to the basement. I'll call you when your coffee's here. And you," I nodded to the newcomer. "Tell me, although I think I already know, who are you?"

The archer puffed out his chest. "I'm called Robin of Sherwood. I command a band of merry men who steal from the rich to give to the poor, and protect the good people of Sherwood Forest from the tyranny of the Sheriff of Nottingham."

"It's nice to meet you, Robin." I rubbed my eyes as a squiggle of orange danced across my vision. "Why did you shoot at Victor here?"

"Just look at him! Those beady eyes, that villainous mustache, that sack of pilfered body parts over his shoulder."

I sighed again. I couldn't argue with that logic.

"I resent that." Victor rubbed his face. "This is a very stylish mustache."

Robin peered around the shop. "I appear to have become drunk on ale and woken up in your strange abode. As I was hunting for my dinner, I noticed him leaving this building with that empty sack, so I followed him, thinking he might be an innocent peasant poaching to feed his family from the King's Forest. Only instead of setting snares, he went to a burial ground and…" Robin shook his head. "I shall say no more. I will not subject such a fair maiden to a description of his depravity. He is a cox-comb of the first order, and I'll—"

"Coffee!" Morrie called. The bell tinkled as the door swung shut.

"Coffee? Is that some kind of sorcery to banish this crooked-nosed knave?"

"Coffee is definitely sorcery, but of the most benevolent kind." I threw my arm around Robin's shoulders. "I have much to teach you. You're a long way from Sherwood now, my friend."

Morrie struggled past carrying two cardboard trays piled high with beverages. A stampede ensued as fictional characters appeared from every corner of the shop and rushed Morrie. Coffee wasn't available to most of them in their books, and they seemed to have developed an addiction. Understandable.

"Okay, so I've got a tall, double-shot latte with cream and caramel drizzle for Socrates..." The philosopher grabbed the milky drink and slurped happily.

"And a triple-shot soy latte for the esteemed Dr. Franken-stein..." Victor accepted his takeaway cup and slouched off toward the cellar. He'd barely emerged from the gloom since arriving at Nevermore three days ago, except to make his midnight trips to the graveyard for reasons I preferred not to ask about. Next, Morrie handed me my drink and set Heathcliff's on the desk for him.

The Headless Horseman hovered behind Robin, and Morrie shrugged as he handed him a cup. "I didn't know what you wanted, mate, so I got you a long black."

Our cranially-challenged friend inclined his stump toward the cup, straightened up, and poured the drink into the air where his head used to be. Coffee splashed into his neck cavity and disap-peared into his spectral body. Morrie collapsed into his velvet chair and brought his own cup to his lips, while Robin swiped Heathcliff's and sipped, his brown eyes widening with delight.

Our first customer of the day was Bernie, a pensioner from the same retirement village Mrs. Ellis now called home. Bernie came each week to browse the Erotica section. We had guys like Bernie in regularly – always men, always bearded, and always in outfits they assumed made them invisible but actually made them stand out a mile as the type of bloke who needed a weekly visit to an erotica bookshelf. Bernie started his search for scandalous reading material in the same place he always did – the railway section, where he removed the dust jacket from a book on GWR rolling stock and folded it over a collection of antiquarian lesbian lithographs. He then sat in the corner for an hour or so with his secret book. I was grateful I now couldn't see across the room, because I didn't know what he got up to over there, but he was quiet and never disturbed the other customers, and he always swapped the dust jackets back when he was done, so we let him be.

A group of Lycra-clad cyclists came in after Bernie. They headed straight for the ordinance map section, unfolded every map and spread them out over the table to plan their route, upturning the stuffed armadillo in the process. After a loud argument about B-roads, they left the shop, leaving me with the impossible task of refolding the maps while they spent a further twenty-minutes blocking the entrance while they fiddled with straps and helmets and drink bottles.

"This is Satan's origami," I muttered to Victor as he emerged from the cellar. "You're good at stitching things back together. I'd appreciate a little help."

"I can't. I'm in the middle of a very precise operation. I only came upstairs to remind you about the plumbing." Victor hiked up the hem of his trousers, and I saw that at least three inches of fabric were completely soaked. "It's awfully difficult to focus on my work with the water level rising down there."

"I'll get to it, Victor. I promise." He'd been bugging me about the leak in the basement ever since he'd arrived. I called Handy

Andy, local village jack-of-all-trades, and he said he'd pop in to take a look when he had a chance, which by handyman standards meant I wouldn't see him until next June. In a village like Argleton, you had to learn to go at a slower pace.

Heathcliff came downstairs after the cyclists left – a blessing, considering the insults he usually hurled at them. He took over counter duties (watching for shoplifters and glowering at anyone who looked like they wanted to haggle) so I could make a quick visit to the Occult room.

I entered the store room – aka, Morrie's makeshift bedroom – and closed the door behind me. Heathcliff had placed strings of fairy lights along the shelves, which I clicked on to help me navigate the cramped space. I located the secret door to the occult books, which we had dubbed our 'war room.' On a blackboard attached to the wall, Quoth had written 'earth boxes' in big, loopy writing with glow-in-the-dark chalk so it stood out to me more than the normal stuff (although it did kind of look like toxic waste). Beneath were two columns – one for us and one for Sherlock down in London to tally the boxes of Transylvanian dirt we'd destroyed.

I made a mark under our column and leaned in close to count up the tallies. I counted three times, just in case I missed one. Sherlock had taken out fifteen around London and Dartmoor, where Grey Lachlan had several properties, and we'd found a further thirty-one scattered around Barsetshire and nearby Loamshire, where the rest of his property portfolio was located. I couldn't believe Grey hadn't thought we'd check his other properties after he caught us at one, but then he'd try to frame Morrie for murder in an elaborate setup just to remove who he perceived as his strongest adversary from the game. He wasn't exactly going to make the Queen's Honors list for intelligence.

We'd destroyed forty-six boxes of earth.

We were so close. And yet, we still had four more to go before we could move against Dracula, and time was running out. We'd been at this for months now and I was so tired of looking over my shoulder all the time. Not when he'd become bold, killing people and draining their blood without a care for the police investigating the crimes. The more he drank, the stronger he'd become.

We knew what Dracula and Grey wanted – the bookshop and access to the waters of Meles. Grey knew about the tunnel stretching between our shop and the basement of Mrs. Ellis' old flat. We barricaded it closed (Handy Andy was supposed to brick it up, but of course he hadn't shown up to do it yet) and bedecked the bookshop with garlic and holy water and crucifixes galore. Dracula needed to enter the shop to access the time-traveling room, but he couldn't cross our threshold without us inviting him in. Unless...the bookshop didn't belong to us any longer.

So Grey tried to buy us out. When we refused to sell, Grey resorted to driving us barmy with incessant construction noise at all hours and blocking access to the shop from Butcher Street with his scaffold to cut off our foot traffic. But if he thought that would break us, he didn't know Mina Wilde.

The Dave Danvers First Annual Science Fiction Convention at Nevermore raked in a ton of money, and the shop's social media presence had become so famous that customers were seeking us out. We wrote to the council and they made him remove the scaffold blocking our front door.

I couldn't help but wonder if littering Argleton with the bodies of dead women was the next stage of the plan. Would Dracula soon have the power to take whatever he wanted from us?

I sent off a quick text to Sherlock, letting him know our current total. We'd started off as bitter rivals, but he wasn't so bad...now that he lived in London and had a new boyfriend. He replied a moment later pointing out that, according to Morrie's app, we'd checked every one of Lachlan's properties. We didn't have a single clue where Grey and Dracula hid the remaining earth.

Great.

I slumped down in front of the plinth and pulled over the clues my father sent – the letters, the scrawled words in the empty pages of the occult books, and the book about the Frog-Mouse War that conveniently appeared while we were dealing with the Terror of Argleton. I flattened out his latest letter and read it over again.

BRING THE WINE

What are you trying to tell me, Dad? Why can't you—
"Mina! Your mother's here!"
Shit.
It was always a bad idea to leave my mother and Heathcliff alone together.

I slammed the books shut and raced out of the room, pushing the storage room door shut behind me. Downstairs, Mum bent over the desk, brandishing a heavy leather-bound volume with a crystal glued on its spine in Heathcliff's face.

"...I don't see why I can't have a teeny, tiny corner of the shop dedicated to my bibliomancy booth. I'm going to be the hit of the festival, and customers will flock here for my accurate predictions, and it's very *on-brand—*"

Heathcliff narrowed his dark eyes at her. "You want to charge people to randomly open books?"

"I'll have you know that the art of bibliomancy has been practiced for centuries by the Greeks, the Romans, and in the Muslim world. It's more than just opening a book at random and using the text to divine the future. I have to channel the inner thoughts of the authors and capture the universe's natural story. It's very complex, and requires a deep, spiritual connection. You couldn't possibly understand..."

"Mum, hi." I shoved myself between them, grabbing the book from her hands before she could whack Heathcliff over the head with it. "What's this about bibliomancy?"

"Mina." She ignored my questions and wrapped me in a huge embrace. "I'm very annoyed at you. Have you been ignoring me?"

"Not at all. I—"

"Because I'm worried about you. Whenever I call you're too busy. You seem to be working all hours and you haven't been over for dinner in weeks. It's not healthy to ignore your mother like this."

"I'm not ignoring you, Mum. It's just been busy here at the shop and getting ready for the Halloween festival and Quoth's art exhibition."

"That's no excuse not to talk to your mother. I wanted to give you this." She scrabbled around in her purse and pulled out a tub of greenish goop. "It's a healing balm made from ground-up Venus flytraps, and it's supposed to have *amazing* properties. The lovely young man who sold it to me said it cured his wife's cancer."

"Mum, I don't have cancer."

"I know, dear, but this *repairs cells*. That's the whole point. It can repair your eyes." She shot me a triumphant look as she thrust the goop toward me, as if she'd just performed an epic mic drop and left every ophthalmologist in the world in awe of her genius.

Ever since my eyesight started to deteriorate, Mum's been determined to find the miracle cure that will restore my retinas. So far, she'd given me a rosehip and carrot eyeball wash, and an entire garden of multi-colored crystals to put under my pillow.

I held the container up to the light, but that made the green look even more disgusting. "If it's so miraculous, why isn't the lovely young man's wife all over the news talking about this stuff?"

"Oh, apparently she died of spontaneous liver failure," Mum

waved her hand dismissively. "But she went to her grave cancer-free."

"Thanks, Mum. That's very thoughtful of you." I dropped the container into my purse, where it would never see the light of day again. "So, bibliomancy? While it's a lovely idea for the festival, we don't really have a lot of space in the shop, so I don't think—"

"What's this?" Mum plucked the small black box from my purse and forced open the latch.

"Oh, it's a..." I scrambled for an answer but came up completely blank. "Well, it's a vampire-hunting kit."

Mum looked at me like I'd gone insane.

"It's just a bunch of garlic, holy water, and communion wafers. Morrie made it for me. It's kind of a joke. I mean...it's not a very funny joke, but it's nice he wants to protect me. You know all those murders in the village, where the victim is drained of blood with the puncture marks in their neck?"

"Of course I know. I've been on the front lines, trying to get the police to take this vampire threat seriously." Mum folded her arms. "Can you believe Inspector Hayes had the gall to say that vampires don't exist? When the evidence is right in front of his eyes. If they don't start taking this threat seriously, then the Spirit Seekers Society will have to take matters into our own hands."

Panic seized me. The last thing we needed was my mother swanning around town slaying anyone with a lisp or taste for rare steak. "Vampire or not, Mum, this is a dangerous serial killer. You need to let the professionals do their jobs."

Like me and Heathcliff and Morrie and Quoth.

"Pffft, fat lot of good they've done so far, with a third girl dead and our beloved historical cemetery looking like a slice of Swiss cheese. Although I must say, I'm grateful that you're taking this supernatural threat so seriously..." Mum fingered the box, and I could see the wheels turning in her head. She wore the look she got when she sensed a get-rich-quick opportunity. But what in my vampire kit could possibly be giving her an idea? I didn't want to guess. She set down the box very deliberately and clapped her hands.

"Well, love, I have to go. I have things to do."

"But don't you want to convince me of the merits of bibliomancy—"

"Oh, what's the point? I'd better go, I've got a Spirit Seekers meeting..." Mum gave me a dismissive wave as she barreled out of the room.

"But you left your bibliomancy book behind!"

"I don't need it," she called back. "Heathcliff's right. It's a bunch of nonsense."

The door slammed behind her.

"Did you hear that?" Heathcliff leaned back in his chair. "She says I'm right."

I nodded. "Of all the bad omens we've received this morning, the fact my mother agrees with you has me the most concerned."

CHAPTER FIVE

"*J*think you'll enjoy this book." I smiled at my bespeckled customer as I rang up his purchase. It was the day before the Halloween festival opening, and he was one of a busload of American tourists who'd stopped in the village for the occasion. He looked thoroughly miserable in his sodden clothing. The skies had opened up – not the best day to capture idyllic village life, but definitely a taste of authentic Britain.

"Thank you, young lady." He wrung out his cap, squeezing a puddle of water onto our already squelchy rug. "I must say, you're more pleasant to deal with than your other salesperson. He's a bit...odd. He asked me all these deep, personal questions, and then gave me a huge lecture about not believing in the gods."

Not again. "Yes, thank you. I'll talk to him."

The tourists filed out, exclaiming in huge voices over every little detail of 'Jolly Old England' and talking excitedly about their pub lunch. I flipped the 'out to lunch' sign on the door, even though it was only 10AM, and went to find my 'salesperson.'

He was in the Philosophy section, of course, his nose buried in Nietzsche. He wrinkled his nose and tossed the volume over his shoulder, where it joined a pile of crumpled books on the floor. "What poppycock."

"Listen, Socrates." I grabbed a volume of Kant's *Critique of Pure Reason* from his fingers before it joined Nietzsche in the crumpled heap of torn pages on the floor. "I know you're trying to help, but you've got to stop this."

"Eh?" Socrates cupped a wizened hand over his ear.

"You can't rip up the books you disagree with, or we'll have nothing to sell. And no talking to the customers."

"Yes, thank you. I do like cucumbers." Socrates turned back to the book.

"YOU CAN'T TALK TO THE CUSTOMERS."

"But how else am I supposed to re-establish my School of Thinking? From these turbid bird-brains I must extract those students who will most benefit from my tutelage." Socrates tossed Kant's book over his shoulder in disgust and picked up another. "I mean, look at these ridiculous notions. What is this nihilism? It means nothing to me."

I had to bite my lip to keep from laughing. "Nihilists reject religion and morals because they believe life is meaningless. I think you'd find it interesting, actually—"

"But not one of these so-called thinkers ever acknowledges that the only true wisdom is knowing that you know nothing. Why, just this morning I was taught an important philosophical lesson by your bird."

I rubbed my head. "You saw Quoth? Where is he? He didn't come home again last night."

"I was gazing out the open window, up at the glorious clouds, and pondering the nature of the universe, when he flew inside over my head and shat on my face. It's an important lesson that all philosophers should spend more time questioning the universe than opening their mouths to talk about it."

"Yes, that's an excellent lesson. But I need you to keep your questions to *yourself*." I took his arm and guided him out of the

Philosophy room. "I know it's difficult for you to understand, but the world is a very different place from the Athens you left behind. No one wants a half-naked old man quizzing them on the meaning of life while they're hunting for the latest Jeffery Archer, got it?"

"But what do philosophers of your time do?" His jaw wobbled.

"They're on social media." I pulled out my phone and showed him how to scroll through Youtube. "Look, this is Peter Jordanson; he's a professor of philosophy and he has half a million followers. If you want to probe the mysteries of the universe, do it in ten-second video content about the war to save our corruptible youth."

I left Socrates happily watching Peter Jordanson videos and went to look for Quoth. I found him curled up in bed, the curtains drawn, his long eyelashes tangled together. I shook his shoulder, but he didn't stir. I left him to sleep and headed back downstairs just as a group entered the shop. I assumed they were another bus tour group (the overabundance of orthopedic shoes was a big clue). But instead of spreading out and exclaiming over the quaint reading nooks and knickknacks around the shop, they marched straight to the counter in military formation. I recognized the woman at the front as Dorothy Ingram, the hyper-religious matron who I'd once thought guilty of murdering members of the Argleton Banned Book Club. We managed to clear Dorothy's name, but she'd never exactly been grateful. I didn't think Dorothy Ingram could be anything other than sour.

"Mina." Dorothy's mouth pursed into a fine line as she rapped her stick on the floor. Her tone implied she'd been expecting to find me cavorting with demons and was a little disappointed I was instead pricing new stock.

"Dorothy, it's *nice* to see you again." I couldn't resist adding, "Are you excited about the Halloween festival?"

"*Hardly.* Mabel has turned our beloved village into a pageant of demonic depravity." Dorothy frowned. "Even our dear new vicar, the Reverend Mosley, has been corrupted. He's actually allowing a Satanic choir to perform in our church tomorrow! Even with all the hellish goings-on in the graveyard."

"Oh, yes, I heard about the grave-robbing. Such a shame." I tried not to wince as Victor crashed around down in the cellar.

"It's not just disturbing the dead! That poor girl was murdered there – by Satanists, of course. The police found a goat skull near the body. There's a Satanic cult in Argleton using the graveyard for their dark rituals. Just last week Hazel saw a man and a woman having *carnal relations* behind the mausoleum. It's positively *depraved*."

"Sounds like a typical Saturday night to me," Morrie piped up from behind the poetry shelves.

"This is no laughing matter, Mr. Moriarty." Dorothy's cheeks flushed red with righteous indignation. "I've read all about these Satanic cults – animal sacrifices, ritual murders, *necrophilia*. And it's all in preparation for their bloody Samhain ritual. Desperate measures must be taken to preserve the poor souls of Argleton from the influence of Satan. I'd like to purchase these books."

She slid a list across the desk. I handed it to Morrie, who read through the titles with a raised eyebrow. "The *Clavicle of Solomon*, The *Book of Soyga*, the *Saducismus Triumphatus*, the *Rohonc Codex*... These are some of our rarest occult books. Are you looking to summon Beelzebub for a little depraved carnal relations yourself?"

"We're holding a book burning." Dorothy sniffed. "We've raised the funds to purchase these books so that we can make sure no innocent soul will lay hands on them."

What?

I shook my head. "You can't burn these. Some of them are important historical texts—"

"They are vile tomes written to corrupt good Christian minds. They are the work of Lucifer and his demons, and they must be burned. But since I know you both clearly have sympathy for the devil—"

I nodded my head. "It's a great Stones song."

"—and I knew you'd never hand over these books willingly, we, the committee for the Defense against Immorality, Adultery, Bestiality, Lucifer and the Occult—" she gestured to her posse "—have raised the money to purchase them. So hand them over."

"You know, your committee name spells DIABLO," Morrie said.

I snorted back a laugh. Dorothy's face went so red I swore steam would come out her ears.

"He's right, Dorothy," Cassandra Irons said feebly. "Defense against Immorality, Adultery, Bestiality, Lucifer and the Occult spells DIABLO—"

"Yes, well, that was a deliberate act to draw attention to the importance of our cause." Dorothy rapped her stick for emphasis. "It highlights how Satan has penetrated every layer of our lives. You haven't got those books yet. Please hurry, I don't have all day."

"I'm sorry," Morrie said sweetly. "We've just this minute sold out of all these books."

"Every single one?" Dorothy narrowed her eyes.

"What can I say?" he shrugged. "It's the Satan-worshippers in this town. They're insatiable for knowledge."

"And you're not just saving them for this Satanic meetup you've got planned?" Dorothy thrust a flyer under my nose. It was one of the advertisements I'd placed in the window, welcoming a visiting occultist for a lecture on necromancy as part of the festival.

"Of course not." I batted my eyelashes. "I've got a whole new batch of evil occult tomes arriving for that."

"This is no laughing matter." Dorothy's stick rapped against the desk. "An innocent woman has been killed in our graveyard by a depraved Satan-worshipper, and yet we're continuing with this heathen festival that invites Lucifer into our midst. Mark my words, Mina – the committee for the Defense against Immorality, Adultery, Bestiality, Lucifer and the Occult intends to do something about it."

She spun on her heel and marched off, her army of disapproving old biddies flocking after her.

I turned to Morrie, barely able to conceal my grin. "Satanic feasts being conducted in the Argleton Presbyterian Cemetery. What is the world coming to?"

"I don't believe them for a minute." Morrie shook his head. "Any self-respecting Satanist knows that Lucifer is sick of eating goat and would much prefer pizza."

*F*or the rest of the day, I was too busy with customers to think about Dracula until Socrates bounded downstairs, his flapping makeshift chiton scaring away a group of teens. He waved my phone in my face.

"It's possessed by a demon," he yelled as a tinny rendition of the Sex Pistols' 'God Save the Queen' blared through the speakers.

"That's just the noise it makes when I get a text message." I scanned the message from my girlfriend Jo. She wanted to meet at the pub after work. My heart skipped a beat. Jo was the county medical examiner, which meant she performed the autopsies on Dracula's victims. Jo didn't know that a real-life vampire was loose in the village, or that I was the daughter of the epic poet Homer, or that Heathcliff, Morrie, and Quoth were actually literary characters come to life. I knew she'd want to chat about work, and I was half excited, half dreading what she might've discovered. She'd be one of the few people who could connect these murders to the body used to frame Morrie all those months ago.

I needed to find out what she knew.

"Mind the shop. I'm going to meet Jo." I slung my favorite red jacket over my shoulders and clipped on Oscar's harness.

"Arf!"

"That's right, boy. We're going to see Jo."

We had to walk around the edge of the village green – the whole place was a mess of tangled wires, half-built booths, and piles of pumpkins. Mrs. Ellis stood in the center, surrounded by her posse of spirited ghost hunters, directing the chaos like a conductor of the damned. Despite everything going on, I felt a little flicker of excitement about the festival. Everything looked amazing. *New York City, eat your heart out. Argleton is where it's at.*

I noticed my mother affixing a sign to a booth, but I wasn't close enough to read what it said.

By Artemis, I guess she's found a new scheme. I hope this one doesn't end with a lawsuit or an Environment Agency fine.

As soon as Oscar and I stepped into the pub, Richard rushed over. "Hi, Mina. Jo's in the corner booth. Do you want me to bring Oscar his water bowl and chew toy?"

"Thanks, Richard." Being infamous in Argleton village for solving crimes did have its perks – namely, that I knew all the local business owners and they were happy to accommodate Oscar. Businesses were legally-bound to welcome service dogs on their premises, but they didn't have to be happy about it. But we (well, Heathcliff) gave Richard so much business, and we solved so many murders in the village, that Oscar was a local legend. I still ran into trouble sometimes when I left the village, but I was getting better at standing up for myself and demanding my rights. It didn't hurt that Oscar was freaking adorable, and I loved his big eyes and cleverness as much as I did the guys.

I directed Oscar to find the booth while Richard disappeared behind the bar to get Oscar's things. If he'd discovered the random horse living in his barn, he wasn't saying anything about it. Thank the goddesses for small mercies.

My friend looked up as I slid into the seat opposite her, her eyes rimmed with red. She'd been crying.

"Jo, what happened?" I reached across the table to clasp her hand. Someone had already placed a G&T in front of me. Even when she was upset, Jo thought about me. She was a great friend and I...I never stopped lying to her.

My lies are for her protection.

Jo shook her head. "He's...he's claimed another victim."

I knew she was talking about the Dracula Killer. We hardly talked about anything else since he started littering Argleton with bodies, which made it all the more difficult to keep quiet the fact that the Dracula Killer was *actually* Dracula.

"That's terrible. Do they know—"

"It's Fiona!" Fresh tears streamed down Jo's cheeks.

My heart stuttered. Jo had been seeing Fiona, a beautiful, statuesque Swedish backpacker for the last three months. Jo was completely head-over-heels in love, and it was the most wonderful thing to see. I'd met Fiona a couple of times at the pub, and she seemed exactly like Jo's type – bubbly and fun and not at all squeamish about dead bodies.

Why did Fiona have to die? Why did Dracula have to take away Jo's happiness?

"Jo, I'm so, so sorry. I can't believe she's dead. Are you okay? That's a silly question; of course you're not okay. Can I help with anything? Oh, by Isis, they didn't make you do her autopsy, did they?"

Jo shook her head. Behind her back, a streetlight on the other side of the window illuminated a dark shadow. The Headless Horseman nodded his stump at me as he glided down the side of the building toward the stables. "They've asked the Loamshire office to handle it. They don't allow us to work on people we're close to. And yes, there is something you can do."

"Anything. I'm here for you."

"Listen, Mina. Hayes is completely stumped over these

murders, and Wilson is so busy sneering at Mrs. Ellis' Spirit Seekers Society that she's not taking anything seriously." Jo leaned across the table. Her fingers gripped mine like a vise. "I'm the only one who thinks there's a connection between Fiona's death and that body Kate used to fake her death. I need you to help me."

"Help you how?"

"Do your thing. Use your murderer-catching mojo. Get Morrie to break laws and Heathcliff to break bones if necessary. I don't care. I need to see this killer brought to justice, and the police aren't going to do it. I'll get you access to any information you need. Just find the bastard who did this to Fiona."

I swallowed. "Jo, you do realize you could get in a lot of trouble if they catch me snooping around?"

"I know that. I'm not asking you because I'm crazy with grief and not thinking straight. Well, I am crazy with grief." Jo reached into her pocket and set a small black jewelry box on the table. "I was going to propose to her at the Halloween festival."

"Oh, Jo." Tears pooled in my eyes.

"Yeah, I was going to tell you today, and you were going to try and talk me out of it and tell me that it's too soon and we're too young and I would've said but we're in love and what's the point waiting when you're in love but now *she's dead*." Jo's hands trembled as she gripped her glass. "I know I'm putting my job and reputation at risk here, but I also know that you get results when the police can't. You're not bound by the same rules as they are—"

You could say that again. I thought of Quoth shapeshifting into his raven form to sneak in an open window when we were investigating Ginny Button, or Morrie starting a business to help people fake their own deaths.

"—and you're a good friend and you'll protect me if you can." Jo leaned across the table and squeezed my hand. Her fingers trembled. My heart broke for her. If something happened to one of the guys, I didn't know what I'd do. I remembered the horrible panic that tore through me when Morrie went over the cliff a few months ago, or when I thought Quoth had been hurt by Christina Hathaway.

My stomach twisted. The truth was, we didn't need an investigation. I knew who the killer was – Dracula. My next-door neighbor. I just couldn't say that to Jo.

I could never tell her who I really was or what was going on. Science ruled Jo's life. She believed in empirical evidence and scoffed at the slightest suggestion of spooky goings-on. If I tried to convince her Fiona was murdered by Dracula himself, she'd think I was crazy or taking the piss. She'd never talk to me again.

If we had access to Jo's autopsy findings and the police reports, we might be able to see a pattern in the killings, learn how he was picking these victims, and maybe stop him before he piled up another body.

"Jo, of course I'll investigate. I'll get the guys on the case. Now, let me buy you another drink and you can tell me everything you know about Fiona and the other victims."

CHAPTER SIX

"*I* can't believe she's gone..." Jo stumbled on the steps, her arms flailing wildly as she struggled to stay upright. "I...*hic*...don't know...*hic*...how I'll live without her."

As I helped a distraught and wasted Jo up the last step to her flat, my mind flicked back to the brief period we lived together. Jo had been an...interesting flatmate. Between the hearts in the fridge and the plague of locusts she unleashed inside the house, we never had a dull moment.

As soon as I entered, I noticed a lingering scent – a floral perfume nothing like Jo's usual smoky blend. I flicked on the lights and noticed batik pillows on the sofa, a travel clothesline pegged with outdoorsy clothing, and Polaroid photographs of sights around Barsetshire tagged to the wall – little touches of the life Jo and Fiona had started to forge together.

"So the last time you saw Fiona, she was heading out to the cemetery?"

"Yes. She came to Argleton because her grandfather is buried in the old cemetery and she wanted to place something on his grave. She wanted me to go with her, but I had to go to work, so I said I'd meet her at the Rose & Wimple after. When she didn't show up, I went to the cemetery to look for her, and there she was." Jo jammed her fists into her eye sockets as fresh tears flowed down her cheeks. "I just don't understand it. Who'd kill Fiona just to steal an old box of dirt?"

"What?"

"Fiona's box wasn't with her body. The killer must've taken it." Jo took out her phone and scrolled through the images. I held the phone up to the light, squinting at the screen to make out the vague shape of Fiona holding a small wooden box with an inlaid lid. "Here. That box is filled with dirt from Romania. Fiona visited her family's old farm there – because her grandfather wanted to be buried there, but they'd had to sell it. It's such a sentimental thing, but that was what she was like, you know? So caring…"

Jo trailed off into more sobs. I took the phone from her hands, staring into Fiona's bright face. She inherited her Swedish mother's looks – the statuesque features, the golden blonde hair, the sunshine smile that was for my Jo. *She had so much to look forward to.*

Dracula killed her and stole this box, but that didn't give us any clue as to where he hid it.

"Tell me about the other victims." I pulled Jo down onto the couch. My fingers searched the table for a box of tissues. I felt around a couple of empty wine glasses and something squishy that I'd rather remain ignorant on, but no tissues. I pulled off my scarf and handed it to her, and she blew her nose on it with a loud honk. That was real friendship, right there.

I turned on my phone's voice recorder and set it down in front of Jo. She hugged herself. "The first victim is Miriam Bledisloe, an office worker and keen hiker. Fiona actually met her a few times at meetings of the Argleton Ramblers. Miriam came back from a hike in the Carpathian mountains a couple of weeks ago, and she was found murdered in her home. There was no sign of a break-in, and the only window open was a tiny one way up high that no human could fit through. The police believe the killer was known to her and she let him in the house, and he locked the door after he left. They didn't find anything missing, but Miriam lived alone so it's hard to confirm."

"Okay." So she'd been to Romania recently, hiking in a remote place. She could have brought some dirt home with her. But how would Dracula know this?

Jo continued. "The second victim was Dana Hill, the archaeologist. She was found in the woodshed behind her place. What the papers didn't tell you is that she's been stealing artifacts from the sites she worked on and selling them online to private collectors. When police searched the woodshed, they found all kinds of coins and things she's pilfered from sites around the world. What they didn't find was a shoebox filled with the skull of an Ottoman, still in situ with some jewelry and pottery shards, in the dirt it was found in. Dana had been trying to sell it online that week."

I nodded along, making a mental note to check if this artifact had any connection to Romania.

"Our third victim was Jenna Mclarey. She was the one found in the cemetery, laying over a grave, the body positioned after death with her arms out, like a crucifix. She works in the village market. She's married; the husband's a bit of a troglodyte." Jo took a shuddering breath. "And then there's Fiona. As far as connecting the victims, we're stumped. They didn't know each other – Fiona vaguely knew Miriam, as I said, and Jenna probably knows everyone in the village from her job, but no deep connections. Both Fiona and Miriam have recently traveled to Romania, but there's no suggestion the other two have any connection to that country. Both Jenna and Fiona were killed in the cemetery, but not the others. Why? The only thing suggesting a serial killer is the method of murder, and the only time I've seen anything like it was the Jane Doe in Kate Danvers' case..."

As Jo rambled on, her drunken thoughts leaping from place to place, I texted Morrie to ask him to find out if Dana Hill's Ottoman warrior came from a Romanian site. I wished I could tell my friend what I already knew for a fact – all four victims were in possession of Romanian dirt, and all of them had their blood drained by a monster so that he could become strong enough to drain the world dry.

And Nevermore Bookshop was the only thing standing in his way. No pressure.

CHAPTER SEVEN

"*I* think I know how we can find the remaining containers of dirt," I announced as I stumbled through the door of the shop.

"Where have you been? You were supposed to call one of us to walk you home." Heathcliff grabbed my shoulders, jerking my body against him. "What if Dracula attacked you?"

Oscar whimpered at the sound of Heathcliff's raised voice. It was too dark to see his face clearly, but Heathcliff's words dripped with panic. His fingers dug into my skin.

"Relax, Old Toothy is hardly about to jump out at me on the town green with all of Mrs. Ellis' minions out there setting up the festival. He won't kill me, because he knows I'm Homer's daughter."

"You infuriating woman," Heathcliff roared, tearing his hands from me and spinning away. "He doesn't have to kill you. He could make you a vampire like him. He could take you away from us."

"I'm being careful." I pulled down the neck of my red sweater, showing him the silver crucifix glittering at my throat. "I've got a purse full of holy water and communion wafers. I'm not some damsel in distress who needs supervision, especially not from a boyfriend who's spent the last few months acting like he doesn't give a fuck."

Heathcliff stormed across the room. He turned his back to me and gripped the side of the desk. The rage rolled off him in waves that shook the room.

"I care." He rasped the words so quietly I barely heard them. "I care so much I can't breathe."

"Then act like it. I don't need someone yelling at me. I need *you*, Heathcliff. I need you by my side, sword swinging. Instead, I get this limp indifference—"

Heathcliff roared, tearing his hands through his hair. "Don't you understand that I cannot live without you? If he took you from me, from *us*, then he'd take my soul along with him."

"How can I believe that when you treat me with such indifference?" I shot back. "And what about Morrie? What if Dracula took him instead of me?"

CRASH.

Heathcliff smashed his fist into the desk. The old-fashioned till toppled off the end, scattering coins and money across the rug.

"Then my soul would die twice." Heathcliff's whole body shuddered.

"Heathcliff—"

I reached for his shoulder. I wanted him to face me, to look me in the eye and tell me why he'd been behaving the way he had. But before I could grab him, another hand plunged out of the gloom and snatched him from me.

I swallowed down a scream as the shadowed figure loomed over us. I caught the edge of Morrie's distinct scent.

"Do you mean it?"

"Fuck off," Heathcliff growled.

Morrie tightened his grip on Heathcliff, shaking him with a

strength I didn't realize he possessed. "Do you mean that you would die twice if you lost us?"

The pair of them glared at each other, but I saw now it wasn't hate that flashed between them like a storm crashing against the cliffs. "There's a coal in my chest where my heart should be," Heathcliff choked out. "You and Mina are better off without me. My love is poison. I won't taint you with that the way I've been tainted."

"That's not true." Tears welled in my eyes. "It's the greatest honor of my life to love and to be loved by you. I love you the way a writer loves a story that refuses to fall from their fingers – I love you because you're infuriating and precious and always just out of reach. I don't want you to save me from loving you. I want to throw myself into your fire and burn up inside it. And it's because I love you that what you're doing *hurts*—"

"This isn't about us, gorgeous." Morrie's words dripped with danger. "I know what he's doing. I never thought I'd see the great Heathcliff Earnshaw give way to cowardice."

Heathcliff snarled. He curled his big hands around Morrie's throat, and for a flicker of a moment I wondered how far he'd go to stop Morrie talking.

"I'm terrified of losing you both, you idiot!" Heathcliff yelled into Morrie's face. "Don't you understand that you and Mina mean more to me than myself?"

"Don't you see, Mina? His heart's not coal – it's made of paper. An origami heart that's torn and frayed at the edges, and he thinks to encase it with glass so it can't be torn again. He wants to save us from having our hearts torn up, too. He doesn't seem to realize that the cuts and the rips and the puncture wounds *are* love. You can never keep your heart whole and safe, but when imperfect hearts join together, they—"

Heathcliff cut Morrie off with a searing kiss – a kiss that no man with a coal for his heart could be capable of. In that kiss, I felt everything I'd feared about Heathcliff flip on its head. It wasn't that he was falling out of love with us. He loved us too much, and the idea of hurting us if we lost him burned so deep that he thought the only thing he could do to save us from that hurt was to make us indifferent to him. As if that could ever be possible.

Heathcliff tore himself from Morrie to grip my shoulders again, only this time he mashed his lips to mine. I gasped against the onslaught of his kiss. On his punishing tongue, I read the torment he'd put himself through these last months, believing he had to make us hate him, believing he could possibly *do anything* that would make us hate him, so we could be safe from the pain of losing him.

Behind me, Morrie pressed his body to me, his long arms wrapping around us both. He tangled his fingers in Heathcliff's hair as his lips pressed against the stubble on Heathcliff's cheek.

"I promise you this," he whispered against Heathcliff's skin. "Nothing you do to us will ever diminish who you are in our hearts."

Heathcliff's body stiffened. His lips fell away from mine to kiss Morrie. Then they were both kissing me and I was kissing them and all I wanted was to fill my lungs up with their breath.

Morrie tugged my lip with his tongue, and I buried my face in Heathcliff's hair, and his wildness drew us deeper under his spell. He fisted my shirt in a huge hand, and Morrie's in the other, and yanked us to him so hard he drove the breath from my lungs.

With a growl, Heathcliff swept his arm across the desk. Papers, books, pens, and all the accouterments of our shop scattered across the floor. Morrie's long fingers dug into my thighs as he nudged me forward so the fronts of my thighs rubbed against the wood.

My heart hammered against my ribs. Heathcliff's chest heaved, as though he'd emerged from the gloomiest depths of the ocean and desperately needed air. "I want to see." He gnashed his teeth. "I want to see the two of you with your paper hearts. I want to see you without me."

I didn't understand, but Morrie did. His fingers danced along my spine. "What do you say, gorgeous? Shall we show him that his black soul cannot break us, that there's room enough for two cocks in that beautiful heart of yours?"

Morrie's hand closed around my neck, bending me over until I lay across the desk. "I saw my love lean over my sad bed," he murmured, quoting a Swinburne poem he knew I loved. He curled his fingers into my hair. "Pale as the duskiest lily's leaf or head..."

His free hand slid beneath my sweater, drawing it up, exposing my flesh with quiet reverence. I lay my cheek against the smooth wood, wet and aching between my legs for both of them to spill their pain into me. From this angle, light from the street outside filtered through the window and cast Heathcliff in silhouette at the end of the desk. He stood straight, alert, the wolf anticipating the call of the full moon – his shoulders tense, his body wracked with need.

Morrie recited the poem with his husky voice as he slid my clothes over the tips of my fingers, down my thighs, chasing the ghost of their touch with his own, drawing a long sigh from deep inside me. Heathcliff sucked in a shuddering breath. His eyes burned deeper than Morrie's touch.

"Smooth-skinned and dark, with bare throat made to bite," Morrie continued. "Too wan for blushing and too warm for white..." His fingers stopped their liquid dance. He seemed to reach a decision, for he turned to Heathcliff and drew him in for a kiss that could have toppled mountains, it was that full of dark hunger. In that kiss, they said all they needed to say to each other, all the things they should have said since the falls but couldn't because they were both stubborn bastards and I loved them, I *loved* them, and I loved them together. I loved us together.

"Please," I whispered. The ache inside me had become a beast, snarling and gnashing for the fire that sustained her.

Heathcliff broke the kiss to move around the front of the table as Morrie kneaded my bare ass with one hand while the other slid from my neck to dance along my spine. Heathcliff bent low to kiss me again, this time with a gentle reverence I never knew possible.

"Thank you," he whispered. "Thank you for never giving up on me, for not leaving me in the abyss alone."

Heathcliff deepened the kiss, using his lips and tongue to tell me just how afraid he was of losing me, or of being lost to me. I raised my hand to spread my fingers over his chest. Inside that beast of a man lived a paper heart, torn at the edges but still beating for me, for *us*.

Behind me, Morrie teased my entrance with his tongue, stoking the ache inside me with a firefly touch I tried to chase with my hips. He circled a finger around my clit, and his tongue dipped inside me until I squirmed and begged with thrusting hips for more.

CLANK. Morrie's belt buckle hit the floor. The sound was a bell tolling the crumbling of the walls we'd built to protect ourselves, and the beginning of something more. I didn't realize I'd been holding my breath until Morrie's warm cock slid inside me. Heathcliff caught my sigh on his tongue, and he swallowed it down like it fed his soul.

Morrie cupped my shoulder, holding me down with a firm grip as he drew slowly out of me before luxuriously sliding back in. "This feels amazing," he drawled with that insouciant sneer of his, and I knew the pair of them were having an intense conversation across the table with their eyes – a conversation they'd needed to have for three long years.

Heathcliff's fingers knitted in mine, his eyes devouring me as I curved my neck back and opened my lips. He kissed my forehead and stood. His trousers hit the floor, and a moment later, I tasted his cock on my tongue.

Above me, I heard the smack of their lips, the wetness of their tongues as they kissed, as they shared me the way they'd always wanted to, sharing a piece of themselves with each other.

It was the most exquisite sound in the world, because I knew in the moment of losing control, when my orgasm washed over me and my paper heart burned up in the fire of their love, that Heathcliff could never again believe himself to be made of coal and indifference. We were him, and he was us.

"*T*hat was quite spectacular." Morrie kissed my cheek as he swiped his shirt from the floor. "I mean, obviously I was brilliant as usual, but you two were adequate. Have you been practicing?"

"Don't talk about it," Heathcliff growled as he fumbled with the buttons on his shirt. "I don't need a performance review."

Morrie slapped his back. "Why not? 5-stars for you, Grenadier Grumblebum. I'd shag you again—"

"I'd give *anything* for you to stop talking now." Heathcliff went to his desk drawer to fish out his whisky.

"Anything, you say?" Morrie's devilish grin was back. "How about I get Socrates in here to show you his latest tweet?"

"You didn't." Heathcliff groaned. "Tell me you didn't show the old man how to use social media."

"Blame Mina." Morrie slid his phone from his pocket. "Apparently, *someone* claimed he doesn't approve of slander, so he's currently using it to mock other philosophers with terrible jokes. For a doddery grandfather who can't keep his dick in his sheet, he's actually rather clever. Look at this one: How many surrealists does it take to change a lightbulb? Answer: Baboon."

"He only found out what a lightbulb was yesterday! You had a hand in this, and if he turns this store into some kind of hipster influencer hangout, you'll pay, Moriarty. You'll pay."

I yawned and tapped my phone. It read out the time – 1:03AM. It was late and we had a busy day tomorrow, but I knew even though my body still buzzed from the incredible sex, I wouldn't be able to sleep unless we'd started our work. "Will you both shut up and listen to me? What I was coming home to tell you is that there's been a fourth victim. It's Fiona, Jo's girlfriend. Jo's completely gutted. She wants us to investigate."

"Jo's giving us actual permission to meddle in affairs best left to our upstanding boys and girls in blue?" Morrie leaned forward. "Sign me up."

"It's not much of an investigation." Heathcliff shoved one foot into his trousers, hopping around as he pulled up the leg. "We know who killed her. He's living right across the street, probably perving on Morrie's pale ass through the window."

"Of course he's looking. This ass is a haunted house; it makes people scream when they're inside it." Morrie wiggled his bare ass at the window.

"More like it's full of demons and things that'll kill you," Heathcliff muttered into his drink.

I rubbed my temples, feeling the onset of a headache. "Jo doesn't know about Dracula, so it gives us the perfect excuse to get information from her. For example, it only took three G&Ts tonight to discover the women who were killed could have all been in possession of Romanian soil. That's four women and four containers of soil. Now he's got all he needs, so we have to find and destroy the last of his stash quickly. I also know that Fiona stored her soil in an inlaid wooden box, and another victim, Dana, was probably trying to sell hers online. Well, not the dirt, but the artifacts in the dirt. It's *wild*—"

"Let's not discuss this down here. We don't know who might be listening at the windows." Morrie leaped to his feet and pointed to the stairs. "To the murder room."

"Sssshhhh." I held my fingers to my lips. "Try not to wake any of our guests. Victor's light is still on under the cellar door, and I saw the Headless Horseman going to visit his horse, but we don't exactly need input from Socrates or Robin. I'll go wake Quoth up and—what?"

Even in the darkness, I couldn't miss the strained look between Heathcliff and Morrie.

"Quoth's at the art studio," Heathcliff said. "He left after dinner."

His words punched me in the gut. I was beyond happy Quoth felt ready to display his work for the art-buying public, and I loved the way he'd thrown himself into the exhibition with his whole being, but I missed him. When he was here he acted as if stopping Dracula was the most important thing in the world, but when he was overcome with his art-making, he forgot everyone and everything outside his own head, including me.

He should be here.

But that wasn't fair. Quoth needed this exhibition. He needed to believe in himself as much as I believed in him. And I wouldn't let Dracula destroy Quoth's chance for happiness.

"I'll text him." I sent off a quick message. If Quoth knew what was going on, he'd want to come home and help, I was sure of it.

We crowded into the storage room. Robin Hood poked his head around the door. "Did I hear you say something about murder? Because if you need men of good character to fight alongside you, I volunteer my bow to help you catch this fiend."

"That's very nice of you, Robin, but it's something we have to deal with by ourselves right now." I wasn't above asking Robin for help, especially since wooden arrow-shafts were basically stakes at high speed. But for now, I didn't want to put him in danger.

"Oh." His shoulders sagged. "But of course, I understand I am but a stranger to your bookshop…"

My heart went out to him. It couldn't be easy to be torn from an adventure story where you were the hero saving fair maidens left and right to become an afterthought in someone else's. But I didn't have time to smooth ruffled egos – I had my hands full with Morrie and Heathcliff. "I promise I'll tell you if we need your skills."

I tried to shut the door, but Robin stopped it with his leather boot. "I wanted to inform you that another fellow showed up. He calls himself Puck, and he speaks in an odd tongue, keeps saying he'll lead me about a round, through a bog, a brush, a brier—"

I groaned. *Great. Just what we need.* "Thanks, Robin. In that case, I do need your help. Make Puck up a bed in the Philosophy room. I showed you where we keep the spare sheets. And if you wake up tomorrow with the head of a donkey, then, um…don't panic."

Robin nodded, his mouth tight with worry. He opened the door a crack to let Grimalkin through, then shut it behind him. I checked the lock twice and pulled a heavy box in front of it to keep out any other problems.

We crowded into the occult room. While Morrie mixed martinis (because we couldn't have a secret murder room without a bar), I pulled up the Argleton Gazette website and searched the articles about each murder. While my phone read out the information and I added the details I learned from Jo, Morrie scribbled notes and Heathcliff looked moody.

"I don't see why we need to do this." Heathcliff grabbed a second martini from Morrie's hand. "We know exactly who murdered these women. All we need to do is march over there and stake his heart and chop his head off—"

"Not until we've got rid of all the dirt," I said. "We have to find these final four caches. We know what Fiona's box looks like and—"

"—and I can confirm that Dana Hill's artifacts are from a Romanian archaeological site. An Ottoman scholar has identified them as stolen from a dig three years ago." Morrie held up an image from an online marketplace. "Look at this – a visual. She's put them all in this scuffed-up *pálinka* box. Some people have no respect."

I refrained from pointing out we were the ones snooping into the private lives of these victims. "What about Miriam? Jo said she'd been hiking in the Carpathians, but it's not as if that means she's carrying around a rucksack filled with dirt."

"One swipe through her social media and I have the answer." Morrie held out his phone in triumph. "Miriam keeps a small glass jar filled with dirt from every place she hikes. She has a wall filled with them in her house. She says she accidentally forgot to pack her glass jar on this hike, so before she left the hiking trail she filled up her shoe with dirt. So we're looking for a smelly shoe filled with dirt. Delightful. The third victim, Jenna, is proving elusive. I'm scrolling her socials now and I doubt she's ever left Argleton, let alone traveled to the misty foreign climes. I'll run a full background check, of course."

"She might not have collected the dirt herself," I remind him. "Someone could have gifted her dirt, or…or…maybe Dracula coerced her into having some shipped here. The other question I have is, how did Dracula know about these dirt stashes? Jo said Fiona hadn't shown the contents of that box to anyone else. She said the only other person who might've seen it was the customs officer who checked the contents."

Morrie swiped his drink back from Heathcliff. "What's that about?"

"Fiona didn't want to risk the airport security refusing her entry for the box," I said. "So she shipped it to herself from Bucharest. Apparently, all she had to do was get a special biosecurity sticker and it was fine."

"How does any of this help us?" Heathcliff had finished his martini and was eyeing up the gin bottle. "It doesn't matter how the boxes got here, only where they are *now*. No new properties have popped up on the app. Dracula could have hidden them anywhere."

"Grey's been so busy being an annoying git, he might not have had time to secrete away these objects," I added. "They might be waiting next door."

Morrie rubbed his chin. "It's worth investigating."

"What is?" Heathcliff glowered.

"Dracula sleeps during the day, does he not? *And* we have a secret passage beneath the shop that will slip us into his lair unnoticed. All we have to do is create a distraction to lure Grey away, then sneak inside, locate the remaining dirt, and neutralize it without them even noticing."

"No."

I glared at Heathcliff. "Why not? It's the simplest plan we have."

"You want to walk right into the lair of the beast? It's suicide."

"Wrong. Suicide is sitting here drinking all the gin." I grabbed the bottle from his hands before he could tip it down his throat. "We're doing this, and we need your help."

CHAPTER EIGHT

"*C*rooooooak?"

Quoth lay on the floor in his raven form, one wing bent at an impossible angle. Blood pooled around his tiny body. His head twisted up toward me, orange-rimmed eyes swimming with pain. He tried to cry out again, but he was too weak; all he managed was a wheezing noise that made him shudder.

"No, no, no." My body trembled as I scooped Quoth into my arms. He was light as a feather and so, so cold. Quoth's head flopped back, exposing his throat. My fingers curled around him as I felt his life ebbing through his veins. *I don't have much time.*

I brought his limp body to my lips and started to drink. His blood filled my mouth, warm and cloying with a metallic tang. I'd never tasted anything so delicious before.

Drip-drip-drip. His blood dribbled from the corners of my mouth, splashing on the floor.

Mina...you can save him, Mina. Join me and you can be with him for eternity...

Drip-drip-drip.

Fuck. No.

I bolted from the dream, my body coated in sweat. I swallowed hard, but I could still taste the metallic warmth of Quoth's blood on my tongue.

Drip-drip-drip.

What was that? I touched my clothes, searching for bloodstains. It couldn't be. It was just a dream.

Drip-drip-drip.

No, not dripping. *Tapping.* Someone was tap-tap-tapping at the attic window.

Groggily, I reached across and flung open the shutter. With many a flint and flutter, a large black bird hopped down from the sill and transformed into a beautiful boy.

Quoth's hair fell across my face as he leaned in to sweep me into a hungry kiss. I cupped his neck with my hand, and my thumb brushed over a vein. His blood pulsed beneath his pale skin, warm and steady and very much alive. To taste his lips now after drinking his blood in my dream felt especially perverse, but in a way that made me press myself harder against him, chasing away the ghosts with his full lips and tangled lashes.

But I hadn't forgotten I was mad at him. Reluctantly, I pulled back. "You didn't get my text?"

"I came as soon as I saw it." He stroked my cheek with paint-stained fingers, tilting his face to the side and giving me this wide-eyed, innocent bird look that nearly made me forgive him on the spot.

I pointed to the window, where the first rays of sunlight peeked over the horizon. "It's morning. You didn't think to look at your phone all night? Even knowing that Dracula is killing women, you didn't think to check in? What happened to 'I'll always protect you'?"

"You're stronger than anyone I know." Quoth's fingers cupped my neck, sending fire through my skin. "And you have Heathcliff and Morrie here. I didn't think I'd be needed. If something serious happened, you would have told me."

"How? You wouldn't have seen my text. If I called, you wouldn't hear it. You're in another world when you paint, and I love that about you, but we've got a serious situation here and you don't seem to care."

"I care." The bed creaked as Quoth slid in behind me, his naked chest fitting perfectly into my back. His hands circled my knees, squeezing me against him like he wished he could crawl inside my skin. I touched his skin, feeling the bumps and changes in texture where he hadn't scrubbed off the paint.

"I miss you." I leaned back against his shoulder, peering up at him. From this angle, I got this whole new view of him – I could see up his nostrils and the pointed line of his chin, the way his cheekbones cut back to reveal the dark, feathered lashes at the corners of his eyes. Evidence that any view of Quoth is a good view.

He sighed. "If you said the word, I'd quit the exhibition."

"That's not what I want at all." I cupped his chin, pulling his face down to mine. "You deserve this. You *need* this. But you can't abandon the world just to paint. You can't stay out all night when we need you. Dracula killed Jo's girlfriend. We figured out most of the clues to get the final four boxes of dirt, but we needed your help. We still need your help."

Quoth pressed his lips to my neck, just above my collarbone. His whole body shuddered. His hair fell over my face, a pleasing sensation as it brushed my skin. "I'm sorry I disappointed you. And I'm sorry Jo lost Fiona. Please, tell me what happened and how I can help."

He listened with eyes drooping and fingers dancing fire on my skin while I told him everything that happened last night, and how we intended to search Dracula's house for the remaining dirt. "It sounds like you didn't need me after all. You figured out all this without me."

I squeezed his hand. "That's not true. When you didn't come, I felt...alone. You *are* needed. Jo missed you, too. She said she could have used an Allan hug. You give the best hugs."

He hugged me now, so tight and wistful and arresting. He was so light in my arms, I wondered, as I often did, how he didn't just float away. How it was that I got to be with this wonderful, kind man who didn't ask anything of me but loved me unconditionally, who loved with a love that was more than love, who loved as only the child of Edgar Allan Poe's pen would know how to love.

"Once," he said, his face nuzzled in my hair, "I flew away."

His words sent a chill down my spine. I knew behind them was a pain he seldom spoke over. I waited for him to continue.

"Heathcliff and Morrie were downstairs, bickering. That kind of bickering they always do that is more about the things they could say to each other but don't. And I realized how deeply they needed each other, that if one of them were to go missing, the other would batter down every door in the village, turn over every stone, just to find them again. But I never felt that same connection with them. They were kind, but they had their world and I had mine and we crossed paths at awkward moments on the way to the shower. I pretended that's how I liked it, that I didn't need friends who would burn the world for me, that I could fly over the earth without actually touching it, slip through every gap, and be apart from it all because I didn't belong. But it wasn't true." His voice cracked. "I wanted more than anything to have a connection like that, to be wanted by someone the way I desperately *wanted* – a wanting that filled my whole body right down to my toes. Bit by bit, the wanting ate away at me until I was an empty shell, until I was nothing but desolation.

"So I flew away. I thought only dark thoughts – they didn't want me, no one wanted me, I was a broken soul, a cursed wretch that should not exist, they'd be better off without me, they wouldn't even notice I had slipped away. I flew deep into King's Copse wood. I followed the stream, flying low enough to dip the tips of my wings in the water. I stopped in the crook of an ancient oak and I thought..." his shoulders shuddered. "This is a nice place to die."

"No..." I whispered, squeezing him tight.

"I burrowed into the hollow of the gnarled old tree and I thought if I closed my eyes for long enough, I would fade away back into the pages of my poem, and there I at least would return to my true purpose – as the grim, ungainly, ghastly, gaunt, and ominous bird of yore. Even being a carrier of woe would be better than what I was in this world – a ghost, a hidden thing, a lonely, loveless wretch."

"Quoth, what happened?"

"Morrie." Quoth laughed. "It turns out he'd put a tracking chip into my wing one day when I was asleep, and they followed it into the forest until they found me. Just in time. I hadn't eaten in so long, and it was so cold that night the tips of my wings had frozen."

"Quoth..." I crushed him against me, gripping his arms in mine. I looked up into those deep brown eyes with the burnished edges, like a forest ablaze. His hair draped over his shoulders, collecting and reflecting the sunrise, painting the strands in fleeting shades of color – indigo, lavender, copper, gold.

Tears rolled down my cheeks. I couldn't imagine the world without Quoth in it. I didn't want him to ever feel that way again.

"Thank you for telling me this," I whispered. "You should never feel alone."

Quoth pressed his nose into my hair. "I can smell them on you, both of them. Now that Heathcliff and Morrie have found the missing pieces of themselves in each other, the three of you fit together like pieces of a puzzle. I don't fit. I will never fit. But I'm okay with that as long as I have you."

My tears splashed on the duvet. "Please don't say that. You fit. I know you fit because just thinking about losing you makes my heart hollow." I sniffed. "My turn to tell you a story. I remember when I first got my diagnosis. I hated myself. I felt like it was my fault somehow, that I'd done this to myself, ruined my own life. I thought my life was over, and at the time, it was. I felt as though when I walked into a room, people could *see* that I was different. I sensed them pulling away, like they didn't want to catch my rotten luck. It was all in my head because I was afraid and lonely, but knowing that now doesn't help for back then." I shook my head. "There was a party for Marcus' fall campaign where I ended up on the balcony overlooking the city, and I thought how easy it would be to just jump."

Quoth squeezed me tight, pressing his cheek against mine so our tears mingled together. I kept going. "Those thoughts followed me every day, especially after Ashley did what she did. I thought, 'how could anyone ever love me?' I kept waiting for a silver lining, and then I lost my best friend and it felt like the universe punching me while I was down. It's partly why I came home to Argleton – I needed to find out who I was without vision. But the point is that I don't feel like that anymore. Marjorie says it's the barriers, attitudes, and exclusion of society that make us disabled, not our eyes or our...*feathers.* The world isn't set up for people like us, and that can be lonely sometimes. But we don't have to be lonely anymore, either of us. Because we have each other, and Heathcliff, and Morrie, and our friends and our art and our lives. It's like Heathcliff says, 'What doesn't kill you gives you unhealthy coping mechanisms and a wicked sense of humor.'"

Quoth laughed, the sound so soft and warm and musical. How alike we were – only we knew what the other needed. I nuzzled his cheek and he nuzzled mine. "I can't wait for you to see my paintings."

"Show me now. Maybe it will make you feel better."

He shook his head. When he spoke again, his voice was all velvet and darkness. "I'm so tired. I haven't slept all night. Do you need me right now for Dracula-slaying duties, or can I catch a few winks?"

I lay him back against the pillows. His eyelids fluttered shut, his impossibly-long lashes tangled together. I kissed his eyelids. "Sleep well, my prince. I'll wake you when we need you for sneaking."

CHAPTER NINE

*T*he problem with planning a stealthy attack on a vampire's lair during broad daylight was that we needed a free window of time where we could get in and out without anyone noticing. And one thing could foil even the best laid secret plan – customers.

Okay, also, fictional characters. Between Robin, Socrates, the Headless Horseman, and the newly-minted Shakespearean sprite Puck, we had no hope of keeping a low profile while we went about our shady business. But today of all days, the customers could foil us.

The grand opening of Mrs. Ellis' Halloween festival kicked off later today with a performance of Halloween music by the village choir (not Satanic, as Dorothy Ingram feared, although their medley of Cure songs was quite diabolical) over at the Presbyterian church. Even though the show didn't start until 1PM, by nine the village was teeming with people in all manner of crazy costumes. For some unknown reason, they all wanted to buy books.

Maybe it was the four-foot ghostly sign I made for the top of Butcher Street and the monster footprints I drew on the pavement leading to the store, but from the moment I flipped over the sign, a steady stream of people entered the shop looking for their next spooky read.

Heathcliff wanted to close the store for the day to focus on our dirt-finding mission, but Heathcliff wanted to close the shop every day, and I refused to give in. With Grey's construction site making Butcher Street unappealing to strolling shoppers, we needed all the sales we could get. And besides, I'd seen Grey outside supervising his workers. We couldn't do anything that would make him suspicious, and closing the shop on a day with so much foot traffic would definitely raise eyebrows.

So I was stuck behind the desk while we waited for our chance to strike. A woman wearing a fur stole and an impossibly tight pencil skirt strolled up to the desk and placed a paint swatch in front of me. She jabbed a color named 'Divine White' with a perfectly-manicured nail. "I'd like a book to match that color, please."

"You…what?"

She lowered her glasses on her nose to peer down at me like I was a simpleton. "I want you to find a book to match this color. I'm redecorating my living room and I like things to match."

Even though I couldn't see him, from across the room I could feel Heathcliff's ire growing into a black cloud that would consume us all.

"I'm sorry, I'm afraid I'm blind, so I'm not going to be very much help." I handed the swatches back to her. "Why don't you just choose a book from our discounted table and paint the cover in this color?"

"Discount table?" Her eyes lit up. "I could have a whole shelf of Divine White books. That's an excellent idea."

While the woman happily sorted through the stacks of Dan Brown hardcovers we were desperately trying to offload, Morrie came over with a stack of biology books he'd found on the fiction shelves and a flyer advertising today's performance.

"That's our window," Morrie whispered, jabbing at the paper. "Everyone in the village will be at the performance. We can put a sign on the door saying we're attending as well, but no one will notice if we're not in the crowd. It's the perfect time to sneak over to Dracula's abode and do a little snooping. We just have to make sure Grey's out of the house first."

"But how do we do that?" Heathcliff emerged from the poetry stacks.

"Easy." I grinned as I noticed a familiar pink feather boa bob past the window.

A moment later, the shop bell tinkled. The familiar waft of hyacinth perfume announced the arrival of one of my favorite visitors.

"Mina." Mrs. Ellis bustled toward me, dressed as a full-blown wicked witch with a lace gown (it was her wedding gown. I helped her dye it a couple of weeks ago), a wide-brimmed witch's hat, and a giant hooked faux nose, complete with a realistic-looking boil on the tip.

"Hello, darling." Cynthia Lachlan peered out from behind Mrs. Ellis, in her own witch's outfit which consisted of a Morticia Addams dress with a plunging neckline. She must be literally freezing her tits off outside. I let her air-kiss my cheeks to oblivion.

They were with a third woman. When they stepped aside, I recognized Deirdre, the village postmistress, in her own suitably witchy attire. She looked all around the room. "Hullo, Mina. Is your shop bird here?"

"No, he's...eating some berries upstairs."

"Oh, that's a pity." She pulled a packet from her purse and handed it to me. "I wanted to give him these bird treats. Our raven absolutely loves them."

"Your raven?" Mrs. Ellis turned to her friend.

"Yes, didn't I tell you? We've had a bird friend visiting the post office. I wondered if he might be a friend of your chap, although he seems better trained – he hasn't defecated on any customers yet. He just sort of hops along the windowsill in the mailroom and waits for his treats."

"Oh, well, thank you." I shoved the packet in my pocket. "I'm sure our bird will love these treats."

"Do you like our outfits?" Cynthia giggled as she gave a spin. "The Spirit Seekers Society are stepping out in Halloween style."

"You all look fantastic!" I beamed. "Although, obviously, I'm biased. How are things looking over at the church?"

"Oh, stunning. That new vicar – Reverend Mosley – is such a good sport. He let us put up all kinds of autumnal decorations, even a few jack-o-lanterns lining the church steps. And he's quite handsome."

"Blond hair and ocean-blue eyes," Cynthia said dreamily.

"So tall," Deirdre gushed. "With those *shoulders*. He could bowl for the village cricket team."

"And that Irish brogue," added Mrs. Ellis. "It has me all aflutter."

"Just keep your hands to yourself during the service," I warned with a smile. "The good reverend has already attracted the ire of Dorothy Ingram's new society. I wouldn't want him to be chased out of the village by an angry mob for impropriety."

Mrs. Ellis waved her hand dismissively. "If you ask me, that Dorothy Ingram needs to play a little hide the bishop of her own, then maybe she wouldn't be sticking her nose into everyone else's business. She's only lashing out because she's afraid of the Dracula Killer. Everyone is, of course, but they don't feel the need to go round spoiling everyone's fun."

"My Sally joined her little group," Deirdre added. "What's their name again?"

"Defense against Immorality, Adultery, Bestiality, Lucifer and the Occult," Morrie piped up. "It spells DIABLO."

Mrs. Ellis tossed her head back with a wild, honking laugh. "Oh, dear me. I bet Dorothy was spitting tacks when she found that out. Listen, Mina, we wanted to visit you because we wondered…"

"Yes?" *Here it comes. I knew this wasn't just a social call.*

"I know you've already got a stall at the Halloween fair tomorrow, and the darling Allan has his exhibition, but I wondered if you might consider commissioning the Spirit Seekers to do a little paranormal investigation of the shop as part of the festival."

"Oh, gosh, well…"

"Pretty please with a sexy vicar on top?" Ms. Ellis clasped her hands together. "With all the vampiric murders around these parts, we're absolutely swamped with business from local families. But we're ready to expand. Go bigger! We want to audition for *Strictly Come Ghosting.*"

"What?"

"*Strictly Come Ghosting.* It's the hottest new reality TV show, dear." Cynthia said. "We'd compete in various paranormal challenges with different ghost hunting teams from across the country. We truly believe the Spirit Seekers could take out the grand prize and put Argleton on the map."

"But we need a location to shoot our audition video," Deirdre cut in. "We need to demonstrate our abilities during a real, live paranormal investigation. All you'd need to do is let us stay in the shop overnight, and we'll set up our equipment and do our thing. You'd barely even notice we were here."

Wait, what? "Oh…um…" An orange light squiggled in front of my vision. I could feel a migraine coming on, but I didn't think it had anything to do with my eyes. "What about Lachlan Hall? That place is ancient. There's bound to be a few ghosts wandering about up there."

"Puh-*lease.* Every other team will be doing some old, crusty hall." Mrs. Ellis waved her hands around. "We want to be different. We want to *stand out.* And just look at this place – it's a balefire for supernatural beings, mark my words. I've been doing some research, and I discovered there has been a bookstore on this site since the Doomsday book! And with all the grisly murders that have happened here, there must be some juicy paranormal activity to uncover. And we intend to uncover it."

I shifted my weight from foot to foot. "I'm not sure about this. We're having some plumbing issues at the moment, and until they're fixed it could be dangerous allowing you free rein in the store after hours. Health and safety, you know."

And there's the little matter of the shop bringing literary characters to life, and the time-traveling room upstairs. Oh, and the bloodthirsty vampire living across the street trying to get his hands on Nevermore's magic. All important health and safety considerations.

As if on cue, there was a bang from the cellar, followed by a low-pitched moan. Mrs. Ellis grinned at me as if to say, *I told you so.*

"Not to worry, we're set up for all that." Mrs. Ellis drew from her carpetbag a sheaf of papers. "We have all the paperwork – waivers, site safety, indemnity insurance. All council-approved."

"We took a course," Deirdre added. "Frightfully dull, but the tutor was a dish."

"And we use only the latest in scientific ghost-tracking methods," added Cynthia. "We have all the ghost tech we need – EMF meters, infrared thermometers, Geiger counters, ultrasonic motion sensors. We take our work very seriously. In fact, we've already banished a banshee from the Argleton Arms Hotel and put paid to a pesky poltergeist in the retirement village puzzle room. And now your mother and Sylvia have joined the team, we'll have even more spiritual power behind our investigations."

I should have known my mother couldn't resist the pull of the Spirit Seekers Society. This was the last thing we needed, but I couldn't think of an excuse that would get them out of my hair. And besides, I needed Cynthia on our side.

I sighed. "Sure thing, you can do a paranormal investigation in the bookshop."

Heathcliff threw up his hands and stomped upstairs.

"Thank you, Mina," Mrs. Ellis threw her arms around me. "I knew we could count on you."

I turned to Cynthia. "You'll have to check with your husband to make sure he's not working. The noise can be terrible, even at night. I wouldn't want it to mess with your scientific equipment during the big audition."

She screwed up her face. "I will. I'm so sorry, dear. My husband is a perfectionist – he won't rest until that poxy block of flats is ready for sale, and damn all those who get in his way. His health is suffering – you must've seen him around, Mina. He's not well. He doesn't even come home at night anymore, just stays at that dirty construction site."

Or in a coffin next to his master, I thought but didn't say.

I smiled at her. "I think you should drag Grey out to the concert. He needs a break."

"Yes, Cynthia, that's a wonderful idea." Mrs. Ellis squeezed her friend's hand. "Grey should be able to step away for an hour to see the concert with you. He's been ignoring you long enough."

"But Grey wouldn't be interested in—"

"It's not about the music." I gave her a nudge toward the door. "Let him see it as an opportunity to perv at you in that gorgeous dress. Or maybe you should flirt with Mr. Handsome Reverend a bit, make him jealous. Go on, don't let Grey take no for an answer."

"You're exactly right. Thank you, Mina." Cynthia waved goodbye to Mrs. Ellis and Deirdre and scampered across the street to surprise her husband.

As soon as the rest of the Spirit Seekers had tootled on over to the church, Morrie and I pressed our noses up to the window. A moment later, Cynthia emerged from the construction site, dragging a protesting Grey behind her, an enormous, wide-brimmed straw hat pulled low over his face, no doubt to protect his sensitive, vampire-ish skin from the flaccid British sunshine.

"Heathcliff, darling," Morrie yelled upstairs. "It's time."

Heathcliff stomped back downstairs, muttering under his breath. We checked the shop was empty of customers, then Morrie went upstairs to fetch a sleepy Quoth while Heathcliff flipped the sign and I banged on the basement door.

"Victor, we need the basement for a bit."

"Um…" a distracted voice called back up. "See, the thing is, I'm right at the most critical part of my experiment—hey, unhand me."

"Outside, Poindexter." Heathcliff dragged Victor from the basement by his collar. "You too, green man," he yelled at Robin Hood, who hung over the balcony, peering down at us while twirling an arrow shaft in his fingers. "And take the fairy, the Insta-whore, and the quiet one with you."

One by one, our resident fictional characters filed out the front door of the shop. When Puck passed by Heathcliff, he sneered in his face, "My mistress with a monster is in love…"

"Nope." I shoved him toward the door. "No turning Heathcliff into a donkey, or a walrus, or a delphinium. No turning anyone into anything, or I'll make you share the bed with Socrates. Got it?"

The fairy poked his tongue out at me as he skipped after the others.

At least they're dressed appropriately.

Morrie flicked on the basement light, but the dim bulb barely penetrated the gloom. Quoth settled on my shoulder, his talons reassuringly sharp against my skin. Morrie went first, and I followed with one hand resting on his shoulder, the other trailing along the stone wall. I'd left Oscar upstairs in his doggy bed – no way would I risk his life in Dracula's lair. Although I missed him now as I stepped blindly into the gloom behind Morrie. Oscar wasn't a pet, he was my eyes, and I hated how helpless I felt without them.

No, I'm not helpless. I can see things in this basement Morrie doesn't notice, only in a different way. For example...

"Look at this." My foot kicked an extension cord, which I held up for Morrie to see. The cord was damp in my fingers. "That cheeky bugger's been using the shop's power to supply his experiments. With the pipes leaking, he could start a fire down here."

"If HSE ever inspects the shop, they're shutting us down for sure." Morrie's foot splashed into the water that flooded the cellar floor. "Victor wasn't kidding about the water. This is going to ruin my favorite brogues."

Even my impervious Docs took in a little freezing water as I splashed across the flooded floor behind Morrie. He held up the flashlight on his mobile phone, and I could just make out a lumpy shape on a table in the corner, covered by one of my good white bedsheets and surrounded by strange machinery. I didn't want to see what was underneath.

Morrie and I shifted the stacks of chairs and old bookshelves we'd used to barricade the entrance to the secret passage, then pried off the sheets of plywood Heathcliff nailed up months ago. We left the garlic and magical sigils in place, in case anything decided to follow us back through.

Morrie's fingers slipped into mine. Quoth nuzzled my cheek with the top of his head. I planted a kiss against his feathers as he spread his wings and took off into the darkness. He returned a few moments later, settling onto my shoulder and nodding his head. "Croak."

The tunnel is empty, and I'll head out to the street to help Heathcliff keep watch. Be careful, Mina.

"You too." I stroked his head. He let out another *croak*, then flew back up the cellar stairs.

Morrie and I sloshed our way down the tunnel, moving carefully to avoid the low arches that held up the roof. Our feet splashed and squelched through the water, which grew shallower as we moved away from the bookshop – the ground had to slope upward a fraction. We reached the stairs on the other end and moved up them as silently as we could. The walls I touched turned from stone to wood. We were between the walls in Mrs. Ellis' old flat.

Dracula knew about this tunnel – it was why Grey Lachlan purchased the property. I knew he wanted to get his hands on Nevermore's Bookshop's magic, although how he thought he'd use it when none of us knew why the shop did what it did was anyone's guess. Now that Dracula was drinking blood in earnest, he'd soon become stronger than ever. Strong enough to break through the protections we used to guard the shop? I didn't want to find out.

Morrie stopped, and a moment later I heard a click, followed by a slow *creeeeak* as the secret door swung outward. I squeezed Morrie's arm as we stepped down into a small room.

The last time we'd been inside this room, it had been decorated for Mrs. Ellis' niece, Jonie. She'd had the walls painted yellow and covered with posters, her clothes and stacks of Christmas presents she'd stolen from the village charity Christmas tree all over. Now, the room had been nearly completely stripped. Instead of the yellow, the walls had been painted a cool midnight blue that swallowed the light from Morrie's torch. In the corner stood an iron candelabra holding three taper candles that cast a dim glow across the room, just bright enough that I could make out the dark object in the center.

A gleaming mahogany coffin.

CHAPTER TEN

I swallowed. I could *feel* the weight of the malevolence that waited on the other side of the lid.

Dracula's inside.

I'm in a room with a literal vampire.

So far, we hadn't encountered our enemy's face. We knew him only as a black bat hanging in the window across the street or a menacing shadow described by my father in his letters and hidden behind the creepily deteriorating face of Grey Lachlan. I didn't need to see Dracula to know him, because I'd loved Bram Stoker's book as a teen, and because his malevolence visited me in my dreams every night, making me do horrible things to the people I loved.

But the coffin made everything *real*. We truly were in the lair of the slumbering beast.

"I could open it right now." Morrie held up the wooden stake he brought with him. "This would all be over in moments. We could wait until Grey came back and found him, and follow him to where they've hidden the dirt."

Part of me itched to lift the lid and come face-to-face with the monster who had plagued my thoughts for so many months. To put a face to this fiend would render him knowable, conquerable. He would be in his daytime slumber, dead to the world and unable to sense our presence.

I swallowed, pulling away from the coffin. "It's too risky. We'll have lost the benefit of surprise. We're so close. Let's stick with the plan."

As we passed around the coffin, I pressed my back against the wall. I didn't want to be in the room with it any longer.

There was a narrow, winding staircase leading up to the first floor. It came out in the breakfast nook – Mrs. Ellis usually had the entrance covered with a crocheted wall hanging, except when Jonie was staying. We stepped into the nook and took in the narrow kitchen and living room across the hall. Without Mrs. Ellis' knickknacks crowding every corner, the space echoed with our footsteps. Enough light penetrated the building paper covering the windows that I could make out a small table and a couple of chairs stacked with tools, blueprints, and lunchboxes for the construction crew. A few lone objects were lined up on a high shelf in the kitchen.

Morrie pulled over a step ladder and reached up onto the shelf. "Does this look familiar?" Morrie handed down an object.

The light was too dim for me to see properly. But I ran my fingers over the surface, feeling wood engraved with a swirling design. "It's Fiona's box. Open it."

The latch clicked. "There's dirt inside," Morrie whispered, handing it back to me.

I tucked the box under my arm. "What about these other objects?"

"A shoe…also filled with dirt." Morrie dropped it onto the counter. "It smells positively *delightful*. Definitely the shoe of someone who's hiked across the Carpathian mountains. And there's a shoebox stuffed with dirt and…what looks suspiciously like tiny bones and bits of coin and jewelry."

I collected the objects from Morrie, wrinkling my nose. He

was right – Miriam's shoe definitely retained the aroma of her last hike. "What else is up there? What about Jenna's object? He must've taken something from her."

"There's nothing." Morrie jumped down and started pulling the lids off the coffee and tea canisters. I noticed Mrs. Ellis' old cow-shaped cookie jar on the end of the countertop.

"It's got to be here somewhere—"

"Oh, Mina Wilde." Grey Lachlan's voice called from the front of the house. "Come out, come out wherever you are. I know you're in here. I think you and I need to have a little talk."

CHAPTER ELEVEN

S hite.

My fingers flew to my purse, fumbling for my stash of holy water and communion wafers. I didn't know what Grey planned to do to us, but I'd destroy the dirt before he had the chance.

"H-h-how did you get away from your wife?" I called into the gloom. Morrie moved in front of me, placing his body between me and Grey. My fingers closed around the holy water bottle, and I slid my nails under the cork to work it free.

Please, by Hera, let this work...

"Cynthia's sudden interest in this insipid Halloween festival made me suspicious." Grey staggered toward us. He flicked on the light. I couldn't see him behind Morrie, but I could hear the glee in his voice at finding the two of us in his master's lair. "It's lucky I got back here to catch you trespassing. I have a mind to call the police, but I think we can settle this between us. I'll have my property back."

"These aren't yours." I turned away from him. The cork popped off the bottle. *Yuss.*

"Finders keepers." Grey's fancy shoes clapped on the bare wooden flooring as he moved closer. Morrie moved with him, keeping his body between me and Grey. "Their owners don't need them any longer, but my master has use of them. You should give up your efforts now – there's no way you'll find all our stashes of earth. I've hidden them too cleverly."

We've covered our tracks well. He doesn't know about the houses Sherlock hit in London or the others we've destroyed near Argleton. He doesn't know all of Dracula's dirt is useless now.

Except for the remaining four boxes. I slid my nails under the lid of Fiona's box, trying to pry it open. *Come on, come on...*

I dared a glance up at Grey. He advanced on us, his hand outstretched, a look of cold cruelty marring his broken features. This close, I saw that he was in worse shape – his clothes torn and coated with construction dust, his eyes bloodshot, his gums pulled back from his teeth. "Hand them over, Mina. And I will consider sparing your life."

"Stay away from her." Morrie brandished his stake. Grey ducked under it with ease, but Morrie dug something else from his pocket and thrust it in Grey's face. A silver crucifix. Grey staggered back, his hands swiping at his face as Morrie pressed the metal cross into his skin. While Grey howled with pain, I sprinkled the shoe with the holy water, dropped it on the floor, popped the lid off the shoebox, and got that one done, too. Behind me, I heard grunts and crashes as Morrie and Grey fought. The latch of the box was still stuck. I wrenched it every way but it wouldn't unlock. *Doubleplus shite.* "Morrie, let's go."

There was another crash. Morrie's fingers slotted into mine, placing my hand into the crook of his arm. "Follow me, gorgeous."

From somewhere on the floor, Grey groaned. I didn't stop to see what Morrie had done to him.

We raced back down the staircase and dodged around the

coffin. Behind us, Grey cursed as he pulled himself to his feet and stumbled down the staircase. Morrie yanked me around the coffin and into the tunnel. We crashed down the steps. My boots splashed in the water as we entered the tunnel. I cried out as my arms scraped against the bare brick walls, but I didn't stop, didn't look back. Footsteps splashed in the water behind us, close and getting closer.

With a yell of triumph, Morrie stepped into the cellar and helped me through the tunnel entrance. I turned around to face our pursuer. Morrie aimed his flashlight at the tunnel just as Grey's face burst into view, his features even more ghastly in the snatched light. "Grey, you look terrible. When was the last time you've been home? Cynthia misses you terribly."

Grey stopped just shy of the tunnel entrance. Was it my imagination, or did his face pinch at my mention of his wife? "She does not understand, and she does not care to understand what I am doing here, the empire I will build for my master. She should stay away from me, so I don't..."

His words trailed off. Before I had the chance to wonder what he had started to say, Grey surged forward with a cry. He tried to step through the tunnel entrance into our cellar, but as he shoved his leg forward past our protective spells, something sizzled.

Grey howled. A burned smell reached my nostrils.

"His skin's burning," Morrie said. "It's like BBQ-property developer, which I must admit is how I prefer my developers. Dracula must be drinking from Grey, too, because the garlic is giving him a lovely color."

Grey staggered back into the tunnel, gripping the walls as he breathed hard. I noticed he no longer put weight on his other foot. "You think I mind a little pain?" he gasped out. "I'll do anything to serve my master. *Anything.*"

With a yell, he surged forward again, slamming his body into the entrance. His limbs flailed as the garlic repelled him, but instead of falling back, he growled and grunted and pushed his way forward. The air sizzled with the sound of boiling flesh, and the smell of pork BBQ made me want to puke. A horrible scream tore from Grey's throat as he crawled along the floor, one hand over the other like he was pulling himself through quicksand. The water soaked his clothing and splashed in his mouth, cutting off his next scream into a spluttering couch. He was doing it. Inch by inch, he crawled forward into the cellar.

"Well, that's something." Morrie flattened us against the far wall. I hugged Fiona's box to my chest with one hand while the other felt along the bricks. My fingers brushed Victor's extension cord. A desperate idea came to me. I dropped my hand from Morrie's and followed the cord along the wall, feeling for the dangling plug. When I found it, I stooped to pick up the other end. It had been dragging in the water. I wiped it dry on my t-shirt. *Please, don't let this kill us all.*

"Morrie," I yelled. "Get above the water."

"You won't escape me." Grey sent up great waves of cold water as he crawled toward us. Now that he was past the garlic, he seemed to gain strength even as steam rose from his smoking skin. He grabbed the edge of Victor's table and gripped it as he tried to haul himself to his feet.

Morrie appeared beside me. "Toast him, gorgeous," he whispered.

I jammed the plugs together. A light flickered overhead as a surge of electricity hit Victor's machine. Sparks flew across the room, and I screamed and dropped to my knees as Morrie bent his body over mine to protect me.

Lights burst to life along the edge of the table, and a whirring, sizzling noise drowned out Grey's cries. As I watched, horrified and transfixed, the lump on the table shot upright, the sheet falling away to reveal a human-like figure.

He looked exactly the way I expected Frankenstein's monster to appear in the flesh – more terrifying than any horror film could do justice. Everything about him screamed *wrong*, from the wide, flattened forehead, the ill-fitting snub nose and beady eyes, to the places where the flesh hadn't stretched properly over bone and organ. From the neat rows of stitches crisscrossing his patchwork skin to the pair of industrial-sized bolts sticking out from his neck.

"Wh-wh-what is that?" Grey stared at the monster. The monster turned to Grey, its beady eyes rolling and swirling and focusing on Grey with a kind of naive curiosity. It reached out with hands like tractors and grabbed Grey's shoulders.

"Please," Grey begged. He didn't get to finish his plea.

With a roar, the monster flung Grey across the room. He crashed into the wall with the sickening *SNAP* of bones breaking.

"Good thinking, gorgeous." Morrie shoved me toward the stairs. "Now, run!"

I scrambled up the steps, throwing myself from the cellar and across the rug as the monster roared behind us. Morrie slammed the cellar door shut and drew the bolt across. He leaned his back against the door and breathed an audible sigh as crashes and snarls and pleas for mercy shook the shop.

"My creature!" Victor cried, falling to his knees. "You've woken him before he was ready. What have you done?"

"Mina saved all our asses." Morrie sank to his knees, clutching his stomach. In this moment, my Napoleon of Crime didn't look very sure of himself. Downstairs, Grey screamed, and I heard the roar of the monster receding as it chased him back along the tunnel.

Victor glared at me. "You've set him loose on the village, and he cannot be controlled."

"One more monster in this place won't make any difference." I loosened my grip on Fiona's box, letting it fall into my lap. I sucked in a deep breath, then another, trying to calm my racing heart. My fingers fumbled with the latch but now, without panic blinding me, it opened easily, revealing a thin layer of dirt on the bottom. Heathcliff tossed me a fresh bottle of holy water, and I sprinkled it inside.

"It's done." I let my head fall back against Morrie as Heathcliff and Quoth sank down beside me. "We've only got one more box of earth left to find, and then we can destroy Dracula once and for all."

ARGLETON GAZETTE

FOREIGNER IN FRANKENSTEIN COSTUME
PICKED UP BY POLICE

A stranger was picked up by officers in the early evening shuffling across the motorway while traffic swerved to avoid him. Luckily no one was seriously injured, and the man was escorted off the motorway for his own safety.

Due to movie FX-grade makeup and the realistic-looking bolts sticking out of his neck, the officer was able to deduce our stranger was bound for Argleton's Halloween festival.

It transpired that the man, who police believe to be a foreigner with a speech impediment, is a guest of Heathcliff Earnshaw, resident at Nevermore Bookshop, 22 Butcher Street. This reporter is unsurprised to find the bookstore proprietor keeping such peculiar company. The stranger has been returned to his home and Mr. Earnshaw given a verbal warning by police not to allow his houseguests to break council bylaws.

CHAPTER TWELVE

"*J*'ll take this book, thank you." A dour-looking woman handed over a copy of *The North Staffordshire Railway in LMS Days, Volume 2*. "Do you gift wrap? It's for my husband's retirement party. He's an avid railway enthusiast."

"Of course." I rang up her purchase and unrolled the purple wrapping paper across the desk. Gift-wrapping was one of those little extras I'd introduced that set Heathcliff's teeth on edge. The service was much in demand, as long as I was the one doing it – Heathcliff threw books at anyone who asked for gift-wrapping and Morrie liked to hide little presents inside the paper (usually notes with mysterious and vaguely threatening messages for people to puzzle over). Quoth was excellent in human form, but he preferred his raven form around the shop, and ravens can do many things, but gift wrapping is not one of them.

Besides, it's not as if Quoth is here to help. I tried to push away the negative thought as I folded over the edges of the paper. Quoth had been out all night again. He flew in just before sunrise and was upstairs, sound asleep. Still, at least he'd been here yesterday when Morrie and I broke into Dracula's place. *I can't wait until the exhibition is over and we can go back to normal – as normal as anything ever is around here...*

The woman tapped her foot impatiently. Just as I tied the bow, I heard a familiar 'croak' that warmed my heart. A moment later, a heavy bird swooped down the stairs and perched on my shoulder.

I'm hurt. Wounded. Deeply offended. Quoth picked up the edge of the paper and tried to fold it with his talons. *I'm an excellent gift-wrapper.*

His talon poked through the paper, tearing a long rip right through the center. The woman huffed. I slid the book out of the wrapping and cut off a new square of paper.

Okay, okay, maybe you have a point, Quoth's voice landed in my head. *I can't stay long. I need to get over to the studio. But I wanted to surprise you before I left.*

This is the best surprise, I thought back. *Now, stop trying to help me with this so we can get this grumpy old biddy out of here.*

"You shouldn't allow birds inside the shop," said the woman as I handed her a package. "What if he defecates on customers?"

Is she giving you trouble, Mina? Quoth lifted one leg and waved his talons menacingly. *I ate some lovely berries earlier. I can give her a wee present to remember me by.*

"Have a nice day." I thrust the package into the lady's hands. Thankfully, she bustled out of the shop before Quoth could make good his promise. I stroked the raven's feathers as he peered around the shop. Seeing we were alone – Heathcliff was shuttered in his private office – he hopped around the room, pulling the curtains closed with his beak. He hopped onto the till and transformed. A moment later, a very naked, very beautiful man leaned over the desk and pressed his lips to mine.

"Surprise," he whispered, his breath warm against my lips.

Mmmmm, and what a lovely surprise it is. I wrapped my arms around Quoth and drew him close, loving this stolen moment between us. It was one of those perfect kisses, where our mouths fit perfectly together and our tongues knew exactly what to do to draw out a moan or gasp or sigh.

It was also...not like Quoth at all. Despite the closed curtains, the shop was still open. A customer could walk in at any moment, or one of our resident fictional characters. Victor was banging away down in the basement again, and Robin and Puck were just upstairs, trading stories about magical forests and maidens fair. Not to mention Heathcliff and Morrie were around somewhere, and if they walked in on us things could get loud and dangerous...

Quoth wasn't like Morrie – he didn't get off on the thrill of doing filthy things in the daylight, unless he was in his bird form, watching from a place of safety.

I don't know what had inspired this dangerous streak in him, but I craved more of it.

"Do you want me to put clothes on?" Quoth's fingers slid up the hem of my skirt.

"Quoth, I..." All my questions died away under the intensity of his gaze.

He smothered my lips in his, his fingers teasing my clit through my knickers. *By Isis, we shouldn't be doing this. Someone could walk in at any moment. I should have him stop. I will make him stop. Any second now.*

Yes, I'll pull the plug.

Right now.

Right.

Now.

Yes...um...

Quoth kissed a trail along my neck, his teeth scraping my skin as his fingers worked inside me, and I completely forgot about stopping as an orgasm teased the edges of my nerve endings—

"Mina, are you in there?" Jo's voice rang through the shop. "I really need to talk to you."

"Ow." I jerked, and Quoth bit down in surprise. We sprang

apart like two teenagers caught snogging behind the bike shed. Quoth dived behind the desk, his cute pasty arse sticking up as he tugged open the drawers in search of the spare clothing he kept down here for this exact purpose.

I rubbed the bite mark on my neck and smoothed down my skirt just as Jo staggered in. "Jo, are you okay? You sound upset."

"I—I—I—" Jo's words dissolved into a wretched sob.

I ran to her. Quoth swore as he struggled into his trousers, but Jo didn't seem to notice him. I led her over to the leather sofa under the window and sank down beside her. Quoth pulled a Blood Lust tour t-shirt over his head and collapsed into the cushions on the other side of her, wrapping his arms around her in that embrace he knew she needed. Jo rested her head on his shoulder.

Morrie poked his head in, took one look at Jo's stricken face, and with the understanding of a true British gentleman, headed off upstairs to fetch the tea.

Jo's limbs trembled, and she kept trying to speak but couldn't seem to find the words.

"Take your time. I'm here." I knitted my fingers in hers. "You don't have to tell me if you don't want to."

"It's not that I don't…" Jo shuddered. "It's that I can't even explain it. I was just at home, packing some of Fiona's things to send home to her family, when the office called me. I thought it might be the results of the autopsy, but…it was the Loamshire examiner, wanting my professional opinion on the death. He said he made the incision in Fiona's chest and she leaped off the table."

No. Oh no.

"I just don't understand. I found her myself. I checked all her vitals. She was *dead*, Mina. The EMTs confirmed it. So then how did she shove Dr. Spencer and walk out of the morgue with a scalpel still sticking out of her chest?"

"Um…" How could I tell my best friend that her girlfriend was a vampire? "Have they found her yet?"

Have they contained her?

Jo shook her head. "They have her on camera running into the King's Copse woods. The police are out combing the area for her. I came here in case she… I thought maybe if she was looking for me, she might come to you…"

The Headless Horseman chose this moment to float through the wall, drift across the room directly in front of me and Jo, and pass through the door to the office just as Heathcliff flung it open.

Jo's hands flew to her mouth. She made a strangled sound.

"That man…that man has no head."

CHAPTER THIRTEEN

"*H*eathcliff, get him out of here," I hissed. I held Jo against me as Heathcliff picked up his broom.

"Go. Go on, off with ye." Heathcliff shoved the Headless Horseman into the Children's room and slammed the door.

"Mina." Jo's chest rose and sunk as she sucked in deep breaths. "Why did that guy have no head?"

I faked a laugh. "You're freaking yourself out. It's obviously his Halloween costume."

"That's not a costume." Jo's chest heaved. "You know it's not. That bloke *came through the wall,* and he's wandering around the shop without a head like he's familiar with this place, like he's another one of Heathcliff's kooky chums. But that's impossible."

On the other side of Jo, Quoth twitched uncomfortably. He dropped his arm from Jo's neck as a couple of black feathers tumbled through the air. *He's stressed, and when he's stressed, he gets very feathery.*

Shit.

Quoth, you can't shift now. Please, Jo is freaked out already.

I met his eyes, pleading with him to be strong. He was focusing so hard I couldn't even hear his voice inside my head.

Quoth's lips parted, the word 'sorry' had started to form before it was torn away as his lips snapped and elongated into a hard beak. His arms went next, the fingers extending and the elbows twisting in a way no human elbow should twist. Black feathers shoved through his skin as his bones crunched and his body shrunk into itself, depositing his haphazardly-applied clothing into a heap on the floor.

Jo stared, her eyes wide with shock, as the man who'd been comforting her exploded in a flurry of black feathers.

A moment later, a raven hopped along the counter and peered up at Jo with curious, fire-rimmed eyes.

"Croak?"

To Jo's credit, she didn't scream. She just kind of stared at Quoth, her head bobbing as she swallowed again and again and again.

Heathcliff sighed as he moved toward the hallway. "I'll flip the sign. I'm guessing we'll be closed for some time."

When he returned, he pulled a bottle of Scotch from his desk drawer and poured a generous lug into a glass. As he held the glass out to Jo, she swiped the bottle from his hands.

"Hey! That's mine."

"Thanks." Jo sucked on the neck of the bottle like she was a baby with a pacifier. Quoth hopped onto her lap, and she stroked his feathers. Even in bird form, he had the power to calm her.

Although...maybe that was the whisky.

When Jo set the bottle down again, a significant portion of it was gone. She turned to me, and I didn't need perfect vision to see she was freaked out. "I suppose you'd better tell me what's going on."

"I...I...don't know. Quoth just turned into a bird, it's crazy! I've never seen anything like it before."

"Mina." Heathcliff looked mournfully at his rapidly-declining whisky bottle. "Jo needs the truth."

"Yeah. I know." I sucked in a deep breath and poured out the whole story, how the bookshop brought fictional characters to life, how Quoth shifted between raven and human forms, and how I was the daughter of Homer and somehow responsible for it all. "The murders we've solved over the last year have just been the tip of the iceberg. There's been a much greater mystery ruling over us all – Nevermore Bookshop and why it brings fictional characters to life."

Jo glared at Heathcliff. "So you are Heathcliff Earnshaw, that stroppy, skeleton-hugging bastard from *Wuthering Heights*?"

Heathcliff nodded. She whirled around to face Morrie. "And you're James Moriarty, the Napoleon of Crime from Sherlock Holmes."

Morrie takes a deep bow. "At your service."

"And Quoth is…"

"Croak?" Quoth tipped his head to the side.

"The raven from Poe's poem," I said in a small voice. "We have no idea why he can shapeshift. But I'm grateful for it."

Jo gestured at Socrates, who appeared at the top of the stairs, eating ice cream out of a tub as he yelled obscenities at the presenters on BBC One. "And those jokers upstairs are…"

"…characters from Classical literature the shop has brought to life in the last month," I shrugged. "There have been others, too. Remember Lydia? She was from *Pride and Prejudice*. And Morrie's old boyfriend Sherlock…"

"Right." Jo swallowed again. "The shop brings fictional characters to life. And you're saying that Fiona…"

"—was drained of her blood by Bram Stoker's *Count Dracula*, so he could steal the Romanian soil she kept in her box. Yes, that's what I'm saying." I reached across to hug my friend, but she shied away. "I'm so, so sorry, Jo."

Jo gives a barking laugh. "I mean, I can't say it's entirely a surprise." She tipped the bottle in his Heathcliff's direction. "I can easily believe you're the famous Heathcliff, and the way the raven reacted whenever anyone quoted Poe…and Morrie and Sherlock,

I mean every fan fiction writer has been shipping that couple since the stories first made it to print. I feel so stupid for not figuring it out."

"Don't feel stupid. You're the smartest person I know."

"Hey!" Morrie protested. One look from me and he shut his trap.

Jo looked up at me, and I read the hurt behind the fear in her eyes. "You should have told me, Mina."

"I know. I wanted to tell you so many times, but I didn't think you'd believe me. And I didn't want to lose your friendship." I stared nervously at my friend. I hated all the lies I'd had to tell her over the last year. "I've spent my entire life watching people look at my mother like she's insane. Which she is. But I couldn't stand it if you looked at me like that."

"If you can get justice for my Fiona, I don't care if you're the queen of bloody Sheba." Jo clenched her fists at her sides. "That bloodsucker hurt my love. He dies tonight."

"It's not as easy as that. Which reminds me, we found Fiona's box. I think she'd want you to have it." I nodded to Heathcliff. He rummaged around behind the desk and pulled out the box from whatever crevice he used to hide it and handed it to Jo. Her fingers trembled as she took it from his hands, and from the way her shoulders heaved I knew she was dangerously close to crying again.

"Thank you." She caressed the inlaid design. "This means the world to me. Now, what were you saying about the bastard who did this to her?"

As succinctly as I could, I recapped the plot of the book and reminded her that we needed to destroy every one of the fifty boxes of dirt before we could go after the vampire. We only had the dirt he took from Jenna Mclarey left to find.

"What if he uses more than fifty boxes?" Jo asked.

"We thought of that, but we don't believe he will. Dracula's habits are ingrained from centuries of life between the pages.

He's not going to veer from the plot and suddenly change things up just because he's in our world. Plus, Grey Lachlan made it clear they don't know we've destroyed all the other dirt. He'll assume fifty is more than sufficient."

Jo slumped back in her chair. "So what do we do?"

"We didn't find Jenna's dirt with the others at Dracula's house, and we don't even know the vessel it's stored in. If we can figure out where she got it from we'd be closer to an answer—"

"I mean about Fiona." Jo's lip trembled. Right, of course. In the chaos of Jo discovering our secret, I'd almost forgotten why she came here in the first place – her girlfriend rose from death and was wandering the woods. "How will we find her?"

"Easy," Heathcliff said as an ambulance tore through the village, sirens blaring. "We follow the trail of destruction."

CHAPTER FOURTEEN

"*T*hat bitch is crazy." Wilson coughed. "She was high on something, but I've never seen drugs do that to a person."

"What did she do?" I handed Wilson the glass of water on the nightstand. Jo and I followed the ambulance to the hospital while the others had driven out to the woods to see if Quoth could locate Fiona. When I heard it was DC Wilson who'd been hurt by Fiona, I didn't expect her to see us. But I must've endeared myself to her more than I realized. Or, more likely, she and Jo were friendly through work and Wilson wanted to warn her about her homicidal undead girlfriend.

"Fiona had these wild, crazy eyes. She moved incredibly fast. I've never seen anything like it. She flung herself into the bushes and plucked out a rabbit. And then she bit off its head, just like that! She looked up at me with rabbit blood dribbling down her chin. That can't be good for her. Hayes and I tried to restrain her, and the crazy bitch *bit* me." Wilson held up her hand. "I've been shot at, stabbed, and chased with a machete once. But never bitten."

"I'm so sorry." Jo held her hand.

"You should be." Wilson smiled. She tried to take her glass from me, but winced from the pain and let me hold the straw for her. She looked like she'd been hit by a bus, with tape over a wound above her eye and scrapes and cuts all over her body, not to mention the dressings covering the wound to her throat. "Your whole job is deciding how people died. I don't know how you missed a live one."

"It's an honest mistake." Jo did her best to make her voice passive. "You'd be surprised how often it happens. So she's still in the woods somewhere?"

"As far as we know. We've got every officer in the county searching for her. We don't want her to hurt someone else, or herself. Or eat anyone's pet rabbit." Wilson patted Jo's arm, but the action made her wince again. "We'll find her, I promise."

"That's what I'm afraid of," Jo murmured under her breath as Wilson's eyes fluttered shut. We left the DS to sleep. In the hallway, Jo grabbed my arm. "What do we do, Mina? If the police find Fiona before us... I don't want any more people to be hurt. And what about Wilson? Will she turn into a vampire?"

"Wilson will be fine. There has to be an exchange of blood to turn someone into a vampire. Fiona's not skilled enough at being a vampire yet to know how to control her hunger, so she can't make others like herself." I squeezed Jo's hand. "As for Fiona, they won't find her out there. She's Dracula's progeny. She needs his blood to sustain her life. She'll make her way back to him. And we'll be waiting."

"Socrates, get your poxy foot off my hand."

"Tell me, what reason would you give for me to get off your hand?"

"Because I'll kill you?"

"Is that your final answer?"

"Is your arsehole jealous of all the shit coming out of your mouth? *Get off my hand.*"

"I'll get off your hand if you answer my question – *why should I get off your hand?*"

"Because your bony foot is crushing my fingers, and it hurts."

"Ah, but what *is* pain?"

"Pain will be my boot getting acquainted with the inside of your scrotum if you don't *move your bloody foot—*"

"Ssssh." Morrie clamped a hand over Heathcliff's mouth. "There she is."

I squinted at Butcher Street below, but I couldn't see anything in the gloom, and I couldn't move closer because I was hemmed in on all sides by fictional characters. Every resident of Nevermore Bookshop had decided to join me and Jo for our midnight vigil, and the window with the best view of Butcher Street was in Quoth's attic bedroom, which wasn't exactly resplendent with space.

That was, every resident except Quoth, who had gone back to the studio after his fly over the woods earlier. But he had replied to my text with a bat emoji, so that was something.

I heard the *clap-clap-clap* of heels on the cobbles, heading toward Grey's flat. Everyone crowded in closer. Robin's elbow boxed my ear. Oscar stood on his hind legs and pawed the window.

"It's her." Jo's voice cracked. "It's my Fiona."

She scrambled to her feet and dashed for the stairs. Morrie untangled himself from Socrates' sheet. "I'll go with her, just in case. Mina, don't you dare move from this spot."

I stuck my tongue out at him. Heathcliff shoved Socrates off the end of the bed, and I leaned out the window, straining to hear what was happening on the street below. Fiona battered on Grey

Lachlan's door, crying out a long stream of gibberish. Another door creaked open. Jo's wavering voice called out, "Fi?"

Fiona ignored her.

"Hey, Fi, it's me, Jo. You should come inside with me."

Bang-bang-bang.

"Did you hear me, Fi?" Jo's voice cracked. "I'm inviting you inside."

Fiona's figure took a step away from the door. She let out a wail as her arms jerked in both directions – she looked like she was doing battle with herself.

"Fiona, please. I want you to come in."

"No," Fiona said firmly, flinging her body away from Jo. She tore up the street with a strange gait, as if she were still battling with her body to accept Jo's invitation.

Shit. Shit. How come she didn't accept our invitation?

Pandemonium ensued. Heathcliff flung Socrates on the bed and rushed for the stairs. Robin notched an arrow and declared he could bring her down from here, while Puck put a protesting Grimalkin on his head and danced around with glee. I tore down the stairs after Heathcliff, Oscar's lead gripped tight in my hand.

Jo held the door open for me, her face grave.

"She didn't want to come in," she said, looping my free arm through her elbow. "She looked right at me, and her eyes were... not her eyes. But there was some part of her still inside. I think she knew if she came in, she'd hurt me, and she was trying to protect me from herself."

"I think so, too. Did you see where they went?" We raced up the street, my purse of stakes battering against my thigh.

"Toward the pub."

Of course. In a mostly darkened village, the pub was lit up like a Christmas tree. I could hear villagers inside singing along to a karaoke version of 'The Monster Mash.' To a newly-minted vampire, the Rose & Wimple was a breakfast buffet. We moved toward the entrance but then Jo must've seen something, because she tugged me and Oscar into the alley. "They came around here."

"Arf!"

We rounded the corner just as I heard Morrie swear. I found him on his knees on the cobbles, and heard footsteps pattering off between the outbuildings.

"I tripped over a poxy bin," Morrie scrambled to his feet, dusting off the front of his blazer. "I didn't see where she went."

She was *fast*. Not even Morrie's long legs could keep up with her. *We'll never catch her now. We—*

A shadow flew around the corner. Fiona shrieked, the sound so high it shattered the glass in the pub windows. She ran toward us, arms flailing, heedless to the fact we were waiting for her. She looked back over her shoulder at the dark shadow that chased her—

The Headless Horseman.

He reared up, his black cloak silhouetted against the moon as he blocked her escape. The horse snorted. Smoke billowed from its flared nostrils. Fiona whirled away from the shadow, her jacket flapping as she scrambled toward us.

"Got you." Heathcliff dropped from the roof of the stable. Fiona swung around and clipped him around the ear just as he thrust a crucifix into her face.

Fiona hissed – an inhuman sound that drew a sob from Jo. She reeled, staggering backward. Morrie threw a sack over her head. Heathcliff pressed the crucifix to her to keep her docile.

"Fiona, I'm so sorry," Jo sobbed as she helped Heathcliff and Morrie bundle the girl onto the back of the horse. The Headless Horseman glided in front of us, the reins tight in his spectral hand. Fiona kicked and bellowed, but it didn't seem to faze the horse.

As we trotted back across the green toward Butcher Street, Mrs. Ellis popped her head from behind the ever-growing bonfire pile.

"Mina!" She thrust her hands on her hips. Tonight she wore a yellow-and-black striped knit dress and a pair of round wings. A bumblebee, appropriate since she was about to sting our vampire-napping. "Where are your costumes? Richard won't let you on stage without a costume."

"No karaoke for us tonight, Mrs. Ellis," I stammered out. "We were just, um..."

"Walking Heathcliff's cousin's horse," Morrie piped up. "He needs regular exercise, or he starts to eat the books."

"Exactly." I gave Heathcliff a shove toward the horse. He tripped on the curb and ended up draped across its rear end. He bellowed a protest, which thankfully covered up Fiona's cries. "And we stopped at the pub to see all the fun, but you know what Earnshaw men are like around booze..."

"You didn't say Mr. Heathcliff had a cousin visiting. I saw a picture of your other houseguest in the paper, and he had a face like a bag of spanners, but this fellow has the Earnshaw tall, dark, and handsome gene..." Mrs. Ellis patted the horse, seeming not to notice her hand went right through the horseman's knee. "You look particularly dashing in that costume atop your mighty steed, young man, even without a head. Now Mina, don't forget your stall at the Witch's Market tomorrow. I've put you next to—"

"Yes, yes. I'm sorry, Mrs. Ellis, we really have to go. We'd better get these two away from the pub before he ends up legless as well as headless. See you tomorrow."

The Headless Horseman spurred his horse, which took off at a mighty gallop with Heathcliff still draped over its rear end. We caught up with them as the Horseman pulled up in front of the shop.

"Nice save with the cousin thing," Heathcliff glowered at Morrie as he slid off the horse. "You know, you're a lot like Socrates."

Morrie placed his hand over his heart. "I'm the wisest man around?"

"No. You piss everyone off."

"Can you both either get a room or help me with this body?" Jo grabbed Fiona's ankle.

Heathcliff threw Fiona over his shoulder and carried her inside. Robin appeared on the landing, an arrow notched on his bow. "Do you want me to put one between her eyes, M'lady?"

"No!" Jo threw herself in front of Fiona.

"What I want you to do is get out of my way." Heathcliff swung his bulk up the staircase. Fiona kicked, knocking one of Quoth's paintings to the floor.

Victor poked his head from the cellar door. His trousers were wet up past his knees. "Mina, you're back. Good, good. I think I've worked out all the kinks now that my monster is back. Have you had a chance to speak with that plumber yet? It's getting a little biblical down here."

"Not now, Victor!" Books cascaded down on us as Fiona slammed her body against the shelves. Morrie pressed the crucifix into her forehead. She howled, clawing at his fingers to get it off her, but it kept her from destroying the shop.

"Take her to my bedroom," I said. "We need Morrie's restraints."

As we maneuvered her into the flat, Fiona kicked a hole in the wall. Heathcliff held Fiona's arms down while Morrie fastened her to the bed with his best bondage gear. She thrashed and jerked, but the restraints held fast.

"If Dracula's been feeding from her, we need to make sure he can't get in to take more blood," I said. "I'd like an extra layer of protection. We need to vampire-proof this room."

"Luckily, we've still got supplies." Morrie disappeared into the kitchen and returned with a box of garlic. "I was going to make my famous garlic roast chicken this week, but we'll just have to have a takeout curry instead."

As the boys rushed about, bedecking the room with garlands

of garlic and gluing crucifixes to the window, Jo buried her face into my shoulder. "I can't bear to see her like this."

"I'm sure everything will be okay. We'll find a way to reverse what he did to her." But even as I said the words, I knew neither of us believed them. We'd both read the novel. We both knew what happened to the victims who shared Dracula's blood. Fiona had risen from the dead – was she fully a monster now, or did some small part of her humanity remain?

CHAPTER FIFTEEN

*B*etween Fiona's toe-curdling shrieks and Jo hogging all the blankets, I hardly slept a wink that night. I loved my best friend, but I didn't love her bony elbows in my ribcage. Quoth's bed was far too small for two people who weren't lovers, but it was the only sane option. I refused to sleep in Heathcliff's bed because it was impossible to find beneath the pile of junk in his room, and the walls in Morrie's storage room were so thin we'd be kept up all night by Socrates recording his philosophical TikToks.

It didn't help that Quoth didn't come home at all. I called and texted him to tell him what happened, and all he did was send me a gif of *Buffy the Vampire Slayer*.

I didn't want cute pop culture gifs. I wanted my bird *home*, in my arms. I wanted him to *want* to be home.

If I did sleep, it was too fast and too deep to experience one of my Dracula dreams. Which was just as well – I didn't think I could bear living through another night of tasting the blood of my friends or lovers on my tongue.

When I checked on Fiona in the morning, she'd settled into a fitful sleep. My room smelled like an Italian restaurant.

"Coffee." Morrie materialized at my side, holding a tray bursting with togo cups. He didn't look like he'd slept much better.

I accepted a cup. "It's a pity you can't hook this to my veins."

Downstairs, I packed up our book selection for our Witch's Market stall – fun children's books like *Meg and Mog*, some classic horror fiction, spooky short story collections, Emily the Strange novels...anything that fit the Halloween theme. I stacked one box into Oscar's cart, and Morrie helped me carry the remaining boxes across the green. Stallholders set up around the perimeter, while in the center stood the towering bonfire, unlit until the final eve of the festival. On top of the pile of sticks and wood, someone had crafted a crude figure of a man from lengths of wicker. It was vaguely unsettling, but burning wicker effigies was part of British folklore, and I knew the toasted marshmallows would taste amazing.

While I arranged our table, Quoth fluttered down from the tree and settled into one of the boxes. "Croak?"

"Yes, I'm fine, thank you." I slammed down a stack of books. "Why didn't you come home last night? Jo needed you."

I needed you, I thought, but then remembered he could hear my thoughts.

I'm sorry. I truly thought you wanted me to text. Professor Sang was showing me this new brush technique. If you'd asked me to come home, I would have, but you didn't ask. You were asking between the words but I was too sleepy and distracted to see it. I truly am sorry.

I sighed. I couldn't stay angry at Quoth, especially when he apologized so sincerely. *That's my bad, too. I should have been clearer. For two people who can talk telepathically, we need to work on our communication skills.*

It's my fault, Mina. I'm so tired I wasn't thinking clearly. This will only be for a couple more days, until the opening, then everything will be better, I promise.

"I know. I love you and I'm so proud of you." I held open the flap of the box. "Why don't you come out in the sunshine? I'm sure the villagers would love to see you."

Quoth shook his head, burying his face under his wing. *Can I just sleep in here? I want to be close to you, but not deal with people quoting that poem at me.*

"Deal." I set the box down in the shade. Oscar loped over and lay down next to it, peering in at his friend.

"Arf."

"Don't you disturb Quoth. He's sleeping." I patted Oscar's head and returned to laying out my stall. As I straightened the edges of my black-and-orange tablecloths, a familiar and terrifying voice reached my ears.

"...endorsed by the Spirit Seekers Society of Argleton, these will provide portable protection from the Dracula Killer, guaranteed or your money back..."

By Isis, save us all.

I put on my best, most patient smile, and turned around to the nearest stall. "Mum, what are you doing?"

"Mina!" Mum beamed as she set out a row of boxes on the stall next to mine. "You're not doing bibliomancy, are you? I don't think you'll get much business. Heathcliff was right, it's basically codswallop—"

"Um, no, I'm not doing bibliomancy." I directed Oscar to lead me over to her table, where I noticed colorful shoeboxes stacked behind her stall and overflowing the trunk of her car. "I wouldn't dream of honing in on your territory. What are these? Tarot card decks?"

"Really, Mina, I thought you had more business sense. It would be silly to sell cards that make my own services obsolete. Frankly, I'm bored of the whole fortunetelling lark. No one wants vague suppositions about the future where there's a killer in our midst. I realized I needed to offer something special to the good people of Argleton, something no law-abiding citizen should be without." Mum pulled away the cloth covering her stall's sign, and I gasped.

HELEN WILDE'S VAMPIRE VANISHING KITS

"Mum, what—"

"Brilliant, isn't it? You and Morrie gave me the idea." Mum held out a shoebox she'd painted black and decorated with silver stars and crosses. She lifted the lid to show me inside. Nestled on a bed of dried garlic cloves was a set of thin wooden stakes that didn't look like they could spike a pigeon, a small glass bottle with a cork stopper labeled 'holy water,' a couple of wooden crucifix necklaces, and a bullet painted silver. "I was up all last night spray-painting the bullets and decorating the boxes. I've done all different colors and designs to suit every taste. Look." She holds up one completely decoupaged with cats. "Isn't this darling?"

"It's..." I couldn't find the words. Instead, I tapped the vial of water. "Where did you get the holy water?"

Did you have to break into the Catholic church and have Quoth distract Father O'Sullivan by enduring a lecture on hairshirts while you nicked from the tabernacle?

"Oh, that was easy. Father O'Sullivan used to be my best customer back when I was doing the diet shakes...or was it the Flourish patch? Anyway, all I had to do was fill up the bathtub, invite him over for tea and scones, and get him to bless it for me in one go. I've got enough holy water to vampire-proof the whole village."

"You...blessed the bathtub?"

"Mina, *please*." Mum gave me a shove back toward my booth. "Not so loud. I don't want my competitors to learn my secrets. They probably think you have to steal from the tabernacle at church."

"But you can't sell blessed objects. That's been the rule since the Middle Ages, if you sell holy water, you remove the blessing and then it's no use against a vampire."

Mum gave me another shove. "Father O'Sullivan gave me a loophole. Technically, my customers pay for the container, and I haven't included any additional charge for the holy water. Now, you go on off to your stall. I don't want people to think I'm part of your dusty old book sale."

She turned away to fuss with her Vampire Vanishing Kits, leaving me standing there with my chin in the dirt.

For the next couple of hours, I tried to forget about Mum and focus on my customers. The Witch's Market was a smashing hit – it seemed as if the entire village was here in costumes, drinking steaming cocktails from cauldron-shaped mugs and buying witchy-themed knickknacks from the stalls. I waved to my friend Maeve, who'd traveled in from Crookshollow to help her friend Clara run a stall for her crystal and witchy store.

No one was buying books, though. A few people stopped to chat, but most of them were more interested in the Halloween-themed fete games or Richard's cider tent, which...fair enough.

Mum, however, was doing a roaring trade. She had a line of villagers stretching from her stall halfway around the market. She beamed as she presented Richard with a shoebox she'd decorated for him with little pints of beer all over it. She sold out before morning tea time and started taking orders, promising each person she'd create a customized box for their personality.

"I can't believe this." I folded my arms. "She's making money off people's fears. Dracula is out there killing people and all my mum can see is pound signs."

"You're jealous." Heathcliff had left Morrie in charge of keeping the fictional characters out of our hair, and stopped by to deliver me one of Oliver's scones and a steaming coffee. "Decorating customized vampire-slaying kits is the most Mina Wilde business idea I've ever encountered."

I punched him in the arm, but I had to admit he had a point. I didn't like how Mum was exploiting the villagers' fears for financial gain. But unlike literally every other get-rich-quick scheme she'd been involved in, this one was actually kind of fun. And the kits were cool. They'd actually be something I'd consider stocking in the shop…if that wasn't a dangerous proposition to make to my mother.

"Mina, look lively," Morrie called from somewhere across the market. He sounded out of breath. "He's on the run."

"What's Morrie saying?" I was bent over, re-tying my bootlace.

"You need to see for yourself. Morrie's run outside with his shirt buttons all buggered." Heathcliff stifled a laugh. I didn't want to look up, because if the Napoleon of Crime was *that* flustered, it had to be bad.

"Yoohoo, Mina," Mrs. Ellis called out. "That naked gentleman wants to speak to you."

I dared to raise my head just as Socrates vaulted over the edge of the bonfire, bedsheet flapping wildly. He shoved market-goers out of the way as he rushed toward me, waving my mobile phone triumphantly in the air. "He retweeted me," he cried out with glee. "Peter Jordanson retweeted me."

"You're supposed to stay inside." Morrie put his head between his legs, gasping for breath. "I'm not built for physical exertion. That's why the first rule of being a criminal genius is, hire minions."

"Mina had to see this." Socrates thrust the phone under my nose, but he was so excited he wouldn't hold it still so I could look. "Look, right there. I've got over seven-hundred new followers already."

"Go on, you'd better show us this tweet." Morrie leaned over to look at the phone. "Ooh, that's good. I approve."

"Don't encourage this." Heathcliff glared at Morrie. "What does it say?"

"'What do you call a dinosaur who followed all my teachings?'" I grabbed the phone from Socrates and read the tweet aloud. "He was a real philosoraptor."

"That's hardly a joke," Heathcliff said. "It doesn't make any sense. And the punchline is weak."

Socrates whipped the phone from my hand and trained it on Heathcliff. "Then tell me, learned sir, what is a punchline?"

"A punchline is the funny bit at the end of a joke."

"Is it a punchline simply by virtue of being at the end?"

"Um, I guess not." Heathcliff sounded wary, like he sensed he was walking into a trap. "It's got to be something unexpected. I'm not going to *explain* humor to you—"

"But if you know that the punchline is about to arrive, how can it be unexpected?"

"Then I guess there can't be a punchline for any joke, since the fact there's a punchline is always expected." Heathcliff folded his arms. "Are you happy now?"

"That's exactly right." Socrates waggled his finger in the air. "Last night the exact same conclusion was told to me by your mother, while we were having intercourse."

Morrie fell onto the grass, shaking with laughter. From inside the box, I could hear the *nyah-nyah-nyah* of Quoth's corvid chuckles.

"Did you..." I glanced at our sheet-clad philosopher with a newfound respect. "Did you just get Heathcliff Earnshaw with a 'your mother' joke?"

"Yusss." Socrates did a victory jig that had several mothers covering the eyes of their innocent children. "You've been pwned by Socrates. And I got that all on video. Be prepared to go viral. Peter Jordanson will eat my dust."

He proceeded to perform a dance around the village green, flapping his giant feet in all directions.

"Don't mind him," I called out to the distraught market-goers. "It's just...er, Heathcliff's great grandfather. Yes, Heathcliff has some family visiting from the North, and they're a bit...eccentric."

"They're not eccentric – they are of the devil, and so is he. So are all of you!"

I whirled around to the sound of righteous indignation. I wasn't surprised to find Dorothy Ingram and the members of DIABLO standing in front of the church gate, glaring at the Witch's Market like they believed a hole in the earth would open up at any moment and we'd all be swallowed in hellfire.

"Do not think that God isn't watching," Dorothy cried, pointing a shaking finger around the stunned villagers. She was dressed in her Sunday best, including an impressive hat with an arrangement of dried flowers and fruit. "He sees this ungodly festival put on by a known fornicator and her friends who raise spirits from their rest. He sees the bookshop with its blasphemous tomes and its shopkeeper who allows herself to be defiled by no less than three men. He sees this alcohol you drink on his Sabbath and this effigy you've built instead of worshipping at his house. He sees all, and sinners will be punished—what's that crunching noise...argh!"

She spun around, her hands flying to tug her hat from the mouth of a monstrous black horse, which had snuck up on her seemingly from out of nowhere to munch on the fruit. Atop the steed, a headless rider clad in black shadow reached down to pat the horse's mane.

"Cool costume!" someone yelled.

"Can I ride your horse, mister?" A kid tried to tug on the Horseman's sleeve, but his hand went straight through. "Wow, neat effect."

Seeing Dorothy's minions scatter in fright as the horse plucked the tasty hat from her head and munched through the brim sent Mrs. Ellis into an uncontrollable giggling fit. That was the last straw for the now hatless Dorothy, who marched up to Mrs. Ellis and waggled her finger in her face. "It's *you* that has brought this killer to our village, Mabel. You with your demonic festival have opened the gates of hell to defile our church and curse innocent women. And I'm going to prove it."

She spun on her heel and stormed away.

I ran to Mrs. Ellis' side. "What a horrid woman. All you're trying to do is give the village back a bit of light-hearted fun after those grisly murders, and she *dares* to blame you—"

"Don't you worry, poppet." Mrs. Ellis patted my arm. "I'm not afraid of Dorothy Ingram."

I thought of the righteous tremor in Dorothy's voice and remembered how far she was prepared to go last time she'd been involved in a crime in this village. "I think maybe you should be."

hen the green emptied out and the majority of the village moved the party to the Rose & Wimple, I packed up the stall. Quoth had flown off just as the sun had started to set, croaking that he'd see me back at the shop, and I was excited to talk to him again and try to rebuild some of our trust. I managed to fit my remaining books into one box and Oscar's cart, but even so, books are heavy, and we returned to Nevermore at a slow shuffle.

As I passed by Dracula's house, an involuntary shudder rocked my body. The place had such a *vibe* of oppressive danger that I didn't know how Dorothy Ingram hadn't broken down the door and performed an exorcism on the Count already.

"I'm back," I called out as we entered the shop. "How's our patient?"

"Huh?" Socrates leaned around the Aviation shelves, turning his ear toward me.

"HOW'S FIONA?"

Socrates peered at me with concern. "Why in Zeus' testicles would you want to go to Macedonia? Nasty, grubby place."

"I don't want to go to Macedonia! I want to know about—" I waved my hand as something crashed overhead. "Never mind."

I hung up Oscar's harness and climbed the stairs. I flinched at another loud crash, followed by an ear-piercing wail.

Puck met me at the top of the stairs. "Are you certain you do not wish her transformed into an ass?"

"Not now, thank you." I shoved open the door to our private chambers, slamming it shut in Puck's face before he could suggest a drastic spell I might actually consider.

Inside our flat, the noise was deafening. Fiona's cries shook the walls. Oscar whimpered, collapsing on the rug and covering his ears with his paws. Grimalkin sat bolt-upright in front of the fire, and as I dropped my coat, she transformed into her human form for the specific purpose of glowering at me.

"How am I supposed to get the twenty-seven hours of daily sleep recommended for a healthy feline with that racket?" She glanced casually down at her nails, which had been perfectly manicured to a sharp tip. "If this continues, I shall have no choice but to scratch her eyes out, give her something to really cry about."

"You'll do no such thing," I warned. "We just need to figure out how to undo what Dracula's done to her, and then we can set her free. Why don't you do something useful and prowl on over to Jenna Mclarey's old place, see if you can figure out why she might've had a stash of Romanian dirt?"

"And be subjected to the slimeball of a husband? No thank you." Grimalkin licked her fingers, then rubbed her ear. "I met him at the pub on one of my nightly prowls, so distracted by chatting up a beautiful young woman he didn't notice me licking the foam off his beer. But if she so much as talks to another man, he flies into a rage like a jealous tomcat."

"Thank you for that tidbit of useless information. Now, go." I pointed toward the door. Grimalkin pouted, but she did transform back into a cat and stalked out the door with her tail cocked high.

I poked my head into the bedroom, catching a wall of garlic fumes in the face. Heathcliff sat in the chair beside the bed, nose in a book while Fiona writhed and thrashed against her restraints. I covered my ears against her wails. "How can you stand the noise?"

Heathcliff snapped the book shut. "Years of blocking out the incessant chattering of customers."

"She wasn't loud this morning."

"We think she might have built up a tolerance to the garlic over time. We tried to get more, but your mother has bought all the fresh garlic from the market. I sent Morrie to Barchester to see if he can find some at the Sainsbury's."

He stood up, holding his arms open. I collapsed into them, resting my head on the lapel of his thick coat, breathing in the spicy musk tinged with peat and the fresh moss of the moors that defined Heathcliff Earnshaw. "What are we going to do?"

"Close the shop for a few days. If anyone asks, say we've had an infestation of banshees." Heathcliff winced as Fiona let out a particularly high-pitched screech.

"We can't afford to lose that much business. Besides, the Spirit Seekers will be here two nights from now."

"You could just...tell them not to come?" Heathcliff sounded hopeful.

"Have you told Mrs. Ellis not to do something? How about my mother?" I burrowed my face deeper into his jacket, wishing I could crawl inside him and hide forever. "Where's Quoth? He said he'd meet me here."

Heathcliff grunted.

That was all the answer I needed. I pulled back reluctantly, spun on my heel, and stalked into the living room.

"Mina, what are you doing?"

I grabbed my coat and signaled for Oscar. "I'm going to see Quoth."

"I'm coming with you."

"You can't. Someone has to stay behind to watch Fiona."

"Make Robin do it. That annoying little gobshite is desperate to have a purpose, and he'd be grateful for anything to get him away from Puck. That blasted fairy turned his bow into a banana."

I smiled despite myself. Heathcliff growled. "It's not funny. He also transformed my favorite Scotch into sour milk, and despite all my best threats he's yet to return it to its former, more delicious state."

With Robin installed as Fiona's lookout, we headed outside to catch a rideshare. As we crossed over the green toward our driver, I noticed a group of people gathered at the edge of the churchyard, their heads bent together as they whispered furtively. I glanced at Heathcliff. "Who's that?"

"Dorothy Ingram and the members of DIABLO. I wonder what they're planning."

"More interruptions to the festival, no doubt." I directed Oscar to climb in the backseat of the Uber. When the driver saw my dog, he slammed the door. "No animals in the car."

"He's a service animal, and you're legally obligated to—"

"NO ANIMALS." The driver tore off, wheels spinning.

This frustration happened often enough that I was considering forcing Morrie to get his license so we could have our own car. Most of the rideshare drivers didn't know the laws around service animals, and they didn't want dog hair in their cars. There were a couple of local drivers who knew me and would happily welcome Oscar on board, but with the app you couldn't always guarantee who you got. Just another super fun example of something that should be straightforward being made more difficult for a blind person not because of their vision but because of society.

Needless to say, I was in a mood by the time we got a driver who'd accept Oscar to drop us off at Quoth's school. As we exited the car, I heard the excited whinny of another dog. Silhouetted against the headlights of a taxi was a woman with a guide dog of her own. I rushed over to catch her.

"Marjorie, hi. It's Allan's friend, Mina Wilde, and my new guide dog, Oscar."

"Oscar? Oh, Mina, I'm so happy you have your dog now." We spent a couple of minutes introducing the dogs and letting them sniff each other, then I asked Marjorie if she could point me toward the studio where Quoth was working.

Her face twisted in concern. "Allan's not here. I've only just left my office and I checked the studios before I locked up."

"Does he have his own key? He's been working late in the studio a lot recently, pulling all-nighters to prepare for the exhibition."

She shook her head. "That's not possible. We don't give out keys to students, and we don't allow them in the studios after 8PM – it's a health and safety thing. He might have rented a private studio space – some of the students do that if they need a big area to work on their pieces after hours."

"Oh, okay. Thanks." I watched her hop into her taxi and drive off, my heart thundering in my chest. Quoth had told me he'd been in the art studio every night, but he wasn't here. He'd *never* been here.

What is Quoth doing?

CHAPTER SEVENTEEN

*Q*uoth didn't come home again that night. I sent him several texts, asking him to wake me up when he got home so we could talk. But I didn't sleep. Part of it was I didn't want to have another of Dracula's dreams, but the Count's presence pressed in on me from all sides anyway, reminding me that on the other side of the street lurked a man who could hurt anyone I loved.

But as I watched the glow-in-the-dark stars and birds on Quoth's ceiling, letting the lights dance colored squiggles across my vision, I drove myself crazy trying to rationalize Quoth's lies. He'd never lied to me before, not *ever*. I didn't even know he was capable of lying.

But he was. And he did.

And it hurt. It hurt more than a wound not made by a knife or a weapon should ever hurt. It hurt like his lie was flaying my skin. It made me doubt every beautiful moment we shared, every kiss he'd placed so reverently on my lips, every sad and lovely word he'd spoken to me.

Tears rolled down my cheeks. I didn't even care where he was – it wasn't important anymore. I thought we had something special. I thought we were birds of a feather. But if he could lie to me about this, then I...I didn't know what to believe.

When Quoth finally fluttered through the window, the first dappled rays of sunlight danced through the trees. I bolted upright, my fists curled with suppressed emotion. "Where were you?"

He hopped onto the bed and transformed into his human form. I flicked the light on – I wanted to see his face when I confronted him. He gazed up at me through a curtain of shimmering hair. His fire-ringed eyes appeared sunken, bloodshot. He needed sleep.

Well, tough. I needed answers.

Quoth went to take my hand, but I jerked away. "I went to the school to see you tonight, but it was locked up. I spoke to Marjorie in the parking lot. She said you haven't been working late at school. They don't allow students on campus after 8PM. So where have you been going all these nights?"

Quoth's eyes fluttered closed. He pressed his lips together, and his features sank into an expression of such sadness and regret that I almost melted right there. "I'm sorry," he whispered.

"Don't be sorry. I'm beyond sorry. I want an explanation. Where *were* you? Is it another girl? Another...family? You wouldn't have lied like this unless..." I didn't realize until the words were out of my mouth how much I feared them.

He shook his head. "No, no, I would never cheat on you, not with a human or a bird. Professor Sang rented a place so I could put in the extra hours to get the pieces finished. I didn't tell you because...I was embarrassed that I let him pay for it, I guess. I knew you'd think it was weird and I didn't want to ask you for money for it when the shop was struggling—"

"You *should* have asked. We would have found a way. Not to mention dangerous, saying you're at school when you're actually somewhere else. What if tonight was an emergency and I tried to find you but you weren't there? And it *is* weird, this professor paying for your studio space like that. If you needed a place to work after hours, why couldn't you do it at home? At least then I'd know where you were and I wouldn't worry about you."

Quoth nodded to the staircase, where the sounds of Fiona's keening wail echoed up through the attic, joined by Heathcliff and Morrie bickering and random thumps and yells that could be...absolutely anything now that Puck was in residence.

"Okay, fine. I get it. This place is chaos on toast. But you *lied* to me." I sniffed back the sob that threatened to consume me. "How can I trust anything you say now?"

Quoth's bottom lip quivered. "Mina, I—"

I held up my hand. "I can't do this right now. I've got Dracula to worry about, and Fiona downstairs, and Jo's upset, and new fictional characters showing up every day, and a bunch of occultists showing up for a lecture, and Heathcliff and Morrie being...Heathcliff and Morrie. I didn't think I had to do this alone, but you've made it clear where you stand. So go, Quoth. Just *go.*"

He said nothing. His shoulders trembled as he bowed his head, retreating into his own mind to shield him from the harshness in my voice. He didn't move from the bed. I snatched my clothes from the floor and stormed toward the door. I hated hurting him. I hated every step I walked away from him, but I needed him to know that he'd hurt me, too.

"*E*xcuse me." A white-haired lady glowered at me. She looked familiar, although I felt certain I'd never served someone who looked quite this irate before. "I want to return this book. And I demand a refund, plus extra for damages. In fact, I shall be suing you for emotional distress."

"Um, sure, you can try. What seems to be the problem?" I

peered at the North Staffordshire Railway book, which looked perfectly fine to me.

"I purchased this book for my husband's retirement present. But look at the filth I found inside." She flung open the cover and tossed the book down on the counter like it would burn her fingers if she held it any longer.

I leaned in close to see what she was so upset about. I gulped as the pictures came into view. Instead of scenic photographs of LMS rolling stock, I was greeted with woodcut images of naked women interlocked in the most *acrobatic* positions.

"My husband had to open this...this *filth* in front of all his friends," she screeched. "What must they think of us? Father O'Sullivan was there, and he fainted right into the custard creams. You ruined my husband's retirement party, and I *demand* compensation."

Oh, no. Bertie must've forgotten to change the covers back on this one. "Sure, ma'am. I'm so sorry about the mixup. If you hold on a moment I'll be able to locate the actual interior of this book for you—"

I reached for the offending volume, but she snatched it out of my reach. "I refuse to allow you to expose other innocents to this degradation. I'm giving this book to Dorothy Ingram and she'll burn it along with the others."

"What others?" I cried out, but the woman was already stomping toward the door, nearly bowling over Jo in her rush to escape my depraved presence.

"What was her problem?" Jo handed me a breakfast sausage roll. "Did she make the mistake of quoting The Raven to Quoth?"

I told Jo what Bertie had done. She nearly choked on her coffee with laughter. "Hearing about your customers always makes me happy mine are so quiet and well-behaved. Well, except for Fiona..."

She trailed off, her eyes turning toward the ceiling as Fiona's cries wafted down from upstairs. Jo stiffened.

"I'm sorry." I squeezed her shoulder. "At least she's safe here. We're telling customers it's a spooky Halloween soundtrack."

"Right." Jo swallowed. "Are you up for a little crime scene re-enacting?"

"Explain."

Jo held up a stack of papers. "I hold in my hand the ill-gotten police report for Jenna Mclarey's murder. It includes a map of the exact location of the body, as well as the SOCO report and statements from the police interviews. All Jenna's friends say her husband Connor was a sleazebag who tried it on with each of them at least once, but that he was fiercely jealous of her talking to other men. Sounds like a real winner, not that it's much help to us. Although *this* is." Jo pulled out a paper and waved it at me. "I thought we could head over to the cemetery tonight with this handy crime scene map and see if any brilliant ideas occur to us."

"I'd love to, but maybe you should take Morrie instead. You know I don't see so well at night and—"

"Nonsense. Mina, if I'm going to be sneaking around a cemetery in the middle of the night trying to hunt a vampire, then I want my best friend by my side." Jo grinned. "I'll be back for you after closing. Wear your best cat-burglarizing catsuit, and we'll see if we can trap this mouse."

CHAPTER EIGHTEEN

"...$\mathcal{S}$even, eight, nine...here it is." Jo stopped in her tracks. "This is where Jenna was killed."

I dropped my hand from Jo's arm and bent down to inspect the grave. I had to press my nose against the cold stone and hold my phone right next to my face to read the name – GEORGE HACKSTONE – I CAME HERE WITHOUT BEING CONSULTED AND LEAVE WITHOUT CONSENT. "Sounds like old George was the life of the party. Not a relation of hers?"

"Not as far as I can figure," Jo said. "I don't think the placement of the body at this grave is significant. Jenna's murder wasn't like the others. She was killed first, then he drained her blood afterward. Left quite a bit behind on the grass, too, the messy bastard."

"What?" I stood up, dusting off my hands. Oscar sniffed around the headstone. "That wasn't in the papers."

"With serial killers, we try to keep back certain information. Sometimes you don't want the killer to know what you know."

"So she didn't die from exsanguination?"

"Nope. She was done in by a blow to the back of the head – a blunt, flat object. There was a spot of blood on the corner here."

Jo tapped the stone with her nail. "The police thought the killer might've pushed her and she hit her head. That's definitely possible, but…"

"But not if Dracula's our killer." That wasn't how he operated. Dracula used coercion – he prided himself on his mind-fuckery prowess. He didn't go about shoving people in cemeteries.

"Exactly. And there were some other odd things. She was all tarted up – six-inch heels, red dress, sexy lace knickers. Definitely not your usual late-night cemetery-wandering attire. I'd say she'd come to meet someone with amorous intent."

I remembered something one of the ladies from DIABLO said. "Do you think she could have been the woman seen 'cavorting' amongst the headstones? Maybe Dracula seduced her and convinced her to meet him there with the dirt? But it still doesn't tell us about where she got her dirt or what the container might look like…"

I trailed off as I noticed Jo peering over my shoulder, her brow furrowed. "Mina, look."

I turned and tried to focus on the beam of her flashlight, but of course, I couldn't make out what she was staring at. I threaded my hand through her elbow again, and she led me and Oscar over to a low building – the maintenance shed, I guessed. Stacked up beside the door was a stack of old wood. Jo bent down and started to sort through the planks. She held one up.

"I can't believe Hayes and Wilson didn't search here." She pointed to the end of the wood. All I could see were a few bent nails sticking out the end. Jo jabbed at the wood with her thumb. "I'll take this back to the lab to check, but I'd bet my signed Black Sabbath record that this dark patch here is a bloodstain. I'm holding the murder weapon."

CHAPTER NINETEEN

*Q*uoth made a point of hopping onto my shoulder as soon Jo and I trudged in the front door. *I made some hot chocolate. It's on the stove upstairs.*

I knew this was him apologizing, but it was my umpteenth late-night in a row and I did not have the strength to dig into my emotions with him right now. I shut down my thoughts as I trudged up the stairs. Fiona's bangs and shrieks emanated from my bedroom, and Victor stomped through the shop, leaving a trail of squelchy carpet behind him as he muttered about the subpar service of our local handyman, who still hadn't shown up. Jo raced inside ahead of me, eager to sit by Fi's side. I desperately needed a pee and a stiff drink that wasn't tainted apology chocolate.

Mina, please talk to me. Quoth fluttered up the stairs behind me. *I want to—*

"I'm sleeping with Morrie tonight," I snapped, slamming the bathroom door in his face.

*T*he next day, Jo headed off to work early to test the blood on the wooden board we found at the cemetery. Heathcliff had promised Mrs. Ellis he'd run security at today's Halloween Craft-A-Thon at the village hall, just in case DIABLO had any sabotage plans. Socrates co-opted Morrie into starring in a video demonstrating the Socratic Method, and my Master Criminal could never resist a chance to demonstrate his mental prowess, so they were upstairs filming while Robin took practice shots at some old books he'd lined up along the stairwell. Puck stood behind Robin, snapping his fingers to shuffle the books so Robin's arrows always sailed wide. If Puck didn't watch out, he'd find himself riddled with arrow holes like a Shakespearean Saint Sebastian.

The shop was blissfully empty today – everyone in the village was over at the Craft-A-Thon. I spent a little time scrolling through Jenna Mclarey's social media accounts, looking for any possible connection to Romania or dirt, and coming up completely blank. The dead woman smiled at me out of every photograph, reminding me that I couldn't let her death be in vain. Something about our cemetery visit last night was niggling at me, but I couldn't figure out what it was.

I knew there was no point fruitlessly searching – our best chance at a clue would come from Jo's analysis of the murder weapon. I shut down Facebook and opened up a secret file.

My novel.

It was a fictionalized account of the first murder I solved – my ex-best friend, Ashley Greer – and meeting the guys. I'd been secretly working on it during whatever spare bits of time I could snatch. I still hadn't told the guys I was writing it. I didn't know why. I guessed…I wanted this just for myself for now. I was going to tell Quoth first – of all of them, I knew he'd understand. He didn't like for me to see his work before it was finished, but he loved to talk about his paintings with me, his process, his choices for composition and medium and colors, his existential angst when things didn't go his way. At least, he used to talk to me.

Right now I didn't want to tell Quoth anything.

My fingers paused over the keys. I clicked the button to hear my words read back to me. In the quiet of the deserted bookshop, surrounded by the works of all my favorite writers, everything I wrote sounded awful. Cliched. Riddled with errors and tautologies and poxy adverbs.

I slumped over the desk, my head in my hands. *Who am I kidding? I'm a peddler of books, not a creator of them.*

Who knew it was so much harder to write about murders than it is to solve them?

But then I remembered this was how I felt about fashion, too. Whenever I created a piece I'd start with an idea that excited me, but as soon as I laid out the pattern and started cutting, a wave of existential dread washed over me. I felt in my bones that I was making a terrible mistake, but being at school and working for Marcus taught me that I had to work through that fear until I could see my vision emerging from the chaos.

The only way out was through.

I placed my fingers on the keys again. *You can do this, Mina. You lived this mystery. Just write what happened. You can fix it all later.*

I sucked in a breath and drew my mind back to the first day I walked into Nevermore Bookshop. The smell of dusty shelves and leatherbound pages and Heathcliff's peaty, spicy scent. Quoth's voice falling into my mind, as if he'd always been a part of me. My fingers flew over the keys, and my heart soared as the words poured out of me...just as the computer made a defiant *POP* and shut down.

All the lamps in the shop flickered out.

"Victor!" I yelled.

A moment later, the cellar door opened and Victor Frankenstein *squelch squelch squelched* across the rug. "You called?"

"You took out the power."

"It appears so." He peered at the blank computer screen and my phone open on my notes app. "I hope you didn't lose anything important."

"Just my novel." I sighed. "It's fine. It wasn't exactly good, anyway."

"Don't talk like that. Do you think if I stopped the first time I tried to stitch a monster from bits of dead humans, I'd have gotten to where I am today?" Victor beat his chest with pride. "If I'd quit, I wouldn't be Victor Frankenstein, the most celebrated doctor in literature."

"Um, yes, I'm not sure *celebrated* is the right word—"

"Mina, you can't give up every time the answers don't line up perfectly. Art isn't like that. Art is like the human body – it starts with a skeleton to hold everything together. Don't concern yourself with the skin and organs and gristle until you've got the bones in the right places first."

"That's...surprisingly helpful, thank you."

"You're welcome." Victor dripped freezing water over the keyboard. "So, can you get me the power back on?"

"I hope so. We need it to run the shop and power my hair straightener." I picked up my phone. "I'll call Handy Andy."

"Please do, and remind him to fix the plumbing while he's here. Things are getting awfully damp in the cellar." He held up his leg. I couldn't see the fabric, but I heard the *squelch* of soaking cloth. "And sometimes I fancy I see...things in the water. It might be dangerous down there—"

"Hey, Mina! Are you in here? All the lamps have gone out—*ow*."

I held up the flashlight function on my phone and shined it at the doorway. "Jo. Yes, we're having a wee problem with the power."

"I'll say," an annoyed voice called from the top of the stairs. "We were filming a Facebook live and all the lights went out."

"Hi, Socrates." Jo gave the Greek philosopher a fistbump on the way past. "I saw Peter Jordanson mentioned you in his latest video. Awesome stuff."

"You just fist-bumped the father of philosophy." I grinned as she lowered herself into the velvet chair. "You really are okay with all this…bookshop stuff."

"Mina, you're my friend. Everything else is window-dressing." Jo peered at the stairs. "How's Fiona?"

"The same. She isn't screaming as much today. Morrie found some more garlic, and we strung that up and that seems to have helped, but now she's in some kind of Dracula-induced delirium. She hasn't eaten anything we've tried to feed her. I don't know if we should be feeding her blood, or garlic, or what. I wish there was a manual on how to de-vampire someone."

"You and me both." Jo crossed her legs beneath her. "Do you want to hear the results of my tests?"

"Hell yes."

"The plank is *definitely* the murder weapon. The blood matches the victim, and the shape of the wood is a perfect match to the head wound. But that doesn't tell us why the victim was in the cemetery that night or how she came into possession of some graveyard dirt, and where it is now." Jo patted my leg. "So, I invited her husband out for a drink. You want to come with me?"

I held out my phone to view her outfit – a low-cut red wrap dress and blood-red lipstick to match. "Is this official police business or do you intend to seduce this guy into giving you information?"

She flashed me a wild grin. "Three guesses?"

I sighed. "Just give me a second to change. Two wanton harlots always work better than one."

"That's my motto," Morrie called from behind the poetry shelves.

"Arf."

"And Oscar agrees."

"*Y*ou didn't have to come with us," Jo said to Morrie.

"There's a bloodthirsty vampire on the loose. I'm not leaving you ladies unprotected. Besides," Morrie straightened his lapels. "If we're going to seduce this man, we need to cover all our bases. We don't know which way he swings."

"Thirteen complaints of sexual harassment from women in his workplace suggest that we do," Jo said. "He's at the table in the corner. Morrie, you sit at the table behind us. If things don't go well, do something creative."

Morrie snapped his fingers. "One wrong move and his insides move to the outside of his body."

Jo and I slid into the booth opposite Connor Mclarey. In the low light of the pub, I couldn't see his features, but I could *sense* his leer from here. Yep, Jenna's husband was a real winner.

"Mmmmm, two for the price of one. Can I buy you ladies a drink?" Connor leaned across the table, getting right up in Jo's face. "If I knew the police were this foxy, I'd get in trouble more often."

I noticed Jo didn't correct him about his police comment. "We just have a few follow-up questions, Connor. But I thought we'd do it in a more relaxed environment. You're not in any trouble, you understand? We're so sorry for your loss."

She laced her fingers in his. Connor hung his head, his shoulders shaking in faux sobs. "I'm just so...upset...about Jenna. I miss her so much. She might've been a cheating harlot, but she was my girl, y'know? It's so hard being alone, especially at night, especially in our big king-sized bed."

"Tell us all about it, poor boy." Jo stroked his hand. Under the table, she nudged my boot. As much as it made my skin crawl, I reached out and took his other hand, rubbing circles on his knuckles with my fingers.

"We'll sit with you as long as you need, Connor," I cooed.

"All we want to know is if Jenna had any connection with Romania. Maybe relatives? Or a business interest?"

"Romania? You mean like…" Connor formed his hands into claws and stuck his tongue out. "I vant to suck your blood."

"Yeah, that's the country." *I mean, sure, it's also majestic mountains and communist history and Vlad the Impaler and probably all sorts of other interesting things, but let's focus on the book written by the Irish theatre-man who never actually visited Romania.*

"I dunno. She loved those *Twilight* films." Connor's voice darkened. "Maybe that's why she was meeting *him* in the graveyard. She wanted to pretend he was a sparkly vampire. Jokes on her that she got drained by the Dracula Killer instead."

"What do you mean by *him?*"

"The Reverend Mosley. He's the douche-canoe she was cheating on me with." Connor jerked his hands away and grabbed his drink. "That's why Jenna was in the cemetery that night. They met there on the nights I worked late and he didn't have Bible study. They fucked on top of the graves. I think the good father liked slapping her white arse under the moonlight. Jenna thought she was being oh-so-clever sneaking around on me, but she didn't know I followed her and saw it all. *No one makes a fool of Connor Mclarey.*"

"Can you describe this Reverend Mosley?" I glanced at Jo. "We've never met him."

"Tall, longish hair, foppish-looking, with old-fashioned clothes. Real intense eyes." Connor slapped his fist into his hand. "A tiny dick that I'm going to cut off for messing with my girl. I bet he was the one who killed her. He's definitely a freak. Yeah, you should be looking at him."

"Don't worry, we will." Under the table, Jo threaded her fingers in mine and squeezed.

That sounds like Dracula to me.

And we've never seen this new vicar. That can't be a coincidence. Dracula is posing as Reverend Mosley.

So our victim was seduced by Dracula and lured to the cemetery that night. He must've been meeting her there to get the dirt off her. But where would she get Romanian dirt from?

CHAPTER TWENTY

On the day of the festival bonfire, I'd organized for a leading London occultist to give a talk in the shop's event space. I'd agreed to display our occult volumes in the shop for an hour before the talk – a rare chance for those so inclined to peruse these rare works. Even though I hadn't managed to get ahold of Handy Andy to fix the power, we decided to go ahead – the gloom only added to the atmosphere.

From the moment I flipped the sign, Nevermore was abuzz with black-clad men boasting majestic beards and distinctive body odor issues, all chatting politely about the demons they planned to summon and bend to their will. We sold a couple of our rare occult volumes to a guy with a grey beard so long it would make Gandalf jealous, and I endured several incomprehensible lectures about the erotic prowess of various goat-headed deities.

After the talk, when I'd just finished placing every last occult book away upstairs, a spotty man with his hands shoved deep in his pockets came up to the counter. I didn't remember seeing him earlier. "Hi, so I heard about this event on the community notice board, but the lecture didn't answer my questions. I wonder if you have any books about bringing the dead to life again?"

My head snapped up. I gave him my best customer-service smile. "I'm sure you'll find something in our occult section. It's over there behind the man with the Satanic Feminist t-shirt."

The guy shook his head. "I had a look there, but some guy said those books were a lot of nonsense. He said you have some other books. *Powerful* books."

Something glittered on his throat, just visible above the collar of his black t-shirt. I couldn't be sure from this distance, but I was pretty certain it was a crucifix. Either this dude was protecting himself from the Dracula Killer, or he was a member of DIABLO, sent by Dorothy to destroy our books.

I gave him my sweetest smile. "You're right, we do have some antiquarian books upstairs, but they are for viewing by appointment only due to their fragile nature. I can give you a list of titles and if you're interested in a particular book I'll have it brought down for you to view."

He scrambled around in his wallet. I thought he was going to offer me a bribe, but instead, he held out a picture of a scruffy-looking dog. "This is Angus. He died last week and I...I'm not...I miss him soooo much."

His body convulsed with sobs. *By Athena, if this is an act, it's a bloody good one.*

"Can I offer you a tissue?"

He took one from the box I proffered and honked into it. "I want to bring him back from the dead. But I need the spell to be *specific*. Only for dogs – that's very important. He's buried in the garden next to my ex-wife, and I don't want her coming back."

"Oh, Mina," Socrates called from the other room. "This customer wants to know if The Hunger Games is a good diet book?"

"I'm terribly sorry." I gave Mr. My-Ex-Wife-Is-Casually-

Buried-In-the-Garden an apologetic shrug. "I have to help someone else. But Heathcliff here will answer all your questions."

As I made my exit, I heard the familiar scamper of boots as the creepy guy ran for his life from the bookshop, all the other occultists hot on his heels. A moment later, Heathcliff appeared at the doorway, the broom gripped tight in his hands. "This place is even nuttier than usual."

"Agreed. It's something in the air."

"It's this bloody Halloween festival," Heathcliff sulked. "It's turned people crazy. Someone asked me if we had a movie version of the bible with Mel Gibson's face on the cover."

"Speaking of the Halloween festival…" I tapped my phone to read out the time. "We should get going. It's almost time for the bonfire."

"Who holds a bonfire in the middle of the day?"

"People who adhere strictly to the conditions of their council fire permit." I flipped the sign over the door and held Oscar's harness for him to step into. I called out to the others, and from every corner of the shop came hoots and hollers and thumping footsteps as Morrie, Robin, Victor, Puck, the Headless Horseman (sans horse, thankfully) and Grimalkin joined the three of us.

Jo waved to us from my bedroom window. She'd decided to skip the bonfire lighting to watch Fiona. "Have fun. Take lots of pictures for me."

"Will do."

When we arrived at the top of Butcher Street, I realized my promise to Jo might be foiled. I'd never seen so many people crowded around the village green. It seemed as though everyone in Argleton had shown up in their costumes to witness the lighting. I didn't have a hope of seeing over their heads, but the wicker man loomed high above the crowd so I knew we'd still get a great show from the back. I nudged Morrie to get in line for cider, and started hunting out a good snack option from one of the many food carts parked nearby.

Only, someone wasn't having it. "Yooo hooo, Mina." A hand waved from deeper in the crowd. I cringed. I'd recognize that voice anywhere.

"Coming, Mother." I gripped Heathcliff's elbow as we pushed through the crowd. Mum was standing on a chair at the front of the crowd, wearing a Camilla Parker Bowles costume, right on the police tape line that only fire officials were allowed to cross. She had a prime view, but I knew she wasn't there to watch a ritual bonfire. In front of her was a table covered with a small stack of painted wooden boxes. The sign read, NEW: PREMIUM VAMPIRE VANISHING KITS. TAKING ORDERS NOW FOR CHRISTMAS DELIVERY.

I picked up one of the boxes. Instead of a painted shoebox, it was a cute wooden box with brass hinges, lock and key. The edges were beautifully finished. Inside were cushioned dividers for the stakes, holy water, and garlic, and a hand-lettered booklet tucked into the lid offered advice on sigils and spells to ward off vampires and evil spirits. "These are beautiful, Mum. I love the upgrade."

Mum pressed the kit into my hands. "That one's for you, Mina. I made it red and sparkly especially for you. I want you to be safe out there. These others aren't for sale – they're our sample kits."

"What do you mean, *our?*" A familiar sense of suspicion gnawed at my stomach as I slotted the Vampire Vanishing Kit into my purse. "How did you make more kits so quickly? You'd completely sold out the other day."

"Andy helped me." Mum batted her eyelashes. "He's so *handy.*"

Andy? I turned around to see Handy Andy standing awkwardly behind Mum in a matching Prince Charles costume. He blushed when he saw me. "Hi, Mina."

"Andy? H-h-hello." *Why are you wearing a couples' Halloween costume with my mother?* "This is a coincidence. I've been trying to reach you, but you haven't been answering your phone. I need you to fix a few things around the shop. The electricity has gone out, and I think a pipe has burst somewhere because the basement is flooding. And you still haven't bricked up that secret passage for me."

"I'm sorry, Mina." Andy looked to my mother for help, but she was busy demonstrating the Vampire Vanishing Kits to a girl dressed as Wednesday Addams. "I was meaning to pop in and see you in person, but Helen roped me into building boxes and I…"

Helen? They're on first-name basis?

Is my mum *dating* Handy Andy?

I didn't know how I felt about that, especially with the letters from my father burning a hole in my psyche. "That's okay. Just… it's kind of urgent. It's hard to run a bookshop without lights or a computer or a credit card machine, and the Spirit Seekers Society will need it to perform their paranormal investigation tomorrow night."

"Without light, no one will know to heed the KEEP OUT OR WRETCHED CIRCUMSTANCES WILL BEFALL YOU signs I put up all over the flat," Heathcliff added.

"Oh, don't worry about us, dear," Mum piped in. "In fact, it'll probably be better if the power stays off. Shoddy wiring disrupts our sensitive equipment. Now, please dear, stop bothering Andy while he's working."

Andy fitted a hardhat over his Charles mask and stepped over the police tape. I'd forgotten he was a volunteer firefighter. *I think Mum may have actually scored a winner here, especially if I can get him to fix the shop…*

The crowd hushed as the firefighters spread out around the bonfire, hoses at the ready in case things got out of control. Mrs. Ellis stepped out in front of the assembled villagers. Her witch's nose had come unstuck a little at the edge, but she didn't seem to notice. She raised her hands. "Thank you all for being here today. On behalf of the Spirit Seekers Society, we're so grateful you're enjoying the festival. We've got more treats in store for you for the rest of the week, including the much-anticipated Art Walk. Who knows? Maybe there will be a few tricks, as well—"

Behind her, Earl's band struck up a jaunty tune. Robin stepped out of the crowd, dressed in his green woodland garb. The crowd cheered as they recognized him. He raised his bow and dipped the tip of his arrow in something. Andy held out a lighter to light Robin's arrow. Robin drew his arm all the way back to his chin and—

"Stop. Stop this depravity *right now*."

"Arf, arf!" Oscar cried. He wasn't happy.

I spun around to face the voice. It was impossible to see through the crowd, but it seemed to be coming from the direction of the churchyard. People started to scream and cry. My fingers tightened around Heathcliff's arm and Oscar's harness, and urged them forward. We had to know what was going on.

"Mina Wilde, you get back here," Mum yelled after me. I ignored her. We pushed through the crowd as people scrambled toward the shops for cover. When I got close enough to see what was going on, I gasped.

In the middle of the cemetery, someone had stacked a small pile of items. I recognized some of the signs advertising the festival, several of Mum's Vampire Vanishing Kits and…the rare occult books I'd sold earlier today. I'd been wrong about the spotty kid – he wasn't a double agent, he just really missed his dog. The Gandalf-wannabe had betrayed us all. But that wasn't the worst of it.

Tied to a stake on top of the pile was the new vicar, Reverend Mosley. At least, I assumed he was the new vicar because he wore vestments and I hadn't seen him before. He was quite handsome, with vivid blue eyes and long, pale hair that curled below his ears.

But wait a second, if this is the real Reverend Mosley, then did that mean Jenna wasn't meeting Dracula for cemetery sexy-times?

"Somebody help me," he cried, struggling against his bonds. "These crazy women tied me up and they want to—"

"The only person who can help you now is Jesus." Dorothy Ingram stepped forward. "You've been caught red-handed cavorting on sanctified ground. Now, everyone please, turn away from that blasphemous symbol of pagan ideology and feast your eyes on God's true wrath. Starting with Argleton's peddler of profane and Satanic literature, Mina Wilde."

Dorothy lowered something in her hand and pointed it directly at me. It was only when Heathcliff threw himself in front of me that I realized it was a gun.

CHAPTER TWENTY-ONE

"Step out of the way, gypsy." Dorothy Ingram waved the gun at Heathcliff. "I'm perfectly happy to put a bullet through your chest to save this village from eternal damnation."

"No one needs to shoot anyone," I cried out. "Dorothy, can't you see this is ridiculous? You're talking about murdering people. I don't think your god would want you to do that."

"Yes, come now, dear." Mrs. Ellis shuffled forward. "This festival is just a bit of harmless fun. I think what you need is a nice cup of tea."

"Please, Dorothy, darling." Cynthia was inching along the cemetery fence toward Dorothy. "This isn't the way—"

Dorothy spun around, pointing the gun at Cynthia. My hand flew to my mouth. Everyone gasped.

"You...you blasphemers," Dorothy spat. "All this started with your little banned book club. And now you've added Satan worship and witchcraft right here in the middle of our village. Well, we need to clean up this town, starting by burning all the objectionable material." She kicked her pile of books, and a couple of volumes tumbled across the grass.

"That's my Peter Jordanson book." Socrates hopped up and

down. "And my Nietzsche. These are great thinkers. Some might even call them students of my own teachings."

"These so-called philosophers reject the very god who watches over us all. These books are a corrupting influence and must be destroyed to purify our thoughts." Dorothy advanced on Socrates. I glanced around. *Where are the police?*

"This is just like the Assembly of Athens. You're making up nonsense claims of impiety and corrupting the youth to hide the fact you can't handle your own beliefs being questioned. And I thought I left such ignorance behind me." Socrates folded his arms. "What's next, you'll drown us all in a hemlock bath?"

"Socrates, *please* don't provoke her," I pleaded.

"Who are you, anyway? You're another of Heathcliff Earnshaw's relatives. Well, we don't want your sort around here anymore." Dorothy spun back to face Cynthia. "First, I'll sacrifice the rot – this impure priest and the Spirit Seekers Society – then I'll run every person associated with Nevermore Bookshop right out of town!"

There was a clicking noise as Dorothy slid the safety off the gun. I closed my eyes as Heathcliff barreled forward, but I knew he was too far away to stop that bullet from tearing through Cynthia. *By Isis, please, someone do something.*

"I'm afraid you won't be doing that."

Thank you, goddess.

My eyes flew open. I expected to see Inspector Hayes arresting Dorothy. Instead, a hunched and unsightly figure stepped out of the cemetery trees to advance menacingly on her, a wide-brimmed straw hat pulled low.

Grey Lachlan.

CHAPTER TWENTY-TWO

*D*orothy gasped, her hand wavering as she took in the sight of him.

I didn't blame her for her shock. I'd seen Grey just the other day, but that had been in the gloom of Mrs. Ellis' old flat. in broad daylight, he looked like complete shit. The skin of his cheeks hung in tatters, and his eyes and lips were rimmed with red. He shuffled forward with an almost insect-like gait, and even from here I could smell an unpleasant odor wafting from him – an odor of death and decay.

"Grey?" Cynthia cried. "Help me."

Dorothy must've decided someone so hideous as Grey couldn't be a threat, because she continued to point the gun at Cynthia. "No one can stop me doing what I came here to do. I have the Lord on my side."

"That may be true," said Grey. "But the law is against you. As a developer, I know the council bylaws back to front and inside out, and you can't have a bonfire within the village boundary without a council permit."

"That's right. Here's ours." Mrs. Ellis whipped a folded sheaf of papers from her carpetbag and held it up for everyone to see.

"*Exactly.* And I assume the council didn't give you permission for this little effigy." Grey indicated the struggling vicar. "I see at least three council members in the audience. Even if you walk away from this without jail time, they'll have no choice but to issue you with a fine."

"I don't care," Dorothy yelled.

"You'll care because as well as that fine, you'll be forbidden from using council buildings like the community hall. This means the DIABLO committee will have to find somewhere else for their weekly prayer circle. Now put down the gun or train it on me, because you'll only get one chance to shoot before Heathcliff Earnshaw decks you, and the absolute last thing you want to do is ruin my wife's festival or her beautiful face."

I stared at him. Even as corrupted as he'd become by Dracula's power, there was some part of him that still remembered who he was as a human – that he loved his wife. It reminded me of Fiona trying to stop herself from entering the bookshop.

Or maybe this was just Grey's way of manipulating us all.

"Dorothy, the gun." Grey held out his hand. Dorothy's arm trembled as she held out the weapon. She looked like she was trying to control her movements, but her arm moved of its own volition, holding the gun out toward Grey, barrel pointed to the earth.

"Heeeyah!" Wilson sprung from behind the lychgate and tackled Dorothy, swatting the gun onto the grass. Grey went for it, but Hayes barged him with his shoulder and got there first. He ejected the chamber and dropped the gun into the pocket of his trench coat.

"That's it," he barked. "I want everyone to go home."

"But the bonfire!" Mrs. Ellis cried.

"We'll have it another day—" Hayes stepped in front of the remaining DIABLO members, who were all attempting to sneak away behind the church. "Not you lot. You're all coming to the station with us. The rest of you, go home."

The green started to clear out, but Morrie was still stuck behind the crowd over by the cider stall. I gripped Heathcliff's hand. "I want to talk to Grey before he disappears."

He nodded. We stepped through the lychgate and around the villagers who rushed to help the Reverend Mosley down from the stake. Oscar and Heathcliff helped me navigate around the crumbling stones as we headed toward Grey.

A lone mouse skittered across the top of a gravestone, probably heading toward the green to see if anyone had dropped a piece of battered haddock. Grey swiped out his hand and grabbed it, stuffing the rodent into his mouth. The tail hung out the side like a piece of spaghetti.

CRUNCH.

I cringed. "Ew."

Grey slurped up the tail like a piece of spaghetti. "Delicious. You should try it."

"I was coming over here to thank you for de-escalating the situation and demonstrating you still have an ounce of humanity left, but then you went and ruined it. If you're hungry, why don't you stop by the bakery – Oliver catches a ton of mice in his traps every day and we're all sick of Grimalkin bringing them back to the shop and pretending she caught them."

"No thanks. They're no good if they're already dead," Grey smacked his lips together and doffed his hat at us. "If you'll excuse me, ladies, my master needs me."

They're no good if they're already dead...

As I watched Grey shuffle away, the penny dropped. I knew what had been niggling me about Jenna's murder.

I wanted to smack myself. I couldn't believe I didn't see it before.

I turned to Heathcliff. "I can't believe how wrong we've been. I know what happened to Jenna Mclarey."

CHAPTER TWENTY-THREE

"*I*t wasn't Dracula who killed Jenna," I announced to Jo as soon as she came downstairs.

"You're telling me this is an ordinary, everyday, non-supernatural murder," Jo moaned.

"It's right here in the book." I hit play on my audiobook of Bram Stoker's *Dracula*, playing the section where Renfield eats insects. "The blood has to be fresh. Dracula wouldn't drink blood if his victim was already dead."

"Then explain the fang marks on her neck...holy fuckballs, the *nails*." Jo slapped her forehead.

"What?"

"The nails sticking out of the plank of wood were covered with blood. If you inserted them into her neck, it would look like the puncture marks of fangs."

"Of course. Connor knew his wife was meeting someone in that cemetery. He followed her – he admitted that openly. What if he got angry, swung the plank at her head, and killed her? He panicked and tried to make it look like one of Dracula's murders. They've been all over the press – he'd know the details about the bite marks."

Jo shoved out of her chair. "I need to tell Inspector Hayes."

I groaned.

"This is good news, gorgeous," Morrie said. "You solved her murder."

"I guess." I slumped on the desk. "Only, now we're back to square one again. There's one more box of dirt out there, and if we go for Dracula now, we run the risk he'll be able to regenerate. Meanwhile, he's growing bolder. We don't know that Fiona is the only victim he tried to make into one of his own."

As if on cue, Fiona howled from upstairs.

"We'll figure it out." Morrie placed a finger beneath my chin, tilting my head back so I looked up into his face. Every facet of him – his icy blue eyes, his sharp cheekbones, the luxurious quirk of his smirk – portrayed his confidence that we were too clever for Dracula to escape.

I wish I shared his confidence.

"We can't do anything tonight." I yawned. "We've got the Spirit Seekers doing their paranormal investigation, and Quoth wants to show me his paintings before the exhibition opens tomorrow."

Heathcliff grabbed for his jacket. I shook my head. "He asked that it just be me. You know he's too shy to ask for anything, so it's important to him. And we're sort of…going through something. It won't take long, and I'll have Oscar with me. I'll be back in plenty of time to protect you from Mrs. Ellis and my mother—"

"I don't care. You can go into the gallery alone, but I'll be right outside, making sure no bloodsuckers sink their teeth into that gorgeous neck of yours."

Outside, I pulled my collar up to protect my neck from the chill in the air. It was a starless night, perfect for a bonfire – hopefully the weather would be just as good tomorrow. I looped my arm in Heathcliff's and directed Oscar to lead us up to the gallery.

On the green, we passed Mrs. Ellis speaking to Morrie. As we neared them, Heathcliff's body tensed. I knew he still hadn't dealt with his intense feelings for Morrie, even after the other night.

I noticed the corner of a sparkly box poking from Mrs. Ellis' carpetbag. "Hi, Mrs. Ellis. I see you've got your portable Vampire Vanishing Kit on hand."

"You can't be too careful." Mrs. Ellis' eyes sparkled. "It's the time of year, you know. The veil between the worlds is thinnest. I'm just popping over to Richard's stall to buy us a round of mulled wine, and then the Spirit Seekers will head over to the shop. I'm so excited to learn more about the spirits and monsters that might be hiding between the stacks."

You wouldn't be if you knew it was just Socrates dancing without any underwear on.

Morrie glanced at me, and I *felt* rather than saw the questioning in his eyes. He felt Heathcliff's distance still, too. "I think a glass of mulled wine sounds perfect. Nice and *relaxing*." He said that with a pointed nod to Heathcliff. "I'll help you with the cups, Mrs. Ellis."

The art gallery was an old Georgian shopfront on the other side of the square. It was shrouded in darkness – no lights on at all. *That's odd. Quoth knows I need light to navigate spaces. I won't be able to appreciate his work if I can't see it.*

I squeezed Heathcliff's hand.

"Mina, I…"

I waited for him to speak. Silence stretched between us – an uncomfortably long time to go without saying anything. I was about to turn away when Heathcliff spoke, so quiet I couldn't be sure if I'd dreamed it. "I've fucked things up with Morrie."

"Well, yes. You've been pushing us both away. One night of mind-blowing sex doesn't undo that."

"Mind-blowing?" Heathcliff's voice quirked at that.

I swatted him in the arm. "You're focusing on the wrong thing."

"I don't know how to do this!" Heathcliff growled. He kicked a rubbish bin.

"Do what?"

"Be in love! I'm driven mad by the two of you. You crowd out every waking thought. And with Dracula hanging around, just waiting to sink his teeth into your neck...I can't face the thought that I might lose either of you."

"So your solution was to ignore us and treat us like shit?"

Heathcliff tore at his hair. "I thought...you know what I thought! And with you, I can find a way to say the things that I feel, but he...he's not so easy to—"

"Oh, Heathcliff..." I kissed Heathcliff on the lips. "He'll be back with mulled wine any moment. While I'm inside with Quoth, maybe the two of you should have a little chat?"

Heathcliff looked miserably at Morrie, who jogged across the square with three glasses of mulled wine balanced in his long fingers. I squeezed his shoulder then turned away, gripping Oscar's lead more tightly than I needed to as I ascended the steps and knocked on the door.

To my surprise, it swung inward, as if operated by some unseen force. The entire space was pitch black. Oscar encouraged me forward – he could see enough to navigate. My heels clicked against wooden floorboards. The room sounded echoey – I could sense a high ceiling and a half-wall bisecting the space.

"Mina."

Quoth's voice boomed through the space as the lights went up all at once. My head flared with pain as a headache rushed my temples. A squiggle of orange light wandered across my vision. Yup, I definitely needed a decent night's sleep.

"By Isis," I staggered back, rubbing my eyes. "Warn me next time."

"I'm sorry." Quoth stepped out from behind a pillar. "I wanted to surprise you. I wanted you to take it all in at once."

I blinked as squiggles of green and orange light danced across my vision. Through the pain, I started to make out the shapes and colors of Quoth's art.

This was like nothing he'd ever created before. Quoth loved fine detail – complex images that illustrated moments drawn from his favorite stories and mythologies. He spent hours painting gilded swirls onto the spines of books, or getting every feather on a bird's underbelly absolutely perfect.

But these...they were wild. They were expressive slashes of crimson against dark fields, brazen black shapes splashed across electric-blue skies, checkerboards of green that bent and twisted across savage landscapes. They were terrifying and wild and utterly beautiful.

Quoth took my arm and led me and Oscar around the room. Oscar whimpered and tugged on his lead, as if there were something he wanted to show me back in the doorway. Sometimes guide dogs did this – they were dogs, after all. They had good days and bad days, and they could get distracted, especially if they had a full, crazy life like my Oscar.

In the center of the room stood a huge sculpture – upcycled birdcages of various styles and sizes, all painted with a slimy-looking black paint and jumbled together with their doors flung open and empty perches inside. The doors pointed directly at the paintings that dotted the walls – a message about freedom that hit me right in the heart.

We stopped in front of the largest piece – the focal point for the exhibition. Quoth had perfectly positioned three lamps to highlight the crimson arc that soared over the canvas. The paint was thick in places, standing up like cake icing, while in other areas it was perfectly smooth and even, giving the piece a 3D quality.

"I designed these paintings to be touched," Quoth whispered. "I wanted to create something you could enjoy, too."

He laced his fingers in mine and pressed my palm to the canvas. My senses lit up as I caressed the waves and slashes and swirls, feeling my fingers bump over where he'd added something to the paint to make it gritty. He'd captured a story in the texture of this painting that was every bit as bold and vivid as the color.

"Quoth, these are breathtaking." My fingers swept over the surface, following the planes and curves of his lines. He'd made the paintings come alive to the touch – an extra layer of meaning only the two of us shared.

I had so much I wanted to say to him when I walked into this room, about the way he'd been acting, about our fight. But these paintings stole my words – they were Quoth baring his soul to me. His feelings on canvas were more powerful than all the apologies he could give in a lifetime.

"Do you really like them?" Quoth's eyebrow cocked upward. He shifted his weight from foot to foot. Nervous energy rolled off him – Oscar sensed it, because he responded with nervous whimpers and fussing of his own.

"They're absolutely beautiful." I couldn't tear my eyes from the piece.

"They're all for you." Quoth stepped closer, his arms circling my waist, pushing me against him. "None of this would be possible if it wasn't for you, Mina."

His lips found mine. This wasn't like a Quoth kiss at all – it was demanding, all-consuming, desperate and breathless. His hands ran over my body, pulling me closer as if he wanted to crawl inside me. A moan escaped my lips as his hands slid up my shirt, grazing my breasts. Oscar's harness fell from my fingers as Quoth backed me up toward the painting. My back grazed the gritty paint as he ground his hardness against my thigh, and my fingers dropped to his fly to—

My phone rang, piercing the silent space.

Noooooo...

Oscar barked. Quoth's lips grazed my ear. "Don't answer it," he choked out, his words thick with need.

"It's Jo. I have to." *Damn you, Jo.* I held the phone to my ear as Quoth nibbled at my skin. "Jo, I'm with Quoth right now at the art gallery and he..."

I trailed off as Quoth's finger slid into my panties, circling my clit and drawing a deep, keening ache from my belly. Jo's voice shrieked in my ear, but I didn't hear a word she said. My mouth fell open as Quoth stroked the sensitive bud and my body grew warm and then hot and then liquid fucking magma and green and orange lights flickered across my vision.

Quoth slid a finger inside as he continued his relentless stroking. I rolled my hips against his hand, aching for more of him, begging for release.

"Mina? Mina, are you there?"

I swallowed as the heat between my legs burned. Quoth pushed a second finger inside me. "Um...sort of...is it important—"

"As you'd say – by Isis, it's important! I just looked in Fiona's box and it's missing dirt."

I tried to focus on her words, but my legs wobbled and the rising pleasure fogged my brain. "What do you mean?"

"I thought I'd fulfill Fiona's last wish to return the soil to her grandfather's grave. So, I went to the cemetery tonight to sprinkle the dirt. The last time Fiona opened the box for me, it was completely full of dirt. But now it's only got a tiny bit inside."

"But it was like that when we found it..." Quoth ground his palm against my clit as he slammed his fingers inside me. I was so close. I was on the edge, fighting the pleasure as I struggled to figure out what Jo was saying. His fingers swirled, and it was harder and harder to focus on Jo...

"Exactly, Mina. Someone removed dirt from the box before you got to it. Enough dirt to have a second box."

My heart hammered against my chest as Jo's words penetrated the fog of my pleasure.

Oh, no, no, no.

Dracula removed some of the dirt from Fiona's box, splitting it into another container. My blood went ice cold. I remembered Mrs. Ellis' old cookie jar sitting on the kitchen counter in Dracula's house. I bet it was inside there...

"I'll be right home, Jo. I think I have an idea where the dirt is—"

The phone clattered from my hand as Quoth sank his teeth into my neck.

CHAPTER TWENTY-FOUR

"Ow!" I wrenched my body away. My hand flew to my neck, which hummed with pain and a kind of strange euphoria.

My fingers touched something wet, warm, sticky.

Blood. My blood.

Quoth grabbed for me. I ducked under his arm and tried to put some distance between us. But Quoth's grip was stronger than I ever imagined. He wrapped his arms around me, holding me against his body. His teeth sank into me again – deeper, harder. The pain drove the air from my lungs at the same time that his bite hummed pleasure through my veins.

Fog swirled in my mind. I moaned against Quoth. It felt so *good*, the pain and the pleasure of it melding together, battling it out inside me so there was no room for myself inside my skin any longer. I floated above my body, resting on a cloud of euphoria as I watched Quoth sucking on my neck. *He's biting me. Why is he biting me? I have to stay in control. I have to...*

"It'll only hurt a moment, Mina," Quoth whispered, making a suckling noise as he nuzzled against me. "Then we can be together for eternity."

Yes, Quoth. I want to be with you forever.

Pleasure coursed through my veins. I gripped his arms as I rocked against him, giving myself over to him completely. The orgasm that Jo had interrupted rose inside me again, building anew. I wanted this, I wanted to chase the pleasure to its glorious heights. I didn't want Quoth to ever stop.

I glanced down at our chests pressed together, and was dimly aware of a river of blood flowing down the front of my shirt.

I wonder whose blood that is.

The pleasure built and crested, surging through my veins, right to the top of my head and the tips of my toes.

I've never felt more alive. I...

Fuck.

Somehow I clawed back a tiny corner of my mind. And through the haze of ecstasy, the crimson pulses in my vision alerted me to what was happening.

Quoth's drinking my *blood.*

It all fell into place.

The way he'd been sleeping during the day and closing the curtains in the shop. His newfound confidence and forcefulness. The strange paintings that spoke of feelings he'd never before expressed.

All those late nights Quoth spent with his art tutor, Professor Sang – he wasn't at the school, he was with Dracula. We wondered how Dracula was getting information about who had access to Romanian dirt. Deirdre said a raven had been hanging around the mailroom at the post office, and we knew all three victims had their dirt mailed to them...

Quoth was spying on people in his raven form, sneaking into secret places for his master to locate the dirt and...

We took Fiona from Dracula before he could complete her transformation, but all along the Count had been cultivating another bride.

Dracula tried to take my birdie from me.

Oh, Quoth.

The pleasure pressed around my mind, threatening to drive away the truth. Already I could sense the horror of my realization fleeing my veins, replaced by a sense of rightness, of beautiful inevitability. The bite of a vampire immobilizing its prey.

I have to stay strong. I have to—

Quoth made a gorgeous mewling noise as he slurped my blood.

I brought my knee up and slammed it into his crotch.

"Oof." Quoth's face collapsed. His teeth retracted from my skin, and for a moment, the fog lifted and I saw my predicament with terrifying clarity as white-hot pain slammed into me.

I twisted away from him, holding my hand against the wound in my neck. Blood flowed between my fingers. My ears rang. I didn't know where Oscar had gone, and I wasn't even sure where I was anymore. The wild colors of Quoth's paintings swirled around me, and I knew I didn't have much time before I passed out from blood loss or fell completely under Quoth's spell.

"You...you...you..." I backed away. I tried to force my legs to run, but it was like trying to run through honey. "You're a vampire."

Quoth smiled. It was the sweet smile of my beautiful, broken raven boy – a smile that had seen me through some of my darkest days. Under the glowing light of his exhibition lamps, I could see his front teeth sharpened to points.

Fangs.

No. No no no.

Not my Quoth.

"Please." Tears stained my cheeks. "Tell me this isn't true. Tell me you didn't want this, that there's some way to reverse it."

He laughed. "Why wouldn't I want this? I've been trapped in a prison of my own making ever since I was torn from my poem. I've had to watch others live the life I've always dreamed of and give you things I could never hope to give you. I've always been third-best to you, and an afterthought to them even though I've loved them as brothers since the moment they scooped me from the bookshop floor. Well, now I'm the one with the power. One day Morrie and Heathcliff will die. They will become nothing but ashes and memory. But we will live forever, you and I, together."

Quoth lunged. Oscar leaped in front of me, teeth bared. Quoth's lips curled back with a snarl, and he grabbed Oscar by the scruff of his neck and tossed him aside. I screamed as Oscar skidded across the shiny floor. He whimpered as he disappeared into a dark corner and I lost sight of him.

"No, please." My back pressed against the wall, my fingers rubbing the surface of Quoth's painting, searching in vain for something I could use as a weapon. "Don't do this. Don't hurt Oscar. I know you, and you're not a monster. You—"

Quoth took another step toward me, his lips curling back to reveal his sharpened fangs, stained with my blood. My fingers scraped at the gritty paint, scratching at it as if I might be able to tunnel through to freedom. *It feels...*

It feels like dirt.

I realized the truth with a start. *He's mixed the paint with dirt.*

"I'll make you see, Mina. When you're one of us, everything will be better. You'll be stronger. Your eyes will be healed. And we'll be together for all eternity. This is a good thing." Quoth's face twisted, his mouth opening wide as he loomed over me, his obsidian hair shimmering in the light. "I was afraid in the beginning, too, but it's wonderful. It's the most pleasurable feeling in the world, and afterward, you can do anything, be anyone."

The thought of turning my back on Quoth terrified me, but I needed to break the spell. I spun around and grabbed the edges of the painting, lifting it off its hooks. Quoth cried out. I heard a bark and a growl. *Oscar, you're my hero.*

I whirled around as Oscar slammed into Quoth, knocking him back. Oscar sank his teeth into Quoth's leg. I had my chance. I smashed the painting as hard as I could down on the floor.

"No," Quoth cried.

Tears rolled down my cheeks as the beautiful artwork tore down the center, the edges of the canvas curling away. The frame buckled and twisted. I stomped on the edge, cracking the frame in several places. I picked up the edge of the tear and ripped away another piece, destroying it as Dracula had destroyed our love.

"You ruined it." Quoth dropped to his knees, holding up the broken pieces of his work. Oscar took the opportunity to pounce on his shoulders, grabbing for his neck. Quoth shoved him off, his face flashing with uncontrollable rage. Feathers sprouted from his cheeks, and his limbs cracked and jerked as his body transformed. Oscar snarled again as the raven flew from his paws and soared into the rafters.

Oscar ran in a circle, barking and snarling at the circling bird.

"Croooooak." Quoth dived at me.

I threw up my hands to protect my face and ran for my purse. Talons scraped along my back, tearing the fabric of my coat. I yelped and kept running. Behind me, Oscar growled and a fight broke out, but I didn't have time to see who was winning. My fingers closed around the strap. Yesss.

"Help!" I yelled. "Please help me."

Where are Morrie and Heathcliff? Why aren't they hearing all this?

I raced back toward the painting as Quoth circled around the room and made another dive at me. He moved slower, one wing dipping low, throwing him off course. But I moved slower, too. My fingers scrabbled inside my purse, popping the lid off my mother's Vampire Vanishing Kit. I fished out the bottle of holy water and hurled it at the attacking bird.

It hit the wall behind him and exploded. Quoth dropped to the floor, writhing and crying as he flapped his wings listlessly in the puddle of sanctified water, but he was too weak to get up.

Oscar barked as he barreled for Quoth. I grabbed his lead and yanked him back, crying out the instruction for him to sit. *If he gets his teeth around Quoth, he'll kill him, and I...*

I can't say goodbye. Not yet. Not until I know there's no other choice.

Tears streamed down my face. "Quoth, no, no, no." Not my beautiful artist. Some part of him had to survive – the Quoth who painted these images could not want to turn me into a vampire.

Scenes from the Dracula books replayed in my head as I ripped a cage from the sculpture. It was a beautiful old Victorian thing, heavier than it appeared. As I stumbled toward Quoth, my head spun wildly and I had to drop it and put my head between my legs. *I'm going to faint. I can't do this. I'm going to faint...*

Quoth dragged his wings along the floor as he hobbled toward me, making an angry *nyuh-nyuh-nyuh* noise in his throat. Blood smeared across the floorboards, and my nightmare flashed before my eyes in vivid technicolor. Only this was a thousand times worse than my nightmare, because it was *Quoth* under Dracula's spell, his orange-rimmed eyes burning with vampiric hunger.

He unfurled his wings and managed to take off. The holy water had made him groggy, his flight path crooked. His beak opened wide as he dove straight for me.

"I'm sorry, Quoth," I whispered, pressing my back against the wall, waiting for him to get close enough to make my move.

THWACK.

I ducked just in time. Quoth slammed into the wall at full speed. Feathers flew in all directions. He dropped to the floor, stunned. I could practically see tiny yellow birds flying around his head.

He lifted his beak, his eyes narrowed with a malice that didn't belong to my beautiful Quoth. I lunged forward and slammed the cage over his body, scooping him inside and yanking the door shut.

"I'm sorry," I sobbed. I leaned my full weight against the cage as Quoth flung his body at the sides. Oscar trotted over and snarled at him through the bars.

I managed to drag myself to my feet. With the cage in my arms, I cried out for Heathcliff and Morrie as I kicked the pieces of Quoth's painting across the floor until they landed facedown in the holy water. Oscar helped by jumping on them, mashing the paint into the water and making a horrible mess of Quoth's beautiful painting.

We'd neutralized Dracula's final stash of earth. Too bad it had come at such a cost.

While Quoth cried, I maneuvered the cage to the door, kicked it open, and toppled outside into the street.

The light from the gallery cast a rectangle across the front steps, where Heathcliff and Morrie stood, locked in a kiss so intense it could melt ice caps. No wonder they hadn't heard my fight.

I wished I had time to celebrate their moment, but any second now I was going to lose my grip or pass out. "Quit snogging and help me! It's Quoth! Dracula got to Quoth!"

Morrie and Heathcliff leaped apart like someone had set a bomb off between them. Morrie raked his fingers through his hair while Heathcliff sprang into action. He grabbed the cage from me, clasping it against his body to stop Quoth pushing the door open. "I'll get him back to the shop."

"What should I do?" Morrie cried.

"We need more vampire protections." I jabbed my finger toward the market. "What we have for Fiona won't be enough for both of them. Garlic, crosses, everything you can find. Go."

Morrie took off in a jog, his long legs disappearing into the darkness. I hugged Oscar to my chest, burying my face in his soft fur. He seemed to sense what I needed, for he stayed completely still and let me hold him.

"Mina." Heathcliff stood over me. "Can you walk?"

"I can make it to the shop...I think." I gripped Heathcliff's arm, and he half-dragged me across the green. As we rounded the corner, someone stepped out in front of us.

"Good evening, Mina, Heathcliff, Oscar. I'm afraid I can't let you go anywhere near the shop," Grey Lachlan said. He stepped toward us and curled his lips back into a smile, showing off his long, sharp fangs.

CHAPTER TWENTY-FIVE

"*Y*ou should see a dentist about that foul breath." Heathcliff wrinkled his nose.

Grey laughed, the sound completely unhinged. "That gallows humor will get you into trouble one day, my dear fellow. But I really must insist you don't go inside just yet. I'm to wait with you until my master is ready for you."

His words sank in. "What are you talking about? Dracula can't get into the shop. We've protected every entrance with garlic—"

Unless...unless someone invited him in.

As if on cue, a piercing scream cut through the night.

"That came from the shop." Heathcliff lunged forward, but Grey threw out a hand to stop him. I expected Heathcliff to snap his fingers, but Grey must have vampire super strength because he sent my gothic antihero sprawling across the cobbles.

Heathcliff let out a string of curse words as he struggled to keep hold of Quoth's cage. He looked ready to launch himself at Grey again, but I held his arm. "Don't. We can just go through the back door."

We sprinted down the alley between Nevermore and Oliver's

bakery, but as we rounded the bins, Grey stepped out of the shadows to leer at us. "You can't escape me that easily, Mina."

More noises reached me now. Bangs and crashes and someone yelling, "Quick, Sylvia, toss me that garlic…"

My blood ran cold. I recognized that voice.

Mum.

The Spirit Seekers must've gotten into the shop. Mum knew where we hid the spare key. And with me, Heathcliff, and Morrie out of the shop, they wouldn't have known not to invite Dracula inside.

My mum was in the shop at the mercy of the Count.

"It's time to give up this absurd notion that you can beat him, Mina." Grey folded his arms. "My master has his vitality and his full powers at his disposal, and soon he'll have control of the waters of Meles. He'll be able to travel anywhere to feed. He'll be able to change the past and mangle the future. You cannot win against him. You must join with him as his bride."

"If he's so powerful, then why does he need me?" I shot back at him, trying to keep the fear from my voice. "It's the twenty-first century. Dracula doesn't need a bride. Unless…"

Something occurred to me.

"Unless he needs me to use the waters of Meles?" I quirked an eyebrow at Grey. "Unless Dracula can't travel through the waters without Homer's magic?"

Grey bared his teeth, snarling at me. I smiled. *Bullseye.*

"Well, well, well, this is a turn up for the books. Dracula needs little old me." I tugged Heathcliff's sleeve. "I wonder what he'd do to have me? I wonder if I can make him dance like a puppet."

Heathcliff's fingers dug into my flesh. "Mina, don't provoke him."

"That's right, Mina. Listen to your oversized baboon. If you don't come willingly, I'm to take you by force."

He was even faster than Quoth. One moment he was standing in front of us. The next, he'd shoved Heathcliff away from me and his hands were wrapped around my throat. I tried to scream, but he cut off my airway. My ears buzzed. My head filled with fog. I knew any moment I'd be out—

"Just a taste," Grey whispered, sniffing hungrily at the spot where Quoth bit me. This close, his decaying breath soured the air. I tried to twist away, but I had no strength left. "Surely my master won't mind if I take just a sip of Homer's blood? I bet it tastes like roses and..."

Behind him, I heard Heathcliff struggling and Quoth squawking and Oscar growling, but the sounds faded as the buzzing became a roar. The darkness crept inward, and I tried one last time to breathe before everything went black and—

Grey's grip slackened. His body slumped against mine. I stepped aside, gasping for fresh air against his powerful stench. He dropped on the cobbles. A short wooden stake stuck out of his back.

"No one messes with my Mina," a voice barked through the darkness.

"Mrs. Ellis!" I cried, clutching my throat.

My heroine stepped beneath the streetlight, another stake from her Vampire Vanishing Kit gripped in her hand. She planted her orthopedic shoe on Grey's back and kicked him.

"You saved us," I choked out. Every word hurt my throat. Wetness seeped between my fingers. I was still bleeding where Quoth had bitten me.

She dusted off her hands like it was no big thing. "I couldn't very well allow him to devour my favorite ex-pupil and the most handsome creature ever to come from the pages of a book."

I stared at her in shock. "You...you know about Heathcliff being...Heathcliff?"

"My dear, I may be old, but I'm not senile," Mrs. Ellis tsked. "Or blind. I've been reading filthy romance novels my entire life. You don't think I'd recognize Heathcliff Earnshaw if I met him in the flesh?"

"Then why didn't you say anything?" Heathcliff growled as he staggered to his feet, Quoth's cage still held in his arms.

She clapped a hand on my shoulder. "Because you wanted to keep the three of them all to yourself, you saucy minx. I thought it was about time you had some fun in your life. You were always such a highly-strung child. Besides, I think the Spirit Seekers might be able to help you figure out where these fictional characters came from, and maybe we could become the new stars of *Strictly Come Ghosting*. We'd travel around haunted bookshops and introduce ourselves to other handsome fictional chaps. I was rather hoping Mr. Darcy might show up. Or Rochester..." she sighed dreamily. "Yes, I think tall, brooding Rochester is the man for me..."

I burst out laughing, but it hurt. It stung my throat so bloody much. I held onto Heathcliff until my head stopped spinning.

Heathcliff kicked Grey's prone body. "Is he dead?"

I noticed the pool of blood flowing from around Grey's wound. I knelt down beside him. Oscar nudged my hand, sniffing and making little growls. I knew then that he'd been trying to warn me about Quoth back in the art gallery. He sensed something wrong and tried to pull me out the door, but I didn't let him.

I rubbed Oscar behind the ears with one hand. With the other, I grasped Grey's wrist, feeling a faint pulse. "I...don't think so. He didn't disintegrate to dust when Mrs. Ellis staked him, which means he's probably still at least partly human and bleeding internally. We should call an ambulance."

"And get Mrs. Ellis thrown in jail for staking him through the heart? Not happening. This woman is a national hero." Heathcliff reached down and scooped Grey up with his free arm, tossing the man over his shoulder. He staggered up to the back door and tested it, but it wouldn't budge. Another scream pierced the night.

"The bastard's locked us out."

Heathcliff staggered back around to the front door, still carrying both Quoth's cage and Grey's bleeding body. Mrs. Ellis threw my arm over her shoulder and handed me Oscar's lead. I let the two of them lead me back onto Butcher Street just as Heathcliff roared with defiance and battered his fists against the locked door.

"This is *my* shop. Let me in, you poxy bastard."

Mrs. Ellis fished inside her wallet and produced a key. "Helen gave me this. She made a copy when she was minding the shop once, in case she needed to get inside when you weren't around."

"Never have I been so glad my mum is…my mum." I tossed the key to Heathcliff and he fit it into the lock. The door swung inward, just as another grisly scream echoed in the gloom. I reached into my purse and pulled out a crucifix and a wooden stake. "Let's slay a vampire."

CHAPTER TWENTY-SIX

*H*eathcliff stumbled inside, grunting as he struggled to keep hold of the cage with Grey on his back. "Our little birdie's been working out," he huffed.

"Croak! Croak! Croaaaaak!"

"Sharpened his beak, too, hasn't he?" Heathcliff winced as Quoth bit his finger through the bars.

"Dracula's blood has given them super strength." I fumbled for the light switch, but when I flicked it, nothing happened. *That's right, Victor blew the power and Handy Andy has been too busy with my mum's business – and my mum – to fix it yet.*

We were literally going in blind.

Good thing I was used to the dark.

My finger tightened on Oscar's lead. In the darkness, he wouldn't be able to see my hand signals, so I gave him voice commands as we moved deeper into the shop. My chest heaved with fear, but I swallowed it back and focused on what I could control. I couldn't see, but I didn't need to see to know what was going on. I *knew* this shop – I knew every shelf and cobweb and hidden corner. I knew where to stand to avoid the creaky floorboards and to duck when entering the Children's room because the doorway was lower. I knew the scent of fresh wood polish and old leather and ink and the rising damp that came from the flooded cellar and the walls where I guessed the pipes had burst.

I felt, too, the presence of Dracula. He was here, no doubt about it. He'd poisoned the air with his presence, and the shop stank of him. His power and domination rolled off him in waves that crashed against me, making me feel violently ill. Every step I took seemed to confirm this wrongness – as if his very presence broke something fundamentally right and true and good about the universe, and it didn't quite know how to pick up the pieces.

I was the last line of defense against this horror.

Nevermore Bookshop was *my* home, and I'd defend it, and those I love, until my dying breath.

Heathcliff swore as he crashed into a bookshelf, but Oscar kept pushing forward, unperturbed by the gloom. He read my emotions and took his cues from me, so I needed to stay calm. I needed to find what I was looking for. I listened to the footsteps overhead – not Dracula's, they were too hurried – and felt the air shift as someone moved by the poetry shelves.

"Mina, something terrible has happened," Socrates cried from the darkness, his voice muffled by the stacks of poetry books between us. "Some ladies broke into the shop and were passing around wine bottles and strange devices, and then there was a knock at the door and they let in a handsome stranger. And then the screaming started."

Someone nudged my arm. Mrs. Ellis' voice whispered in my ear, "Who's this fellow? He sounds like that clever old scallywag who tried to rescue the philosophy books today. I thought he was rather brave."

Trust Mrs. Ellis to be thinking with her lady boner at a time like this.

"Socrates, it's okay. You can come out." My gaze was drawn to a flickering light that emerged from the end of the poetry shelves and bobbed toward us. Seeing the brightness sent a fresh wave of nausea and pain through my skull, and made a series of orange squiggles dance across my vision. As the light drew closer, I smelled burning.

"You're burning a book." Heathcliff sounded distraught. "What is it with this village and burning books? What have the books ever done to you?"

"I needed some light, didn't I?" Socrates snapped, waving his makeshift torch in Heathcliff's face. "Don't worry, it's only Seneca the Younger's letters and essays. That little rascal thought he could be a Stoic while also acquiring a fortune and enjoying the riches of Nero's favor. The only thing that double-faced ass-kisser ever did stoically was off himself."

"Shut your pie-hole and help me get this lot upstairs," Heathcliff snapped.

Socrates handed me his burning book torch. I held it up for them while Socrates grabbed the bottom of the cage and helped Heathcliff wrangle Quoth and Grey upstairs. Mrs. Ellis, Oscar, and I brought up the rear. From somewhere amongst the shelves I heard frightened footsteps and the oppressive presence of Dracula nearby. At any moment I expected to feel fangs sink into my neck, but he stayed back. He didn't want to hurt me. Yet.

We needed to make Quoth safe from him, and then I would slay his ass so hard he'd be shitting garlic.

Heathcliff and Socrates took their load straight to my bedroom. Fiona shrieked as we crashed into her space. Jo leaped from her chair. "Mina, what happened to Quoth? And why are you holding a burning book?"

As soon as he passed over the salt trail at the door, Quoth quieted. His wings drooped and he turned to me with wide, terrified eyes. "Croooooak?"

"I'm so, so sorry." Fresh tears fell. I touched Quoth's cheek, but he jerked away. My chest ached, but I didn't know if it was from the loss of blood or my heart breaking.

I had to believe Quoth could be saved.

On the bed, Fiona bucked and thrashed. I didn't want to tie Quoth down with her in case she kicked out and injured him. I remembered the hook Morrie hung from the ceiling – the same one he used to handcuff me while he and Quoth did filthy, beautiful things to my body. The memory caught in my throat.

While Heathcliff rolled Grey from his shoulders and dropped him to the floor, I grabbed one of Morrie's harnesses and stood on his desk to clamp it to the hook. Heathcliff grabbed Quoth from the cage and held him while I fitted the handcuffs around his neck and tightened them onto the tightest setting.

"Croooooak!" Quoth found a second wind. He thrashed and bit and scratched as we fought to keep hold of him.

The second cuff went around his middle. By the time we'd secured him my arms were covered in bloody scratches and I could barely see through my tears, but he wouldn't be going anywhere.

I stroked his head. "We're going to find a way to bring you back. I promise."

He thrashed about in the restraints, his croaks high-pitched and laced with pain. I dropped from the chair. Heathcliff caught me in his arms.

"You're still bleeding." He touched his fingers to my neck. I winced as a fresh wave of pain left me dizzy.

"Mina needs a first aid kit," Mrs. Ellis declared from the corner where she was canoodling with Socrates. I guess if you were trapped in a house with a dangerous vampire, there were worse things to do than snogging one of the world's greatest philosophers.

"There's one under the bed, with my collection of novelty butt plugs," Morrie said as he ran into the room.

"On it." Jo slid under the bed.

Relief washed over me as Morrie stalked across the room and wrapped his arms around me and Heathcliff. He was okay. He made it back alive.

"How'd you get in?" Heathcliff snapped. "I've never given you a key."

"I'm a criminal mastermind, remember?" Morrie upturned a shopping bag onto the bed. "I know at least seventeen ways in and out of this building that don't require a key. Do you want me to list them, or should we get on with vampire-proofing the birdie?"

"What have you got?" I peer at the random selection of bottles and jars.

"They were all out of fresh garlic at the market," Morrie said. "Apparently there's been a run on the stuff this week."

I groaned. It was all my mother's fault, stirring up vampire-fever in Argleton. And then I remembered that my mother was in the store somewhere, and my chest tightened in fear.

"But then I remembered the market stalls. I got Mrs. Traverson to sell me her entire stock of extra-garlicky pasta sauce." Morrie unscrewed the lid off the jar. A delicious garlic and basil scent swirled through the room. "I thought we could smear it all over Quoth's body and maybe you could lick it off, nice and slow."

"That's terrible, but it's the best we've got." I unscrewed a lid and reached inside for a big dollop of pasta sauce, which I smeared across Quoth's cheek.

"Crooooooak." He thrashed and spat and nipped at our hands, but we were relentless. By the time we were done, Quoth looked like he'd been mummified by an Italian chef. He smelled deliciously garlicky. Morrie hung a silver crucifix around his neck, and it seemed to sap the last of his strength. He hung in his restraints, croaking softly.

We had to hope it was enough to protect him from Dracula for now.

Jo grabbed my hand and sat me on the corner of the bed. She tossed a bottle of soda into my lap while behind her, Victor held up a bottle of holy water and a needle and thread. Jo pushed the soda into my hand. "Drink that. It'll help replace your sugars. This is going to hurt like a motherfucker, but you need to hold still or Victor will fuck you up even worse."

She was not wrong. I felt every sting of Victor's needle, every tug of my flesh, every splash of holy water like it was scalding hot coffee on an open wound. I guzzled the soda, which sat in my stomach like a lead weight.

Morrie offered the edge of his hand to bite down on, something he usually relished during sex but apparently not when Victor Frankenstein was stitching me up like one of his monsters. Morrie screamed and jerked away, shaking his hand. "Now we're both bleeding. What are we going to do, Mina?"

The Napoleon of Crime's face was drawn. He didn't look sure of himself. He looked like he had absolutely no idea what to do next, and that wasn't something Morrie had experienced before. Through the dwindling fire of our book torch, I noticed him move closer to Heathcliff, their hands clasping together.

I swallowed down my fear. "Dracula is somewhere in this store, and—"

A scream pierced the darkness.

A very familiar scream.

"Mum," I yelled, jerking myself to my feet. "We're coming!"

A wave of nausea and pain nearly kicked me back down again, but I held onto Heathcliff until it passed. Nothing like an immovable wall as a boyfriend to steady yourself.

"You can't go out there unarmed," Jo cried, shoving herself in front of me. "You've seen what he did to Fiona and Quoth."

I swiped my fingers around the rim of the last pasta sauce jar and smeared the garlicky sauce in two stripes across my cheeks. "We're going to war. We won't be unarmed. Where are those stakes Heathcliff sharpened?"

"In the storage room," Morrie said.

"Then we'll have to get to them. Find us anything on this floor we can use as a weapon. We'll head there first." I tugged the

Vampire Vanishing Kit from my purse. Mrs. Ellis did the same thing, and we shared around the supplies of holy water, garlic, and the crucifix charms. "We need to go room-by-room until we find him. Whenever we find one of the Spirit Seekers, we send them back up here to hide out in this room, got it? No matter what happens, my mother is *not* to go after Dracula, is that clear?"

"What about the last box of dirt?" Heathcliff asked as Morrie broke the legs off a wooden chair and handed them around.

"It's gone. I destroyed it." Fresh tears flowed from my eyes as I thought of Quoth's beautiful artwork smashed on the gallery floor. "Quoth painted the dirt into one of his paintings. I broke it and doused it in holy water. It's done. We can now go after Dracula."

Heathcliff cracked his knuckles. "Good. I've been waiting to get my hands on that poxy bastard."

As we made our way out of my bedroom and into the living room, Morrie went ahead into the kitchen and returned with an armload of kitchen knives. He pressed one into my hands. "That's as good as we're going to get. I also found this axe beside the fire."

"That's mine." Heathcliff grabbed it.

"What do we do if we come across the Count?" Mrs. Ellis twirled her knife in her fingers like she'd been slaying vampires all her life, which at this stage I'd honestly believe. "Are we to kill him if we have the chance, or do we need to keep him alive?"

"I—" My gaze swept to Quoth. "I think we need to—"

"Mina...*Miiiiiina...*"

The sound boomed from the air itself. It sank through my body, pooling in my stomach and freezing my heart to ice. My limbs jerked as Dracula bent his considerable power to drawing me closer. He wanted me. He *commanded* me. I'd very nearly fallen under Quoth's spell, and he had only a taste of the Count's true power.

But Quoth... If we killed Dracula, we might lose our one chance at bringing back the people he'd tainted.

"We have to kill him." I swallowed the lump that rose in my throat. "We can't...fuck about, as Heathcliff would say. We can't risk him taking the waters of Meles or hurting more innocent people. Under no circumstances is he to leave this shop or break into the room at the end of the hall."

"I don't know what the waters of Meles are, but you're the boss." Mrs. Ellis slid the knife into her belt.

Heathcliff's hand squeezed mine. "But Quoth—"

"I know," I whispered. "I know. But we have to believe there's a way to save him."

"Right then." Mrs. Ellis brandished her chair leg. "What are we standing around here for?"

I swallowed again. With a last look over my shoulder at my midnight bird who only wanted to be free, then at the shadow-shrouded faces of my friends and my lovers, of two men who'd step into hell itself for me, I raised my own weapon and yelled into the gloom. "You want Nevermore Bookshop? You're going to have to go through us first. Bring it on, bloodsucker."

CHAPTER TWENTY-SEVEN

*W*e checked every corner of the flat first, in case any members of the Spirit Seekers were hiding up here, but Heathcliff's gazillion KEEP OUT signs must've terrified them too much, because we found no one. We left Socrates and Victor guarding Quoth, Fiona, and Grey, and descended the stairs into the darkness. In one hand, I gripped Oscar's harness far tighter than Evie, my guide dog instructor, would normally allow. The other held up the kitchen knife, the blade soaked in holy water.

Morrie strode beside me, holding out a chair leg and a torch made from a burning Dan Brown novel. Finally, the *Da Vinci Code* put to good use.

Something moved on our left. A floorboard creaked. Heathcliff lunged, yelling in triumph as his chair leg hit home.

THUMP.

"Ow. What was that for?" Robin yowled, hopping across the floor.

"Stop dancing around like a medieval jumping bean and help us," Heathcliff snapped. "We need your bow."

"And you have it, sir," Robin yelled with triumph. "Which

arrowheads are required? Flame-tipped? Monster-slaying? Duck-hunting? Apple-piercing?"

"Monster-slaying should suffice." I held out a jar of holy water. "Dip the tips in this water. Have you seen any strange women on this floor?"

"Yes. They had a key and let themselves in, and refused to sit quietly and listen to my stories of bravery and derring-do. When the screaming started, they scattered and hid. We did, too." His voice wobbled. For all his bravado, Robin was afraid. "Puck's on top of the Philosophy shelves. Hey, Puck?" he called out. "Come out now. Mina's here."

The air twinkled as Puck materialized beside Robin. "There is a woman hiding in the storage closet, in violation of the KEEP OUT sign. Should I turn her into a—"

"No." I directed Oscar to lead me across the room. He sniffed at the door and yipped excitedly. My fingers found the handle and I shoved it open.

"Who's in here? It's Mina. I promise everything is going to be okay, but I need you to come out—"

"Miiina…" Dracula's voice echoed inside my head, even as it boomed through the shop. "…I'm waiiiiiiting for you…"

"Mina?" a small voice whispered from behind the shelving. "It's really you?"

"Mum?"

A shadow-cloaked figure moved in front of me. I couldn't see her features, but I recognized her voice, her distinct scent, and the innate comforting *presence* of her.

"Mum." I threw my arms around her. A wave of relief and love flooded my veins, for a moment driving out my Dracula fears. "You're okay."

"Oh, Mina." Mum's body trembled. "It was so terrible. There was a bloke at the door in a flowing cape. He had the palest skin I'd ever seen. He said he was your friend, and he looked like one of those boys in the rock bands you like, so I let him in to wait for you. None of the lights were working, so we didn't see what he did. Only that Deirdre disappeared and he...he...he...*bit* her."

"Sssssh. It's going to be okay, I promise." I slid Mum into Heathcliff's arms. "Heathcliff is going to take you upstairs and show you a hiding place, okay? This is important. Don't come down here for any reason. No matter what you hear. Do you understand?"

She whimpered, but didn't reply.

"Mum, if you're nodding, I can't see you. Do you understand?"

"Yes, yes. Mina, I..." Mum's fingers trembled as Heathcliff dragged her away. "I'm scared."

Me too. "Where's Deirdre?"

"...Miiiiiina..." Dracula called me, his voice pulsing in my chest. It took everything I had to remain beside my mother, to not pick up my feet and run to him.

"She's here, tucked away behind the shelves. She's very weak, and I can't stop the bleeding." Mum's voice trembled.

"That's okay, we'll help with that, too," Morrie grunted as he bent down behind the shelves and picked up Deirdre. Together, the pair of them took Deirdre and my mum back upstairs to the flat, while Puck disappeared in a cloud of sparkles, leaving me, Jo, Mrs. Ellis, and Robin to keep guard in the stairwell, our weapons raised and ready.

I wished more than anything I could stay with my mother, but Dracula's calls grew louder and more fervent. His voice shook the building. Books tumbled from the shelves as he boomed my name through the night. "Miiiiina..."

Heathcliff and Morrie rejoined us, shoving their way through our army to stand at my side. I couldn't see them in the dark but I felt them, their presence as weighty in the air as Dracula's – the forces of good worthy to oppose his overwhelming evil. Heathcliff's spice and peat scent mingled with Morrie's tangy grapefruit and vanilla, tingeing the air with memories that filled my heart with love.

I could do this. With them by my side and Quoth in our hearts, we could triumph.

"For our birdie," Morrie whispered.

"For Quoth," Heathcliff growled.

For love.

At my feet, Oscar snarled at the darkness. I didn't know if he'd refuse to go downstairs, but he tugged on his harness and led the way. Dogs were supposed to be able to sense danger, and it was a testament to Oscar's loyalty and tenacity that instead of dragging me away, he led me right into the lair of my enemy.

We descended the stairs into the silent hallway. Oscar turned left, leading us through the low doorway to the Classics shelves. The air smelled of damp books and cloying, decaying flesh. Morrie thrust the Dan Brown in front of him, illuminating a small circle in front of us.

I *felt* him before I saw him – the concentration of pure evil that waited in the dark like a snake beneath the rocks. My heart plummeted to my knees as his power wrapped around us, stealing away every ounce of bravery I'd fought so hard to keep intact.

Count Dracula stepped forward with malignant silence, and I *saw* him. I saw him in vivid, terrifying detail. I saw the corners of his mouth twist up into a smile, baring long, white fangs. "Mina Wilde, we meet at last."

CHAPTER TWENTY-EIGHT

*I*t didn't make any sense, because Nevermore Bookshop was still pitch black and even if all the lights *had* just come back on, I still shouldn't be able to see this level of detail.

But I wasn't really seeing him with my eyes. He was *inside* my head, giving me this vision of himself so that I *knew.* I understood. He had already beaten us. Standing this close to him, his power washed over me, soaking into my pores. I felt him crawling in my veins and swimming behind my eyes. He held my body frozen. I couldn't move. He could manipulate me however he wished.

Count Dracula was at least as tall as Morrie, but his power made him seem taller still. His features were those of an older man with a hooked nose, a bushy Victorian mustache and pointed beard. He was clad entirely in black, without a speck of color anywhere about his person, so that he seemed to emerge from the darkness itself.

In his hand, he clutched a book he'd plucked from the Classics shelf – a beautiful leather-bound volume of Bram Stoker's *Dracula.* I could see the damp pages crimping at the edges, and a circle of damp on the rug beneath his feet – the broken pipes must have leaked through the back of this wall.

I opened my mouth to speak, but he stole my words, too.

"Listen to them, Mina." Dracula held his hand to his ear as Fiona and Quoth and Grey screamed their madness, their allegiance, above our heads. "My children of the night. They make such sweet music. They can be our children, Mina. We can make the whole earth anew in our lineage."

Quoth's cries filled my ears, and in his distress, I found my voice.

"We have poisoned your earth with holy sacraments," I said. "Every last box of Romanian dirt has been tainted. If you try to use the earth to regenerate, you will die."

"It is no matter." His long fingers turned the book, screwing up the pages. Water dripped from the sodden paper – something else I shouldn't have been able to see. *Something he wants me to see, but why?* "In the waters of Meles I will find my resurrection – true immortality not just in this life, but in all possible lives. Your father tried to lure me away from this bookshop so I would not discover its secrets. Even in his dying breath he did not give you up to me."

"My father is...is dead?" After all the letters and clues he'd left behind for me, after all the time-traveling, I'd started to think of my father as alive but far away where I couldn't talk to him, which was sort of how I'd thought of him my entire life. But now I knew the truth – Dracula had robbed the world of the greatest poet that ever lived. He robbed me of my chance to meet my father. I'd never forgive him for that.

My rage and love bloomed hot inside me, and in that rage I found the strength to defy Dracula's hold on me. I wiggled my fingers. I twitched my wrist. I moved my hand into my purse and searched inside for what I needed.

Dracula smacked his lips together. "Homer tasted *exquisite*. But only after I drained him did I realize I needed him alive to guide me through the waters. But no matter, I have you now, my beautiful bride."

He reached out his hand toward me, and every inch of my body jerked to obey him. Except for my hand. My hand closed around a jar at the bottom of my purse.

I flung the jar at Dracula. It clipped him on the chin, popping the lid off and splattering green goo all down the front of his fancy clothes. He swiped a finger through the goo and held it up, squinting in confusion. "What is this?"

"Um...that's cream made from ground-up Venus flytraps. But this..." I flung another jar. "This is Mrs. Traverson's extra-strong pasta sauce."

The jar hit Dracula in the face, and as the garlic hit his skin the vision of him in my head dissolved. He couldn't hold the magic while he was screaming. And scream he did – an inhuman wail that I knew I'd hear in my nightmares for the rest of my life. Which I hoped would be longer than the next few minutes.

My limbs jerked free of his spell. "Run!"

We thundered from the room. Morrie slammed the door behind him and shoved a chair under the handle. Oscar barked triumphantly at the door.

Dracula roared, his anger shaking Nevermore down to its foundations. Books cascaded from the shelves as the door cracked and groaned under Dracula's fury. Morrie thrust the burning book into Jo's hands and leaned against the door, bracing his long legs against the bookshelf opposite as more heavy volumes rained down on him.

"Run. I can't hold him much longer," Morrie yelled.

"I can't leave you—"

But Heathcliff grabbed my arm and tore me away. "I'll help Morrie. You get away."

His grip dropped from my arm, and I was swept away from him as Jo and Oscar and Mrs. Ellis and Robin all rushed for the stairs. As my feet hit the first step, Morrie's scream tore through the bookshop.

No, Isis, no. Please, not Morrie...please...

But I didn't look back. I wouldn't let Morrie's sacrifice be in vain. I poured on speed, clattering up the stairs after Oscar. Behind me, the doorway slammed against the wall. Heathcliff bellowed as he met Dracula's full fury with his own love-kissed savagery – an unstoppable force meeting an immovable rock.

The moment my foot touched the first-floor landing, Heathcliff screamed.

I didn't know Heathcliff Earnshaw had it in him to scream. The sound rent my soul.

A sob escaped my throat. Beside me, Jo cried. "Mina, what are we going to do? Back there I...I didn't even want to stake him. It's like he took over my *mind*—"

We're not strong enough. I'm not strong enough. But Heathcliff is. He's stronger than anyone on earth. He needs the stakes. We didn't get the stakes.

"Oscar, storage room." I urged him forward. We'd left the door open when we rescued Mum. I found the stakes at the end of Morrie's bed, tied in a bundle with twine. I carried it out to the staircase.

"Heathcliff, catch." I tossed the bundle of stakes over the railing. The knot undid midair and they toppled onto the rug below. Heathcliff cursed as he scrambled to pick them up. My heart surged with hope even as I felt Dracula's power drape over me once more, pinning my limbs so I couldn't move.

Heathcliff let out another bloodcurdling scream.

"Take that," Robin cried, loosing a volley of arrows over the railing as he rushed down the stairs to help. Dracula flew at Robin with impossible speed. Robin sank one arrow into Dracula's shoulder before the Count tore the bow from his hands. When Dracula broke off the shaft, smoke curled from the wound, and his face twisted with pain as the holy water ate away at his insides. But it barely slowed him down. Dracula jerked Robin against his body and sank his teeth into his neck.

"Robin, no!"

A wet, slurping noise boomed through the room, once again momentarily breaking Dracula's spell.

Robin, I'm so sorry.

I sank to my knees, wracked with hopelessness. Heathcliff was trapped downstairs. If Robin's holy-water-tipped arrows didn't slow Dracula down, then our wooden stakes wouldn't do it, either. How would Heathcliff even get close enough to stake the Count? Dracula was too strong, too satiated with fresh blood. We'd never catch him.

"Mina, run," Heathcliff bellowed. I couldn't see him or Dracula anymore, but I heard the desperation in his voice. He'd figured out the same thing I had – that we were doomed, that Dracula would soon overpower us.

"I can't leave you—"

"Get out of here. Now."

But where? We'd have to get around Dracula if we wanted to try for the front or back doors. Swimming through the basement tunnel into Dracula's lair sounded like an easy path to losing my O negative, and Morrie hadn't informed me of his seventeen escape routes from the shop.

But I did know one way.

"Mina." Dracula's face filled my head, his will bent toward finding me. I had a split second to act. *He wants me and only me.*

I needed to lead him away from my friends to give them a chance to escape.

"Run for the door," I barked at Jo. I thrust Oscar's lead into her quivering hand. Before she had a chance to say a word, I spun away from her and raced up the stairs toward the flat.

I *felt* him behind me – his breath hot in my ear, the crinkle of his Victorian clothing as he moved with unhurried ease, the flicker of his tongue against his lips as he licked off the last of Robin's blood.

My lungs screamed for air. I couldn't see a thing. I was guided by muscle memory. All I knew was that I had to stay one foot ahead of him. My feet skidded on the wooden floor as I cleared the top step. I scrambled into our flat and slammed the door behind me. I slid a chair under the lock, grabbed a silver crucifix, and hung that over the doorknob. I knew it wouldn't hold him for long but maybe it would buy me enough time to...

CRACK.

Wood splinters rained down on my face. The door would give way at any moment. I flew into the hallway, barely considering where I was going as I scrambled through the first door into my bedroom. *I have to see him one last time—*

"Quoth, goodbye. I love you."

When Quoth saw me, he gave a terrified CROAK and twisted his body around, somehow managing to free himself from his restraints.

"Crooooooak." He flapped around the room, distraught and in pain and furious. Feathers flew in my face as I reached up to him. My fingers grazed his wing, but he spun away, leaving a smudge of pasta sauce along my arm.

The wall shook as the door slammed against the wall. Dracula's footsteps creaked over the floorboards. "Mina," he rasped, his voice thick and raspy with grave dirt. "Come to me right now. Be my bride. Or I'll kill this woman."

"Mina? Mina?" Cynthia Lachlan called out. "Your goth friend here seems to be deadly serious."

Oh, fuck, he's got Cynthia.

I ducked behind my bedroom door, a hopeless hiding space because he knew exactly where I was. The floorboards creaked closer. He was at the end of the hallway. Quoth hopped across the floor toward him, making his happy *nyah-nyah-nyah* noise at the thought of being reunited with his master.

What do I do? Even if I give myself up, there's no guarantee he'll let Cynthia go. I have to—

"D-d-d-don't touch her."

A dark shape moved on the other side of the room. Grey staggered to his feet and lurched into the hallway. He was death walking, and as he moved through the square of light cast by the moon through the window, I made out the shape of Mrs. Ellis' stake still buried in his back.

"Ah, Grey, my loyal servant. I wondered where you'd got to. Come, we shall share her blood together."

Cynthia screamed.

"I s-s-said, don't touch her." Grey's voice sounded like wet sand. He lunged at Dracula. Cynthia screamed again, and I heard bangs and thumps as the servant turned on his master.

We'd been right about Grey – even beneath all those layers of evil, a piece of his humanity remained. Grey was a class A dick-weasel, but he loved his wife.

"Croak!" Quoth swooped in to help his master, but his battle cry turned into a wail as he was caught in the bloody battle between Dracula and Grey. I cried out as he was tossed onto the hallway rug, his tiny body lolling in a dark pool of his own blood.

"Quoth, no."

And even though I knew I'd lost him forever, even though he was no longer mine, I couldn't leave him there to die alone. I leaped from behind the door, throwing my body over Quoth and trapping him against my chest.

"Crooooooak." Quoth struggled a little, but he was so weak that I held him easily. Warmth spread across my chest as his blood and the pasta sauce soaked my clothes. I shoved Quoth under my arm and ran from the room. I'd lost my knife somewhere in the shop. All I had was another jar of pasta sauce. Dracula and Grey rolled on the rug, slamming into the walls and sending Quoth's paintings crashing down on top of them. I'd have to try and get past them, hope I could find something to finish the job, hope the others had been sensible enough to get out while they could.

My blood rushed in my ears. Quoth squabbled, beating his wings in an attempt to fly to his master. I gripped him tighter as his blood covered my clothes. My mind whirred over something.

Covered in blood...

It was a memory from months ago, a throwaway sentence that I thought mysterious at the time but forgot about in all the chaos of Dracula's arrival and every other crazy thing that happened in my life. But now that phrase slammed into me with the full weight of its power.

Next time I see you, you'll be covered in blood.

I didn't have time to consider if it was a good idea or not. At the same time as Dracula's ice-cold hand reached from the darkness to grip my ankle, I grabbed the handle for the time-traveling room.

As the bloodsucker dragged me backward, I pulled the door open, revealing nothing but oppressive gloom. I didn't know what waited for me on the other side, but all I knew was that it had to be better than here.

"You cannot escape me," Dracula snarled, his icy touch crawling up my leg.

Hold on. My pinkie finger slipped from the door handle. Quoth's beak sank into my wrist. I howled and twisted and cried, but Dracula held me fast. Where was Grey? I couldn't move forward, and soon my grip would fail and...

"Oh, for pity's sake," someone huffed. A hand reached out of the darkness and grasped under my shoulder, warm and mercifully alive. A second hand joined the first. Quoth slipped through my fingers. I screamed as they tugged me forward and Dracula yanked me back. I was being torn in two. Neither would give me up. Something in my spine popped, and pain rushed my ears. *It'll all be over soon...*

"It will never be over, Mina," Dracula roared inside my head. "You'll be mine for all eternity."

"Croak!"

I couldn't see what he did, but Quoth squawked and Dracula hissed and his fingers dropped from my ankle. The last thing I heard before the door slammed behind me was the flutter of midnight wings as Quoth flew through and crashed into the floorboards in front of me.

I lay on my stomach, gasping for breath. It took me a few moments to realize I'd screwed my eyes shut. I didn't want to open them. I didn't know what I'd see. But a bright light pulsed beyond my eyelids and I needed to *know...*

Quoth...is he here...is he alive...

I sucked in a deep, precious breath of air, the edges tinged with blood and ice.

I opened my eyes.

The room was exactly as I remembered – the elegant four-poster bed weighed down with rich linens, the ornate chairs and heavy wooden furniture. The doors leading into the study and the octagonal bathroom above the occult room. But there was one difference – one strange feature that made me certain that I was truly dead, that this was my dying mind playing a last, cruel trick.

I could only see the gloomy spaces because the entire room had been lit up like a Christmas tree, like a Halloween bonfire. Candles and oil lanterns flickered on every surface and burned from sconces affixed to the walls.

"Well, well, well, Wilhelmina Wilde," a dark voice chuckled. Victoria Bainbridge peered down at me from behind her hawk-like nose. "At last we meet."

CHAPTER TWENTY-NINE

"W e've met before," I reminded Victoria as she helped
me into one of her chairs. She set one of the larger
lamps onto the table beside me, giving me a wider circle of light
through which to see. The lantern cast a warm glow over my lap.
She placed Quoth in my arms. My heart leaped as I stroked his
back, feeling the places where his feathers were bent and matted
with blood. He was still alive, cooing quietly, but he was very
weak and bleeding profusely from a wound in his neck. Victoria
slammed a white cloth and a jar of salve on the table in front
of me.

"You might believe that," said Victoria. "But I can assure you,
I've never seen you on this side of the door before. Tea?"

I nodded. Victoria moved to a sideboard and fiddled with a
silver tea service. Her words sank in. "That's not possible. We
came through the door months ago. You found us in your bed."

"Just because it happened in your past, doesn't mean it was in
mine."

As I rubbed the salve into Quoth's wound, my gaze fell on the
window, which faced over the shops next door and gave a view
of the village green. In the center stood a towering inferno. The

Halloween bonfire. Mrs. Ellis' crowning joy had begun without her.

Please, Hathor, Isis, Athena, Hecate, any goddess who'll listen, let Mrs. Ellis be okay. Please let her have got out along with Mum and Jo and Socrates and all the Spirit Seekers.

Oh, Morrie, Heathcliff. I miss you so much already.

It hurt my heart to think about that visit to the time-traveling room – Morrie and Heathcliff and Quoth and I crowded into Victoria's bed, bodies and tongue entwined. I remembered Victoria speaking to me as though she knew me, as though we'd met before. *Next time I see you, you'll be covered in blood.*

Of course. I'd been speaking to Victoria in her *future.* She'd already lived through this meeting with me, but I hadn't. Now, I was the one who'd met her before and she was the one who didn't know what to make of me. But if she wasn't expecting me, if she didn't know who I am, why were the candles lit? Surely she would see this as wasteful and excessive?

I rubbed my temple. "I'm so confused."

"Don't ask me to tell you how time travel works." Victoria set down my tea and offered a small jug of milk. "I'm just the book-seller. But if you want answers, I have someone who wants to meet you. Leave your tea to cool."

I set down the cup and saucer, cradled Quoth to my breast, and let her lead me across the room. She pushed open the door to her bathroom. I heard splashes coming from the bathtub.

I stepped inside.

Candles crowded every inch of space, set into niches in the walls and scattered across the floor, leaving only a narrow path from the doorway to the tub. Through the window, the light of the bonfire splashed an orange glow over the bathtub, illuminating the features of an old man lying in the bubbly water, his head bent back in ecstasy as he washed his underarms with a large sponge.

The old man's face was etched onto my childhood.

Mr. Simson.

His own private joke. Mr. Simson. Homer Simpson.

Homer. The Ancient Greek poet.

It was the eyes that gave him away. Deep green with flecks of gold around the edges. They were the same eyes I'd stared at hundreds of times before.

In the mirror.

They were *my* eyes.

The word caught in my throat. "Dad?"

"My Mina."

I knelt on the floor beside the bathtub. He opened his arms and I fell into them. I fell only a few inches, but it felt like forever. I didn't care that if I turned in the wrong direction I might see more of my father south of the equator than I'd ever wanted to see.

He was my father and he was here in my arms, cradling me and Quoth like we were the most precious things in the world to him.

How many times growing up had I wished for this moment? Mum never talked about him – she left me to build a picture in my mind of this loser petty criminal who walked out on her as soon as he found out she was pregnant. It was why I ran away to Nevermore Bookshop, because I felt as though I could find my father between the pages. Little did I know how right I was.

"My baby girl," Homer whispered into my hair, his shoulders trembling with emotion.

I pulled back so I could look at him again. I raked my eyes over his body, trying to save all his features for future analysis. The broadness of his shoulders, the scattering of fine hairs over his chest, the parchment and leather scent that rose from his skin. "How can you be here? Dracula said he killed you."

"Time, my love." He waved a hand wistfully. "It heals all wounds, even death. I could explain it to you, but we have only a few moments together. Is that what you really want to talk about?"

I shook my head, the words robbed from my tongue. I had so many questions, a lifetime of questions, but they all swirled together and became mush in my mouth. I managed to choke out, "You set up these candles. You knew I wouldn't be able to see you."

He chuckled. "Victoria has an extra stock for when I visit. We may not have the understanding of the disease you have in your time, but we can have a little light to illuminate a situation. How's my mother?"

"This morning she hocked up a hairball into Heathcliff's slippers, so she's the same as usual."

"And Helen?" Now it was his turn to choke on his words. "She is...well?"

"She's happy. She has a business she loves and she's seeing someone." Sadness flashed in his eyes for a moment, but then it was gone, replaced by a beautiful, savage kindness – it was a look I'd seen in Heathcliff's eyes so many times before, a look that said, *I would suffer a hundred times over if you were happy, even if it is without me.*

I was so grateful to him that my mother had a love like that.

"I'm glad." Homer dangled a foot out the end of the bathtub, wiggling his toes. "She deserves to be happy."

"Why? Why...all of this?"

"My dearest Mina, you know why." He held out his hands to me, palms up. I brought them close to my face, noticing the smudges of pigment on his hands, the roughness from where his pen rubbed against his skin. The hands of the most famous writer of all time. "Because the story needed to be told. Because love needed to triumph."

"That's such a *writer* answer."

"Then you understand." His smile could remake the world. "Of course you do. You are your father's daughter."

I thought of my crappy, half-finished manuscript saved on the computer. "I'm nothing like you. I can't write to save myself. It always comes out sounding wrong. You can't possibly think I—"

Again, he made that wavy gesture with his hands. "Let's presuppose that I've been hopping around your life for several years now. I had to make sure my little girl was safe and cared for. And let's just say I've seen you overcome your writers' block and produce something that would make your old man proud. What do you say to that?"

Tears streamed down my face. "Tell me what you saw."

He laughed. "There's no fun in that, my child. What good is a life if you can't live it on your own time?"

"But everything's gone wrong. I think Morrie and Heathcliff might be dead. And Quoth..." I held out the crook of my arm so he could see the injured bird cowering inside. "He's going to die with Dracula's poison in his veins. He'll die not remembering who he was or what he loved in this world. I failed you. I failed everyone. I thought maybe if I came through here we could go back in time together and fix it all."

He kissed my forehead. "Oh, Mina. You could never fail me."

"Mum misses you." I squeezed my eyes shut as more tears threatened to fall. "Ever since you've been gone she's tried to fill the Homer-sized gap in her life. Nothing's satisfied her, not even me. Can't you come back to her?"

He shook his head. "Our love story has already been written. Sometimes, life doesn't give you the happily ever after. But that doesn't mean you can't make a tragedy into something beautiful. Your mother is in every word I wrote, and those words have inspired lovers and writers and artists for centuries. I have a gift for you. But first, hold that towel for me while I get out of this tub. I don't want to scar my daughter for life."

I grabbed a fluffy towel from the stool in the corner and held it out. He slid into my arms, pulling the edges around to cover himself. He felt impossibly light and frail. When I looked into the tub, I saw it was completely empty of water. But it was full only a moment ago. The sleeves of my coat were damp from where they dragged in the water.

"It's that cursed plumbing," Victoria said from the doorway. "The bathtub never stays full for long, and I can't figure out where all the water goes."

Plumbing...

I remembered Dracula holding that sodden book, and something Grimalkin said when she first revealed my father's story. "Wherever and *whenever* the waters of Meles flowed, my son would be able to use them to escape from his enemies."

Plumbing...

I stared at the empty tub as an idea formed in my mind – the final pieces of the puzzle of Nevermore fitting together.

Homer cursed as he hopped around behind me, knocking over several candles as he struggled into his clothes. "Blasted trousers. I much prefer a *chiton*."

"Are you decent yet?" I got down on all fours to right the candles before he burned the whole place down.

"I am."

I turned around. There was my father, wearing an impeccably-tailored Victorian suit, complete with a flocked morning jacket I'd personally kill to own. From his jacket pocket, he pulled a small scroll wrapped with leather. "It's time you had this."

"Could I have your jacket instead?"

He laughed. "I think, on the whole, you'll enjoy this more."

"What is it?" I started to undo the leather strap.

He placed his hands over mine. Warmth flooded me from his touch. "Open it later. You'll understand when you're back in your world."

"I can't go back. Didn't you hear? Dracula's out there. He's killed all my friends and probably Mum, too. And I have no way of stopping him. Your last letter was bloody useless, by the way. *Bring the wine.* What was that about?"

Homer smiled.

"That's his dreadful sense of humor. I have something for you, too." Victoria led me back into the main room, where she lifted a heavy object from behind the bed and placed it in my hands. The lamplight glinted off a shimmering blade.

"It's a Greek *xiphos*, with a vein of silver running down the center of the blade. It's been quenched in the waters of Meles to lend it extra powers." Victoria smiled. "I haven't spent my life hanging around occult masters without learning a thing or two about slaying vampires."

I stared down at the object. "I don't know how to use a sword."

"I think you underestimate yourself," she said gently. "After all, you've been part of a vampire-slaying once before, *Mina*."

Mina.

I swallowed. *Mina*. Mina Harker. The heroine of Bram Stoker's novel.

My father had given me my legacy, wrapped up in my name and my blood and my wonky eyes.

I stepped back from Victoria and swung the sword through the air. It nicked the edge of the bedspread, slicing through the silken threads to leave a tattered gasp. Victoria gave a sharp intake of breath.

"Oops." I shrugged.

My father burst out laughing. "You truly are my daughter."

"Oh, for pity's sake." Victoria shoved me toward the door. "Stop destroying my belongings and skewer that vampire."

"Wait, you haven't told me how to help my friends, and I haven't even said goodbye—"

I only caught the faintest glimpse of my father's sad smile before Victoria yanked the door open and shoved me through. I stumbled forward, holding Quoth's still body against my chest as I toppled into the gloom. I threw my hand out to catch my fall...

...my hand that still held the sword...

The blade slid into something solid like a knife cutting butter.

I opened my eyes to see without seeing the unmistakable figure of Dracula toppling to the floor. The scream that rose from his lips was inhuman, a noise that could tear the world asunder.

His eyes rolled back in his head as his hands grabbed for the sword. But he couldn't seem to touch it. The skin around the wound bubbled and hissed as it burned away, leaving a gaping cavity that smoked and sizzled.

I drew back my hand, sliding the weapon out of his chest. "That was for hurting my friends, and this…" I thrust the weapon forward again, working the blade between Dracula's ribs as his face twisted with agony. "This is for Heathcliff and Morrie."

The burning smell increased as the blade hit home. Dracula's body shuddered as I drove the sword through his heart. His scream was on some other frequency – it wasn't just sound anymore, it had form and mass. It crushed against my ears and squeezed at my chest. It was the greatest sound I ever heard.

"And this," I screamed over him as I drew back the blade. "This is for hurting my little bird."

Dracula's cry cut off abruptly as I swung the blade through his neck, severing his head. His skin shriveled and his eyes and nose disintegrated, and his body crumpled to the floor in a pile of ash and bone.

I collapsed to my knees beside the remains, dropping the sword at my side. I nuzzled Quoth's body to my face as the last twitches of life left his body. My paper heart tore to shreds. *No no no. I have to do something. I can't let him leave me like this.*

Don't leave me in a darkness.

I pressed my lips to his cold head. "Hang in there, Quoth. I love you. I'll find some way to—"

"Nyah…"

Footsteps boomed in the hallway.

No. No more. No one is getting near my Quoth.

I swallowed back my tears and launched myself at the shadow, swinging my blade at my approximation of its head.

"Hey, gorgeous." A strong hand circled my wrist, staying my hand. "You can stop swinging that lump of metal around."

"But Dracula—"

"His head's no longer attached to his body. We're good."

I slumped into Morrie's arms. "Morrie, you're alive."

"Barely," he coughed. I drew back slightly, my fingers tracing the line of his jaw, feeling the blood trickling from a jagged wound in his neck. Wet blood coated my fingers. "The bastard took a good bite out of me, but he had more delicious prey in mind—"

A tiny cry broke through Morrie's words. "Croak?"

"Quoth?" I held him up to Morrie.

"Croooo-aaak."

Mina, Mina... Quoth's voice fell into my head, so quiet and faint I couldn't be certain I didn't imagine it. *I'm so sorry.*

"No." I cradled him against my chest. Morrie stoked his head.

"There's got to be something we can do for him. The after-hours vet—"

"He flew at Dracula to save me." I rocked Quoth. "He was thrown to the floor pretty hard, and he's lost so much blood. I thought we'd lost the real Quoth forever, but there was still a piece of him inside who remembered that he loved me. He saved me, but I can't save him."

"What's in your pocket?" Morrie drew out the scroll.

"It's something my dad gave me..." I didn't care about it anymore. I rocked Quoth and whispered all the words of love I wished I'd told him. I said how sorry I was about our fight. I wished I could take back every harsh word. I wish I had kissed him until we both died of starvation.

Without Quoth, none of it had meaning.

Morrie tore open the leather and rolled out the scroll. I didn't even bother to look at it. What did a bunch of old Greek matter when Quoth was dead? "Mina, this is an original copy of a chapter of Homer's Odyssey. This is *priceless*."

I sniffed. It doesn't matter. None of it mattered.

"It's the chapter where Odysseus goes to the underworld to learn his fate from the blind prophet Teiresias." Morrie frowned as he turned the scroll upside down. "Mina, I think you need to see this."

He thrust the book into my hands. It *shimmered* as I touched it – that was the only way to describe the sensation of the pages vibrating against my fingers. Even though it was too dark for me to read anything on the pages, I *felt* the rows of neatly-printed Greek letters dancing beneath my fingers, and I felt the raised shape of a wine amphorae doodled in the corner, and I *knew* what I had to do.

Something in my chest tugged me to my feet. I held the scroll against Quoth's ruined body and let the invisible thread drag me where it wanted, which turned out to be the kitchen, where I grabbed the bottle of wine Morrie stole from Grey's showhome from the rack.

"Mina, where are you going?"

"I think I know what I'm supposed to do with this." I shuffled to the staircase and descended, one foot in front of the other into the gloom below. Even without Oscar, I knew my way by heart. The steps were ingrained in my muscle memory from the hundreds of happy days I'd spent treading these familiar floorboards.

I paused in the hallway, torn by my desire to look for Heathcliff. But I had to keep going. I passed by the Classics shelves. My feet squelched on the sodden carpet. I flung open the cellar door.

Water lapped at my feet. The cellar had completely flooded. Bitter cold radiated from the surface of the water, raising the hairs on my arms to stand rigid like soldiers marching off to war.

Something clattered on the staircase behind me. Morrie's

breath caressed my ear. "What are you doing, gorgeous? That scroll is priceless. And I was saving that drop for your birthday."

I hugged my birdie against my chest. "Quoth is priceless. That's what my father was trying to tell me."

Tears stung the corners of my eyes. My father had given me everything I needed. I just had to put it together. I was Mina Wilde, vampire slayer, bookstore manager, and – above all else – storyteller.

The invisible thread tugged at my heart.

I had to finish the story.

I tossed the scroll into the waters of Meles.

I tucked Quoth's limp body into the crook of my arm, tightened my grip on the wine bottle, and dove in after it.

reezing water enveloped me. The shock of it drove the air from my lungs. Pain surged across my temples as a migraine took firm hold. I opened my eyes, but it was pointless – green and orange squiggled in my vision, the last vestiges of my overstimulated retinas. I couldn't see the way.

But I had no need of eyes down here. The invisible thread wound around my heart dragged me under. My foot brushed the wooden steps. My lungs burned, and I scrambled for the surface, desperate for a gulp of air. A current from somewhere unknown dragged me down, down, down, deeper than the seven feet of the cellar. So deep that I knew I had no hope of finding the surface again.

My fingers clawed for purchase, scraping along the stone walls but not able to find a grip. I slid away as my lungs squeezed and burned and froze. I had no feeling left in my body, the only sensation the cold clawing at my lungs and Quoth's feathers tickling my skin.

Through the haze, I caught a glimpse of something. A light, maybe? A shape, so impossibly far away that I thought I imagined

it. It was the last flood of oxygen to my brain giving me a halluci-
nation of Morrie in the rectangle of light at the open cellar doorway, reaching his hand out toward me.

Then everything went black.

CHAPTER THIRTY-ONE

*M*y eyes fluttered open.

It made no difference whatsoever. I couldn't see a bloody thing.

I heard water lapping nearby, and a sound that might've been distant thunder. I sat up, running my fingers over the surfaces around me, trying to get a sense of where I was. Sand trickled through my fingers, and my sodden clothes clung to my body.

My head pounded with pain as my eyes sought a single speck of light, some visual clue, but it was too dark. It was darker than dark.

Am I dead? Did I swim through a hole into the center of the world?

I cradled Quoth's limp body to my chest, stroking his feathers, whispering all the things I wished I'd been able to tell him before he was lost to me.

The faintest wheeze escaped his nostrils, and a shuddering movement racked his chest. He was alive, but not for long. I brought his tiny body to my face and laid a kiss on his head.

"I wish...I wish I had a way to save you."

I jumped as light burned across the horizon. A fire blazed on some far distant plane, not close enough to give off any heat, but the light – my eyes burned with the joy of it, to have finally some spark of brightness in the gloom.

A lone figure stood on the plains, silhouetted against the burning sky. He wore a flowing cloak made of midnight.

"Yo." He waved at me. But he was still too far away and too cast in shadows for me to make out.

"I'm sorry," I called back. "I need you to step closer. I can't see in the shadows any longer."

"Forgive me, Mina." The figure stepped forward. In that single step he crossed hundreds of meters so that he appeared only a few feet in front of me in blazing, beautiful detail. He was a handsome, middle-aged man with wavy hair past his shoulders, a prominent nose, a strange outfit beneath the cloak including a brown doublet and little wool cap encircled by a wreath of laurel branches, and a kind, sad smile.

"Hades?" I waved. "Hi. I guess this means I'm dead? I'm—"

"An excellent guess, Mina. But no." The man removed the wreath and placed it on my head. "And I'm not Hades. I'm Dante Alighieri."

"The poet who wrote *Inferno?*" I asked, confused.

"And *Purgatory*. And *Paradise*. But I accept those poems weren't nearly as much fun." He bowed. "I know who you are, Mina Wilde. You're the daughter of my friend, Homer. Welcome to my humble abode. I've heard so much about you."

"You...have?" This was not the conversation I expected to have in the afterlife.

Dante laughed. "Your dad and me, we're old drinking buddies. All the poets hang out together in the afterlife. No one else wants to talk to us. Homer doesn't shut up about you, but at least you're an interesting topic of conversation. You wouldn't believe how hard it is keeping pace with Robert Burns. That man will drink even Lord Byron under the table, and it's impossible to understand a word he says."

I glanced around at the barren expanse. "Do you run the afterlife, then? It feels like I'm inside one of your poems."

"Babe, I don't just run the joint, I *created* it. Your father helped with a few minor details. Like the rivers. He loves himself some rivers, does Homer. It's probably a hangup from that whole 'my mother's a water-nymph who was ravished by Meles' thing. But I came up with everything else. You should see the fields of torment – some really top-notch stuff." Dante beat his chest proudly.

"Um, maybe some other time. I guess I don't really understand why I'm here. *How* I'm here. Am I dead?"

"Far from it. You're here because the story says you must be here." From the folds of his doublet he pulled out a book. I grabbed for it, but he held it out of reach. "Tut, tut, this is not a story for your eyes."

I screwed up my face as Dante consulted his book. Quoth had gone completely still now. Panic rose in my chest. "I don't understand."

"Yes, you do. You know that stories create the world. You work in a bookshop. You know the power of words. Stories are what connect us, shape us, bring us into existence and snuff us from history." Dante gestured around him at the vastness of the plains. "The reality of this, and what's beyond all this, is too complex for the human mind to conceive. But stories give form to the universe, order to the chaos, substance to the unknown. Stories give us beginnings and middles and endings. Stories take our base instincts and weave love and heartache and redemption and pleasure and forgiveness into every word, until we believe ourselves to be essential to the plot rather than being swept along by it. Is it any surprise to you that your story has brought you here?"

"I guess not." I stared around me at the barrenness and figured I could do worse than take a chance. "I guess I've come to ask you a favor."

Dante turned the page. "I assumed so. I owe Homer for that time he got me out of a pickle with Sylvia Plath. Who knew the Ruler of Heaven had such a sore spot about oven-roasted chicken?"

"Wait, Sylvia Plath is God? I mean, obviously, but—" I shook my head. "No, wait, it's not important. So yes, I'd like to cash in Dad's favor. I even brought this wine, which I assume is some sort of libation? Do I have to dig a trench like the Odyssey and pour it in—"

Dante swiped the bottle from my hand and popped the cork. "Don't you dare waste a drop. It's impossible to find a good bottle of plonk in this place. Well, out with it – what favor am I granting the great Mina Wilde?"

I held out my arms, revealing Quoth's lifeless body. "Dracula turned him into a vampire, and now he's..." I couldn't even say the words. "Can you bring him back to life? Only, can he come back to life as Quoth? Not as a vampire."

"Is this what you want?" Dante takes a swig from the bottle. "I have the power to restore *anything* you wish. Wouldn't you like to be healed of your blindness?"

"No, thanks. I really just want my friend—"

"I can make your eyes new again, better than new. I can give you visions of the future. I can give you dreams that divine the fortunes of the human race. Or, what about the power to fly? Or what about superhuman strength?" He took another deep swig. "You have endless possibilities."

I shake my head. "I don't care about any of that. What's the point of having eyes if Quoth isn't in the world with me? So if you could just fix him—Oh, and Fiona and Grey Lachlan and all the others bitten by Dracula back on Earth."

Dante wagged a finger at me. "That sounds like more than one favor to me."

"Please? I promise I'll throw a few extra bottles of wine into the water once I go back—"

"Sold." Dante rubbed his hands together. "And you've definitely decided?"

"I have."

"And you definitely don't want new eyes? Or to be able to walk through walls? Or the ability to fly?" He looked mildly disappointed. "I've always wanted to make someone wings."

"No thank you. Just my friends healed is all I need."

"No take-backsies?"

"No take-backsies." I shook his outstretched hand.

"Well, then. Since you asked so nicely." Dante took Quoth from my arms. He poured the tiniest dribble of wine over his forehead, then took him and washed him in the water before handing him back to me.

"Quoth?" I peered down at his broken form. He still felt cold and hollow and *gone*—

One wing flapped.

I thought I'd imagined it. My stomach twisted up with hope and horror. I leaned down, brushing my lips against Quoth's tiny head. His body convulsed, writhing and snapping and twisting in a way no bird's body should twist.

"Crooooooak?"

I glared at Dante. "What's happening? What did you do?"

Quoth's cry tore at my soul. He was dying all over again, and I was dying with him. I closed my eyes and I wished and hoped and begged as his body twitched and jerked in my arms. *Please, Quoth. Don't leave me in this abyss without you. Not the angels in Heaven above or the poets down under the waters of Meles can ever dissever my soul from yours.*

Please, please, please...

"Careful, Mina," Dante tsked. "Poe could sue you for copyright infringement, and trust me, you don't want that depressing bastard in your face."

I opened my eyes. Two orbs of deep brown ringed with

orange flame stared back at me from behind a curtain of shimmering midnight hair.

"Mina?"

Quoth.

My beautiful Quoth.

He threw his long arms around me, rolling me over into the sand. I felt as if I weighed nothing at all, as if my heart was about to flutter out of my chest and fly away. He laid kisses on my lips, my eyelids, every inch of my face. He still had pasta sauce smeared across his chest and back. I stroked his soft, warm, *living* skin and I couldn't believe he was here, alive, with me.

"My Mina," Quoth whispered, burrowing his head into my neck to kiss the place where he'd bitten me. The wound had now mysteriously vanished.

"I thought I lost you." I stroked my fingers over his cheek. I couldn't stop touching him, marveling at how warm and good he felt.

"You did for a while there." Quoth sat back, and in his fire-rimmed eyes I saw all the pain and regret of what he'd done. "I don't deserve you. I don't deserve this second chance. I was weak. I should have been able to resist him. Can you ever forgive me for hurting you?"

"You weren't yourself. He corrupted you."

"But how much did I fight? How easy was it for him to take me away from you?" His eyes fluttered closed, the long lashes tangling together. "I don't know if I can forgive myself. I hurt Oscar. I attacked you. I spied for him and gave him all the information he needed to get the dirt and kill those women. He said if I didn't he would hurt you. I completely understand if you never want to see me again."

A single tear rolled down his cheek.

"No, no." I wiped his tear with my finger. "That wasn't you doing those things. It was Dracula. It was his poison inside you, his will moving your limbs. He's the one responsible. And I know that because of how hard you *did* fight it. At the end, you escaped. You turned on him because no matter what he did to you, he couldn't take your humanity from you."

Quoth shook his head, his hair streaming over his shoulders. "It's not enough."

"It's everything." I brought my lips to his. In the kiss I laid bare everything I'd been too afraid to tell him all these months I'd been with him. That I'd never known it was possible to love someone so utterly, with my whole heart and body and mind. That in him I'd found a twin soul – someone who understood the creative spark inside me and nurtured that flame until it burned as bright as his own bright flames. That I'd never known what the word home truly meant before I'd found him in a little attic in Nevermore Bookshop.

When we both came up for air, we were a mess of tears and swollen lips and red-ringed eyes. I laughed and kissed him again and again, until Dante cleared his throat behind me and tossed the empty bottle into the sand beside us.

"Time's up, Mina." Dante glanced at his wrist, and I saw he wore a snazzy gold watch with nine faces. "I've got an appointment at the river of blood and fire I don't want to miss."

"Will I see my father again?" I asked. "I know Dracula killed him, but that was only in my time, right? So he could step out of the time-traveling room and be in my life again?"

Dante shook his head. "You know that's not how it works. But you do not have to be sad. Old storytellers never die. They simply disappear into their own tales." Dante touched his hand to mine. "It's your turn now, Mina Wilde, daughter of Homer. Write the next chapter. And don't forget to drop off my wine."

Dante strode to the edge of the water. He kicked out a foot, sending up a splash that swirled in the air in complete disobedience to the laws of gravity. The droplets formed a shimmering doorway, and I felt the familiar tug of the invisible cord around my heart, pulling me toward it.

My fingers laced in Quoth's, and together we waded through the water. We leaned in and kissed each other one final time before walking through the doorway into the unknown.

CHAPTER THIRTY-TWO

*T*hrough the doorway, all was in darkness. We stumbled through the gloom together, Quoth's hand never leaving mine. I held my other hand out in front of me, feeling for the moment when the freezing waters of Meles receded and my fingers brushed cool, damp stone. My feet splashed on wet cobbles.

I blinked as a bright light rushed toward me. Quoth's arms flew around me, and I met that light with my eyes open and my heart whole. If it was the freight train coming for me, then I was ready.

"They're here. The bastards are alive."

The torch clattered on the cellar floor as Heathcliff rushed me, enfolding me and Quoth into his enormous, powerful arms. He crushed us both against him, as if he hoped to smush us through his pores and absorb us into his body.

"Will you look at that." Morrie's voice carried down from the top of the steps. "The whole family is back together."

"Not yet," Heathcliff growled. He broke away from us and raced up the stairs. Morrie cried out as Heathcliff tossed him over his shoulder and stomped back down the stairs. Heathcliff flipped Morrie off his shoulder into the middle of our circle and crushed us all to near-death again.

"Can we do the family reunion somewhere else? This damp will reap havoc on my brogues—hey!" Morrie's complaint was silenced by Heathcliff's lips meeting his.

Heathcliff's hand dragged my collar toward him, and then he was kissing me, and Morrie was kissing Quoth, and we were laughing and hugging and kissing each other, high on being alive and together and wildly, ecstatically in love.

I was filled with a joy I didn't know was possible. We'd done it. The four of us had defeated Dracula and found each other in the process.

And we would never, ever lose each other in the dark again.

There was a sound from the top of the stairs. I tore my lips from Morrie's to squint up at the darkness. Victor poked his head inside. "Mina, I don't know if this is a good time, but there's a man here to see you. He says he's come to fix the power and the plumbing."

I couldn't help it. I burst out laughing.

CHAPTER THIRTY-THREE

"**A**re you sure it's okay to use a regular plumber?" I asked as I ran the mop over the floorboards at the base of the Classics shelves, trying to sop up every last drop of the waters of Meles. "These aren't exactly ordinary pipes."

"Oh, I'm sorry. I must've missed the page in the Yellow Pages for 'magical plumbers,'" Heathcliff grumbled. "The water doesn't seem to hurt people. It's our books that are in danger from your father's shoddy pipework."

He wasn't wrong there. We spent all week clearing out all the books from the Classics shelves so Handy Andy could get into the wall behind them to fix the pipes. When we pulled them all out, the damage was worse than we realized. Most of the books were completely soaked through. Now, several of the less-damaged books were laid out across the radiators around the shop, their pages drying out. Many were beyond saving, and we couldn't risk them going home with customers and bringing fictional characters to life outside the shop. But we had a plan for them.

Now we'd solved the mystery of Nevermore Bookshop. At

least, part of the mystery. When he fitted the shop with modern conveniences, my enterprising father had decided to use the waters of Meles to supply the water to the building, perhaps thinking he'd save on utility bills by tapping the ancient spring deep beneath the house. The shoddy Victorian pipes had started leaking years ago, slowly allowing water to turn the wall to sponge behind the bookshelves and then soaking the pages of the books with magical water and bringing the characters within those pages to life.

It explained why there had suddenly been this huge increase in the number of fictional characters. The pipes were a ticking-time-bomb – at any point during the last ten years they could've blown. They chose to blow a couple of weeks ago, slowing the water pressure to a trickle, soaking the Classics shelves, and flooding the cellar. It was a complete coincidence. A plumbing leak. Nothing to do with Mina Wilde and her wacky book magic.

I wasn't controlling the chaos that was Nevermore Bookshop. I was still an ordinary wonky-eyed girl with three boyfriends and a killer wardrobe. And I couldn't be happier.

I'd rid the world of Dracula and saved Quoth and the others from his spell. Jo had Fiona back and the pair of them were adorably, obnoxiously in love. The Spirit Seekers got some amazing footage from the night that the television people are convinced is fake, but they still want to give Mrs. Ellis her own spinoff show. Dorothy Ingram was off to a special facility where she'd hopefully get the help she needed. And we got justice for Jenna Mclarey – Jo and I presented Hayes with our evidence and – after rebuking us for taking the law into our own hands – he arrested Connor for her murder.

The good ended happily, and the bad got a stake through the heart. That's life in Nevermore Bookshop.

"Does this mean there won't be any more fictional characters showing up in Argleton?" Jo asked as Handy Andy carried the last of his tools up from the cellar. It had taken him over a week to locate the worn pipes down there and replace them with brand new ones, and he had a lot of work still to finish. Luckily, the insurance I'd insisted Heathcliff take out on the shop had covered it all.

"I don't think so." I flipped a copy of Shakespeare's plays over the radiator to dry. Although I was kind of sad that I wouldn't get to meet any more of my heroes and heroines from literature, it was worth it to keep the world safe from the likes of Dr. Jekyll, or Grendel, or Moby Dick or – Isis save us – Edward Cullen. Besides, the fictional characters in my life caused enough chaos and mayhem as it was.

The last of the books set out to dry, I collapsed into Heathcliff's chair, resting my boots on the desk. I was beyond tired. My phone buzzed. 'Incoming call from Helen Wilde' the screen read out. I kicked the phone off the edge of the desk. I was so grateful that my mum was alive, but I didn't need to hear about how in love with Handy Andy she was.

Every child of parents who'd split up had that secret wish they'd get back together. Homer and Helen were written in the stars...but maybe Dad was right, and it was my turn to tell the story.

Morrie picked up a battered copy of *Silence of the Lambs*. "I for one don't want to run the risk of this Hannibal Lecter creeping into my life. There's only room for one criminal mastermind in this bookshop."

"Besides, we're going to have a devil of a time finding homes for all our pox-ridden houseguests as it is." Heathcliff made a dramatic nod at Socrates, who had grabbed my phone off the floor and had fitted it to his selfie stick so he could review loudly Peter Jordanson's latest book for his Instagram followers. "Mina, it's time."

"Arf," Oscar agreed.

I sighed. "Yes, you're right."

Everyone followed me and Oscar upstairs and piled into the living room of the flat. A stack of waterlogged books sat beside the fireplace, and I knelt down and placed the last books from today's clear-out on top.

Heathcliff knelt, stoking the logs on the fire into a roaring blaze. He handed me a leather-bound volume. "You first."

I peered down at the title, my heart catching in my throat. *Wuthering Heights*.

The very volume that had brought Heathcliff into my life. The words that had so stirred my soul were now blots of ink on the ruined pages.

I looked up at Heathcliff with surprise. He smiled at me. "Toss it. I'm not the person I was inside those pages. Because of you, I'm a better man. My story isn't finished. *Our* story isn't finished."

I thought of Dante's offer to me, and how easy it was to cast aside the one thing I thought I'd wanted most in the world a year ago to bring my family together. How it wasn't really a choice at all.

I threw the book into the flames. Fire licked along the spine, wreathing the book in a halo of orange light. The pages curled and fell away, returning to the earth as smoke and ash.

Far from the fear-based 'librocide' Dorothy Ingram had sought to enact, this book burning was about *saving* books – about keeping stories in our hearts instead of running around the streets hurting people. We needed to set these characters free to live their own lives within the pages.

I sucked in a breath. Even though I knew this was the right thing to do, there was something sacrilegious about watching a book burn. I almost expected Ray Bradbury or the goddess Sylvia Plath to float from the heavens and smite us all.

But no, Goddess Plath had better things to do. She knew, as I now knew, that we were the writers of our own stories.

Heathcliff tossed a book to Morrie. "Your turn."

Morrie caught the book in one hand. I didn't have to look closely at it to know it was a collection of Sherlock Holmes stories. He leaned over to press his lips to mine as he tossed the book over his shoulder. That was Morrie for you – he didn't need to look back.

Soon we were all joining in – Quoth squawking with glee as he dropped tomes from a great height into the spitting flames. Socrates practiced his underarm bowl. Jo tossed a few in with a careful flick of her wrist. Morrie passed around marshmallows and skewers.

"What's going to happen with this lot?" Jo gestured to the crowd of fictional characters jostling for a space in front of the fire to toast their mallows.

"I'm already hard at work." Morrie tapped his phone. "Victor will be working at Madame Tussauds, and his monster has a job as the bouncer at a London club. Robin is joining a medieval living-history troupe near Nottingham. The old man just landed a sponsorship deal from a luxury clothing label, so he's going to give up his sophist ways to become a consumer whore. The Headless Horseman will be haunting Lachlan manor, just to remind Grey that we're thinking of him during his early retirement."

Grey Lachlan had only just come home from hospital, where he'd been recovering from internal injuries after the doctors removed the stake from his back. His experience as Dracula's servant had shaken him so baldy that when Morrie offered (or, in true Morrie fashion, made it clear there was no choice) to purchase Mrs. Ellis' old flat for a fraction of the asking price, he'd signed the papers that very day. He'd decided to get out of the property development game and devote the rest of his life to treating Cynthia like a princess, a vocation of which I heartily approved.

This meant Morrie now owned the shop across the street, and we were still deciding (aka arguing) over what to do with it. Morrie was thinking of luxurious living quarters, I had my eye on it for an event space, Quoth saw it as a potential art gallery, and Heathcliff wanted to put a KEEP OUT sign on the door and fill it with books and whisky and a big, comfortable bed.

I turned to Puck. "What about you? Sam from Wild Oats Wilderness Retreat says he's keen to train another wild food forager."

Puck grinned at Morrie. "Actually, I plan to roam hither and dither about Argleton a while longer. I saw in the pub that next on the village social calendar is the annual Shakespeare Festival."

The Argleton Shakespeare Festival. A month-long celebration of the bard's work, with plays, musical troupes, and absolutely no murders whatsoever. And everyone in the village would have a role to play.

They didn't just need actors, but set and prop designers, costume department, and all the other backstage roles. I thought of the now-empty Classics shelves, imagining a display of beautifully-bound Shakespeare editions, maybe some themed teas...

Yes. The future of Nevermore Bookshop looked very bright indeed.

THE END...OR IS IT?

Nevermore Bookshop Mysteries will have 3 more books. Quoth struggles with his guilt, Mina finishes her novel, and Puck unleashes chaos at the Argleton Shakespeare festival in *Much Ado About Murder* – get your copy now:

http://books2read.com/muchadoaboutmurder

Can't get enough of Mina and her boys? Read a free alternative scene from Quoth's point-of-view along with other bonus scenes and extra stories when you sign up for the Steffanie Holmes newsletter.

http://www.steffanieholmes.com/newsletter

FROM THE AUTHOR

Welcome back to Nevermore Bookshop. I know it's been a while since we stepped through the front door to meet a grumpy, loveable giant, a suave and cheeky criminal genius, and a beautiful and kind raven – and let us not forget the stuffed armadillo.

You asked, and I am making it happen – Nevermore Bookshop Mysteries will have three more books, starting with *Much Ado About Murder*. Be prepared for silly costumes, Shakespearean insults, and an ever-growing body count. Get book 7 here – http://books2read.com/muchadoaboutmurder.

And if you need something to read while you wait, I've got you covered. Check out my Briarwood Witches series – it's complete at 5 books, so that's 400,000+ words about a science nerd heroine who inherits a real English castle complete with great hall, turrets, and 5 hot English/Irish tenants. She also inherits some magical powers she can't control (also, there is MM). Grab the collection with a bonus scene – http://books2read.com/briarwoodwitches. Turn the page for a teaser.

If you're enjoying the literary references in Nevermore, check out my reverse harem bully romance series, *Manderley Academy*. Book 1 is *Ghosted* and it's a classic gothic tale of ghosts and betrayal, creepy old houses and three beautifully haunted guys with dark secrets. Plus, a kickass curvy heroine. You will LOVE it – http://books2read.com/manderley1.

If you want to hang out and talk about all things Nevermore, my readers are sharing their theories and discussing the book over in my Facebook group, Books That Bite. Come join the fun. And for updates and a free book of cut scenes and bonus stories, you can join my newsletter – http://steffanieholmes.com/newsletter.

A portion of the proceeds from every Nevermore book sold go toward supporting Blind Low Vision NZ Guide Dogs, and I'm always sharing cute guide dog pictures and vids in my Facebook group.

I'm so happy you enjoyed this story! I'd love it if you wanted to leave a review on Amazon or Goodreads. It will help other readers to find their next read.

Thank you, thank you! I love you heaps! Until next time.

Steffanie

WANT MORE REVERSE HAREM FROM STEFFANIE HOLMES

Dear Fae,

Don't even THINK about attacking my castle.

This science geek witch and her four magic-wielding men are about to get medieval on your ass.

I'm Maeve Crawford. For years I've had my future mathematically calculated down to the last detail; Leave my podunk Arizona town, graduate MIT, get into the space program, be the first woman on Mars, get a cat (not necessarily in this order).

Then fairies killed my parents and shot the whole plan to hell.

I've inherited a real, honest-to-goodness English castle – complete with turrets, ramparts, and four gorgeous male tenants, who I'm totally *not* in love with.

Not at all.

It would be crazy to fall for four guys at once, even though they're totally gorgeous and amazing and wonderful and kind.

But not as crazy as finding out I'm a witch. A week ago, I didn't even believe magic existed, and now I'm up to my ears in spells and prophetic dreams and messages from the dead.

When we're together – and I'm talking in the Biblical sense – the five of us wield a powerful magic that can banish the fae forever. They intend to stop us by killing us all.

I can't science my way out of this mess.

Forget NASA, it's going to take all my smarts just to survive Briarwood Castle.

The Castle of Earth and Embers is the first in a brand new steamy reverse harem romance by *USA Today* bestselling author, Steffanie Holmes. This full-length book glitters with love, heartache, hope, grief, dark magic, fairy trickery, steamy scenes, British slang, meat pies, second chances, and the healing powers of a good cup of tea. Read on only if you believe one just isn't enough.

Read now
books2read.com/earthandembers

EXCERPT

THE CASTLE OF EARTH AND EMBERS

*E*njoy this short teaser from book 1 of the Briarwood Witches, *Earth and Embers. http://books2read.com/earthandembers*

*R*owan showed Maeve around the kitchen, pointing out the spice racks and explaining his stupidly complicated fridge-stacking system. Maeve listened attentively, and she didn't laugh or poke fun of any of Rowan's OCD tendencies. The tension slipped from his shoulders. She was affecting even him.

"What are you making here?" Maeve peered into the baskets of produce and empty preserving jars on the island.

Rowan's face reddened and his shoulders hunched back up again. I winced. That didn't last long. Maeve looked at Rowan's face as his jaw locked. He stared at his feet and twirled the end of a dreadlock around his finger.

"Rowan, is something wrong?" Maeve's voice tightened with concern. She reached out a hand to him, but he stepped back, leaving her arm hanging in the air. The awkward tension in the air ratcheted up a notch.

Time to save this situation. I stepped forward and grabbed Maeve's arm, doing my best to ignore the tingle of energy that shot through me when our skin touched. I'd have to get used to ignoring it. I dragged her across the room.

"This is really cool," I said, opening a door at the back of the kitchen to reveal a narrow staircase. "This was installed when the castle was a grand stately home so the servants could rush meals up to the bedrooms without being seen in the main part of the house. It comes up near the staircase that goes up to your bedroom, so it's a good shortcut down to the kitchen if you fancy a nightcap."

"Duly noted." Maeve sashayed across the room and peered up the narrow staircase. "Are the bedrooms upstairs? Can I see?"

At the word *bedroom* passing through her red, pursed lips, my cock tightened in protest. *Don't think about it.* But that was like telling Obelix – the pudgy castle cat – not to think about all the delicious birds sitting in the tree outside the window.

"Sure." I gestured to the staircase. "After you."

Maeve started up the narrow steps, her gorgeous arse hovering inches from my face. I made to follow her, but something heavy slammed into my side, knocking me against the wall. I cursed as my elbow scraped against the rough stone of the wall.

"Sorry mate," Flynn flashed me his devil's grin as he leapt past me and followed Maeve up the stairs. "I didn't see you there."

"I believe you," I mumbled as I followed them up. "Millions wouldn't."

At the top of the stairs, Maeve pressed her hands against the wood panel. "How do you get this open?"

Flynn tried to reach around her to unlock the clasp at the top of the door, but this time, I beat him to it. As I reached around Maeve, she turned slightly to press her back against the wall and her breasts brushed against my shirt, setting off a fire beneath my skin.

Her lips formed an O of surprise, and I couldn't help but

mentally fill in that O with the shaft of my cock. I blinked, trying to stop thinking about her like that, trying to remember that it was the magic making me into this *animal.*

The air between us thinned, and an invisible force drew my body forward, my arm brushing hers. A few inches more, and my lips would be pressed against hers—

No. You can't do this. You can't encourage her to choose you.

"Well, isn't this intimate?" Flynn shimmied his way through the gap so that he had his back against the opposite wall, his hands falling against Maeve's hips. If he wanted, he could slide her back so her arse rubbed against his cock, and even though that was totally cheating, I wouldn't even blame him. I was cheating just as bad – my face in hers, my eyes begging for her touch. All I'd have to do was lean forward, press my lips to hers, and it would all be over...

Start The Briarwood Witches series today.
http://books2read.com/earthandembers

MORE FROM THE AUTHOR OF
SHUNNED

**From the author of *Shunned*, the Amazon top-20 bestselling
bully romance readers are calling, "The greatest mindf**k of
2019," comes this new dark contemporary high school reverse
harem romance.**

Psst. I have a secret.

Are you ready?

I'm Mackenzie Malloy, and everyone thinks they know who I am.

Five years ago, I disappeared.

No one has seen me or my family outside the walls of Malloy
Manor since.
But now I'm coming to reclaim my throne:
The Ice Queen of Stonehurst Prep is back.

Standing between me and my everything?
Three things can bring me down:

The sweet guy who wants answers from his former friend.
The rock god who wants to f*ck me.
The king who'll crush me before giving up his crown.

They think they can ruin me, wreck it all, but I won't let them.
I'm not the Mackenzie Eli used to know.
Hot boys and rock gods like Gabriel won't win me over.
And just like Noah, I'll kill to keep my crown.

I'm just a poor little rich girl with the stolen life.
I'm here to tear down three princes,
before they destroy me.

**Read now:
http://books2read.com/mystolenlife**

OTHER BOOKS BY STEFFANIE HOLMES

This list is in recommended reading order, although each couple's story can be enjoyed as a standalone.

Nevermore Bookshop Mysteries

A Dead and Stormy Night

Of Mice and Murder

Pride and Premeditation

How Heathcliff Stole Christmas

Memoirs of a Garroter

Prose and Cons

A Novel Way to Die

Much Ado About Murder

Kings of Miskatonic Prep

Shunned

Initiated

Possessed

Ignited

Stonehurst Prep

My Stolen Life

My Secret Heart

My Broken Crown

My Savage Empire

Manderley Academy

Ghosted

Haunted

Spirited

Standalone novels

Poison Malice Twisted

Briarwood Witches

Earth and Embers

Fire and Fable

Water and Woe

Wind and Whispers

Spirit and Sorrow

Crookshollow Gothic Romance

Art of Cunning (Alex & Ryan)

Art of the Hunt (Alex & Ryan)

Art of Temptation (Alex & Ryan)

The Man in Black (Elinor & Eric)

Watcher (Belinda & Cole)

Reaper (Belinda & Cole)

Wolves of Crookshollow

Digging the Wolf (Anna & Luke)

Writing the Wolf (Rosa & Caleb)

Inking the Wolf (Bianca & Robbie)

Wedding the Wolf (Willow & Irvine)

Want to be informed when the next Steffanie Holmes paranormal romance story goes live? Sign up for the newsletter at www.steffanieholmes.com/newsletter to get the scoop, and score a free collection of bonus scenes and stories to enjoy!

ABOUT THE AUTHOR

Steffanie Holmes is the *USA Today* bestselling author of the paranormal, gothic, dark, and fantastical. Her books feature clever, witty heroines, secret societies, creepy old mansions and alpha males who *always* get what they want.

Legally-blind since birth, Steffanie received the 2017 Attitude Award for Artistic Achievement. She was also a finalist for a 2018 Women of Influence award.

Steff is the creator of *Rage Against the Manuscript* – a resource of free content, books, and courses to help writers tell their story, find their readers, and build a badass writing career.

Steffanie lives in New Zealand with her husband, a horde of cantankerous cats, and their medieval sword collection.

STEFFANIE HOLMES NEWSLETTER

Grab a free copy of *Cabinet of Curiosities* – a Steffanie Holmes compendium of short stories and bonus scenes – when you sign up for updates with the Steffanie Holmes newsletter.

http://www.steffanieholmes.com/newsletter

Come hang with Steffanie
www.steffanieholmes.com
hello@steffanieholmes.com